C000264291

THE TRAIN

A PILGRIM ODYSSEY

First Published in Great Britain 2018 by Mirador Publishing

Copyright © 2018 by Allan Ramsay

All rights reserved. No part of this publication may be reproduced or transmitted, in any form or by any means, without permission of the publishers or author. Excepting brief quotes used in reviews.

First edition: 2018

Any reference to real names and places are purely fictional and are constructs of the author. Any offence the references produce is unintentional and in no way reflects the reality of any locations or people involved.

A copy of this work is available through the British Library.

ISBN: 978-1-912601-09-7

Mirador Publishing
10 Greenbrook Terrace
Taunton
Somerset
TA1 1UT

The Train

A Pilgrim Odyssey

By

Allan Ramsay

Contents

"My train of thought felt rebellious, but also... organic. Cleansing. Like that was what men were supposed to do. Be seekers of the answers and the truth. To be above the influence and opinions of the outspoken."

— ***Nadine Brandes, Fawkes***

Reflections

Does Life Have Meaning? That was the title of the book I had just finished reading. I was intrigued by the title, as the author no doubt intended, but I should've known better. Like many passengers on long train journeys, I had sought refuge in a book to pass away the hours. I had started reading the book a few days earlier and had boarded the train early in order to finish reading it. As the overnight train to Aberdeen pulled out of London Euston Station, I put the book on the empty seat beside me and looked out the window.

There wasn't much to see as it was dark outside. I watched the streetlights of Hertfordshire flash past. I could see my reflection in the window.

Look at you, I thought. How would I describe me? Medium height. White. Single. Clean-shaven. Wavy brown hair. Slim build. Mid-forties. Stylish dresser. Expensive leather jacket. Trendy casual shirt. Not bad looking either. But you're still not happy, are you, little man? You should be but you're not.

It must've been that book that had put me in a reflective mood. Maybe my resistance to the haughty overtures presented by a book with such a pretentious title had been lowered in recent months. It could have been due to the incessant onslaught of bad news in the media – I mean horrific terrorist atrocities, sadistic slayings of innocent people, and gruesome road accidents. Over the previous few months, the spectre of my transient mortality had seemed to gate-crash into my consciousness like an unwelcome guest. Had this constant barrage of evil tidings got to me causing me to be attracted to any source that claimed to know what was happening? Does life have meaning? Does anybody know? I didn't. Does anybody care? I thought I did.

It was probably naive of me but I had hoped for some sort of answer to the question posed by the title of the book. But I felt let down. It didn't supply any clear answers; only theories, possibilities and analogies.

The Train Journey Analogy

One such analogy compared our journey through life to a train journey. The idea had a certain appeal as I had been reading it on a train, even though the comparison did not seem particularly original. But as I didn't have anything better to do, I let my mind dwell on the idea. The theory basically proposes the concept that we board the train when we are born and for a while we travel with our parents and any brothers and sisters. But then our parents leave the train when they die. In time we come into contact with others as they board the train – friends, spouse, children, colleagues, and so on. They come and go. Some of them we miss when they go. Some of them we don't. We don't even notice that some of them have gone until we see their empty seat. Sometimes we don't even get to say goodbye. Others move to another compartment of the train. Sometimes they return, sometimes they don't. We encounter all kinds of emotions on this train ride – love, joy, fear, anger, loneliness, jealousy, hope. The great mystery is that we never know when it will be our turn to leave the train. When we do, the train will journey on without us. Then what? Good question. What's the answer? It was no good looking for an answer in the book I had just read. I supposed the title, Does Life Have Meaning? was intended to get people like me to buy the book and read it. I began to feel sorry I had. I felt I had been duped.

Asking Questions

I consoled myself with the thought that many people, maybe even most people, must have wondered whether there is any meaning to life. I concluded that some of them found that meaning in religion and others supposed there was no meaning. Yet without an answer, how could anyone have any peace? Surely I wasn't the only one who found the concept of life as being meaningless to be profoundly depressing? We are born, we work, we love and we die. And that's it? Well if that's all there is, then however wonderful and exciting life can be at times, it's ultimately futile. A bit of a joke. But then I felt I should rebuke myself for coming to such a negative conclusion about life. I had so much of everything – money, property, job, family, health. All the things that are supposed to make you happy. Yet if there's no purpose to life, what's the point? How can anyone be truly happy if this life is all there is? It couldn't only be me who was afraid of the bleak uncertainty of everything but death. I began to ask questions that I would normally dismiss as silly or unknowable. Basic questions.

Who am I?

Who am I? Some might have called it a stupid question but I wouldn't have done. There must have been many people who have asked that question through the ages. Maybe most of us give up and conclude that we don't know where to find the answer or else we don't have the time to look. Who am I? I am me. But who is me? What makes me me? Where did I come from? How did I become me? Am I defined by my race? My gender? My job? My appearance? Must I define myself by such things? Who am I? Does asking the question say something about me? Insecure perhaps? Struggling with my identity maybe?

I wish I knew who I was. I knew my name. That was the easy part. My name was Simon Godfrey. I had read somewhere that the name Simon is a Hellenized version of the name Simeon which comes from a Hebrew verb meaning, to hear or to listen. I liked that. I could live with the name Simon. I had always prided myself on being willing to listen to other peoples' views, however strange they seemed to me. I had also read that my surname Godfrey came originally from a Germanic name meaning, peace of God. As I thought on some incidents in my life, I concluded that I hadn't been able to live up to my surname very well. It had never suited me. I'd never really been at peace. Certainly not the peace of God. But it was a nice idea. Something to aspire to. Everyone's name means something nice, doesn't it? Nobody has a name that's nasty or rude or embarrassing, do they? If anyone did have a name like that they would surely think about changing it. On the other hand, people don't usually have names that reflect their personalities. Wouldn't it be interesting if they did? Maybe I should've been called Simon Seeker because I supposed that's the kind of person that I've turned out to be. I've always looked for answers to life's big questions. I was a lecturer in engineering at my local university. So I had read a lot and I knew a little about a lot of things. But beyond knowing my name and address, some sketchy information about my family background, and what I did for a living, I didn't really know who I was. The question that came to mind was, who am I? I wished the question would just go away. It bothered me.

What am I?

What am I? Now that was another thing I didn't know. Yes, I am a human being but what exactly is a human being? A collection of cells that are made of molecules that are collections of atoms – cells that contain proteins and DNA and RNA – cells that contain complicated molecular machines that perform a vast array of different functions – cells of different kinds that work together to make me the human being I am? I had seen a computer animation of the cell and I knew how complicated it is. This prompted more questions to come tumbling into my brain. Is that all I am? Am I merely a tool-making, tool-using, reasoning animal? A naked ape? The only animal that laughs and weeps and speaks and reasons and blushes and uses complex tools and contemplates death? The only animal that is never satisfied?

What is human consciousness anyway? Is it just an illusion caused by chemical reactions in my brain which ceases when those chemical reactions cease? If so, did any of my thoughts really matter? And what about all the emotions I had experienced? Were all the emotions I've ever felt merely the result of chemicals in my brain? All the love and happiness and fear and jealousy and anger and guilt? What were they all about? What is my personality all about? Is it really me or is it just a mask intended to impress others and to hide the real me?

What am I? A being made in the image of God? God! Is there a God? If there is, that would change everything. But if God exists, shouldn't it be obvious to everyone? If He exists, is He hiding from us? Did I want God to exist? Yes I thought I did. I thought it would make life more interesting. And if He does exist, what is He like?

Does Life Have Meaning?

Does life have meaning? Does the question posed by the book have meaning? What does "meaning" mean anyway? Does it imply a divine purpose? Religious people talk about a spiritual component called a soul. But the thought of something immortal within my frail body caused me to be besieged by questions that I could not answer. Do I have a soul? Or am I only matter? Matter that in the grand scheme of things doesn't matter at all.

Is there an afterlife and, if there is, what will it be like? I felt a hunger for some assurance that there is a purpose to life. I concluded that the only thing that really mattered in the end was whether or not there is a God. If God doesn't exist, then there is no meaning to life and we are free to live as we please. If God does exist, then there may be some meaning to this life and we may be required to live in accordance with His will. Memories of my early religious teaching came to mind. I was surprised how much of it I still remembered.

Then I began to feel emotionally drained and tired, really tired. Maybe it was all the thinking. I decided to retire for the night and headed for my cabin. I got into my pyjamas and pulled down the window blind. I had been having trouble sleeping at that time. As I had a busy day ahead in Aberdeen, I had taken a packet of sleeping pills with me. I seldom took sleeping pills but I needed a good night's sleep so I decided it would be a good idea. I took two pills with a glass of water. As soon as my head hit the pillow I fell into a deep sleep.

The Observation Carriage

Meeting Luke Watchman

The Observation Carriage was at the front of the long double-decker train and I stood looking out at the pleasant countryside as it flashed past. The idea of an Observation Carriage being at the front of a train seemed strange to me because I had always understood that Observation Carriages are at the rear of trains. The top floor of the Observation Carriage had a raised viewing area and large windows which afforded panoramic views through 360 degrees. I gazed transfixed at the variety of scenery – mountains, rivers, lakes and meadows. I was spellbound by the range of colours – the various hues of green and the contrasting blue of the sky. I was engrossed by the variety of animals I could see – cattle, sheep, horses and birds. It was as though they were especially on display for me. The scene from the window was constantly changing. I thought on the last line of the poem by Robert Louis Stevenson, *From a Railway Carriage* that I learned at school, "Each a glimpse and gone forever!"

What a beautiful world this is! I thought. *So marvellous and mysterious and magical.*

It seemed to me to be perfect in every respect. It looked idyllic and tranquil and serene and majestic. Words failed me to adequately express my sense of wonder. Yet the natural world appeared to contrast starkly with mankind. While we humans may be the pinnacle of the natural order, it seemed to me that our nature is blighted in some strange way. How else can one explain mankind's proclivity for greed and strife? Our ruinous nature had caused some of the natural world to be stained with our pollution. The natural order appeared to me to be too good for mankind to live in, something we didn't deserve.

It was while I was thinking about such things that a stranger came up and stood next to me. He said, 'Hello. You seem to be deep in thought as you observe the world going by.' His tone was jovial.

I turned to see a smiling stranger. He was tall. Just over six foot I would say. He looked to be in his mid-fifties with a blue open-neck dress shirt with a grey nylon bomber jacket. He had short, blond hair, delicate features and a kind face.

'My name is Luke Watchman. I like to watch the world going by too,' the stranger said.

'Hi. I'm Simon.'

'Simon what?'

Before I could reply, he said, 'Don't tell me. People should always be called by a name that suits them, especially a surname. Now I would say that you're the type of fellow who is inclined to look at things and to wonder and to ask questions and to seek out the truth. You are what I would call a seeker. Am I right, Simon?'

'Eh, well, I suppose so.'

'Then I will call you Simon Seeker. I think that's a good name for you. What do you think?'

'Well it does have a certain ring to it,' I replied with a shrug.

'Can I ask what you were thinking, Simon Seeker?'

'Well for one thing, I was wondering why the Observation Carriage is at the front of the train. Aren't they always at the rear?'

'Only if it's a steam train you're talking about. And this is not a steam train, it's powered by electricity. That gives the train designers the option of having the Observation Carriage at the front or rear. Personally, I think they've made the right decision because I like to see where I'm going rather than where I've been. Besides, there could be another Observation Carriage at the rear, and another in the middle, for all I know.'

'Oh, I see.'

'Now that we've cleared up your question about the position of the Observation Carriage, what else were you thinking?'

'I was thinking of what a wonderful view I could see and what an amazing world this is. So much variety and colour and complexity in animal and plant life! So much interdependency! It fills me with wonder. I'm struggling to find words to adequately express my feelings.'

'I can see that you are a perceptive fellow, Simon. The world that you and I observe from this train is indeed wonderful beyond words to describe. To those with eyes to see, it speaks of design and order and planning.'

'Eh, yes. You could look at it that way, I suppose.'

'There's no supposing about it, Simon. What we are looking at is a grand creation, my friend. And a creation requires a Creator. It didn't just happen, it has been designed. A design requires a Designer, simple as that.'

'Are you talking about God?'

'Yes, Simon, I am talking about God.'

I didn't reply but something about my expression caused him to ask, 'Don't you believe in God?'

'Well, I suppose I do but why is it that so many people today don't believe in God?'

'Because they don't want to believe in God, that's why. They don't want to believe in the existence of a God to whom they might have to give account someday. They want to be free to indulge themselves in whatever they want to do without worrying about the prospect of some future judgement.'

'But some of them quote scientific facts to back up their views, Luke.'

'Those so-called facts are not scientific facts at all they are fiction, pure fiction, Simon. Any facts that disagree with their ideas are mocked and summarily dismissed without due consideration. Believe me; the decision to reject the concept of God has nothing to do with true science. It is a philosophical decision, nothing more, nothing less. And by the way, not all scientists reject the existence of God.'

'But doesn't it bother you that some of the most highly educated people don't agree with you?'

'The higher up one goes in the education system, the more anti-God it is. So that doesn't bother me at all.'

'You appear to be in a small and declining minority, my friend. Have you ever thought that one day you might have to reconsider your views?'

'The whole media system on this train is biased against God – radio, TV, internet, newspapers, all of it. The system is liberal and permissive yet it militantly denigrates anything it finds objectionable. What it finds most objectionable is the concept of a God who has something to say about morality. It's today's opinion formers who should reconsider their views.'

'But, Luke, don't you care that many people probably regard you as old-fashioned and naive and might even laugh at you behind your back?'

'In a word, no. Anyone who believes in the true God in this society makes himself a target. That's just the way it is today.'

I found it hard to know how to respond to Watchman's emphatic view of reality and the status quo. A silence ensued as we both turned again to watch the changing scenery.

'What else does this view make you think of, Simon?'

'It makes me think that mankind is not worthy of such an amazing world.'

'The Observation Carriage is one place where we can take the time to observe things in the natural world and to think about what we see. We're all so busy most of the time that we don't have time to think. I agree that we humans don't deserve the world we observe out there. I would say that you have just made an astute observation, my friend.'

This comment led to another thoughtful silence which was broken by an announcement on the train's sound system.

'We are now approaching Futile, where we will make a service stop.'

'A service stop,' I said. 'What's that?'

Watchman looked at me oddly, as though he was puzzled that I had to ask the question.

'These are routine stops for the train to stock up on groceries, medical supplies and other necessities. The bodies of those who have died on the train since the last service stop are deposited too. This particular stop is at a place called Futile.'

A large consignment of big wooden containers, each one labelled with what it contained, had been placed on the platform. Some men alighted from the train and dragged, pulled and lifted the various containers onto the train.

'Who left these goods on the platform?'

'I don't know, Simon, but it happens at every stop. Somebody keeps placing everything we need right there where we can reach it.'

'This is crazy, Luke. Somebody must know who keeps leaving this stuff lying around for the train to pick up. But there doesn't seem to be anyone around on the station to ask.'

'No, it looks deserted.'

'But the passengers must wonder why everything we need just happens to be there on each platform we stop at.'

'Look, Simon, you've been around long enough to know that we humans have a proclivity for blanking out what we don't want to think about, even when it should be obvious. We have a tendency to focus only on the here and now. People in general don't want to think about anything outside this train. But to me, it's another indication that there's a Somebody out there who is looking after us.'

We watched in silence as the cargo on the platform was loaded onto the train.

Then, hundreds of bodies in body bags were unloaded from the train. As I looked at all the dead bodies carefully laid out on the platform, I became suddenly gripped by the fear of death. Death was one thing I couldn't deny and wouldn't be able to avoid. One day, I would be in one of those body bags.

Life Outside the Train?

'What do you think happens to all these dead bodies, Luke?'

'I don't know. Maybe they just lie there and rot or maybe someone comes along and buries them. I don't really care what happens to them because I believe that there's more to us humans than just flesh and blood bodies.'

'Do you mean a soul?'

'Yes. I think we each have something called a soul inside us that is not physical. It doesn't die when our body dies and it's eternal. It's the essence of who we are.'

'Are souls conscious?'

'Yes.'

'If we each have an immortal soul inside of us that is released when our bodies die, where do you think these souls go when the bodies die?'

'There are only two possible destinations for the human soul – Heaven or Hell. Whichever destination a soul goes to, it goes there for all eternity. In one destination, there will be perpetual joy. In the other, there will be eternal sorrow.'

'So you believe that Heaven and Hell are real places?'

'Yes.'

'Okay, where exactly is Heaven, geographically speaking?'

'Geographically speaking, it is somewhere north of Earth and way beyond the reach of our telescopes. However, I believe Heaven will one day come to Earth and then King's City will be transformed and it will become the capital city of the whole Earth. And all indications are that it may happen quite soon.'

'King's City? Where is that?'

'It's located in the centre of the Earth's landmass and it's built on seven hills.'

'And where is Hell?'

'I don't know and I don't ever want to find out.'

I thought about what he had told me for a few minutes, trying to process the information, trying to categorise it, trying to know how to respond.

'By the way, why is the train going so slowly?'

'Because there's no need for it to go faster. The train will arrive at its destination at the appointed time. No earlier and no later.'

'So where is the train headed anyway, Luke?'

'The main part of the train is bound for Hell.'

'Hell? You're kidding, right?'

'No, Simon, I'm not kidding.'

'So we just have to sit tight and do nothing and we'll end up in Hell?'

'That's right. Hell is the default destination of everyone on the train.'

'Let me get this straight. You're telling me that our souls will go to either Heaven or Hell when we die but the train is heading for Hell anyway? Doesn't that mean that the souls of all those who are judged to be consigned to Hell and who die before the train reaches Hell will arrive there before the train does? Is that what you're saying?'

'Yes.'

'Hmm. This is very serious. Do the passengers on the train know about this?'

'Some seem to suspect it but most of them don't care. They prefer not to think about such things. If they think about it at all, some would say they believe that we're all going to end up in Heaven eventually. Others think we're all going to a place called Oblivion, where we will simply cease to exist.'

'And what about Heaven… eh, I mean King's City? Suppose I don't fancy going to Hell, how do I get to King's City instead?'

'Like the soul, this train will journey to two alternative destinations but they are not the same two destinations. As I said, the main part of the train is bound for Hell but the End Section of the train will be de-coupled and will go to King's City instead.'

'Where will this separation take place?'

'At a place called Calvary Junction.'

'Will it happen soon?'

'As soon as it's meant to happen.'

'But I don't want to go to Hell. I want to go to King's City.'

'King's City is only for those who accept The Message during this lifetime, Simon.'

Hearing about The Message

'The Message? That's an ancient religious document that claims to be inspired by God, isn't it?'

'Yes and I believe it was inspired by God.'

'I've heard of The Message, Luke but I don't know much about it. I remember learning something about it in the religious education class at school but we were taught about all kinds of religions and philosophies. Isn't The Message like one of those?'

'No, The Message is completely different from any other religious teaching.'

'I remember learning something about The Message. I've only ever read short extracts of it. It seems to me to contain some interesting things, but things that can't be understood.'

'Then you are like many people who have never taken the time to read The Message right through from beginning to end as you would read any other book. Of course, the fact that people have never bothered to read The Message doesn't stop them from having an opinion about it. The Message does indeed contain interesting things as you say, Simon but these things are much more than merely interesting. They are vitally important and they can be understood by those who really seek the truth with all their heart. The Message says that all people are bound for Hell unless they accept what it teaches.'

The Communications Centre

'Why is it that whenever I hear The Message being mentioned, it's usually negative?'

'That's because people on this train have been born with a nature that resists any thought of the supernatural. The irony is that they are being biased against The Message by invisible supernatural forces that they are unaware of.'

'What kind of invisible supernatural forces?'

'Just as God is an invisible supernatural force for good, there is also an invisible supernatural force for evil. The leader of this evil force is called Prince Nicholas Rebel. You might have heard him referred to simply as Nick

Rebel. He has an army of former angels who are usually called demons. It is these invisible demonic forces which are behind the constant barrage of fake news that is put out every day on the train's various media outlets by the Communications Centre.'

'Fake news? What do you mean by fake news?'

'In this instance, I mean secular propaganda.'

'Hmm. And what about this Nick Rebel? I've heard of him but isn't he just a myth of a bygone age when people believed in supernatural things?'

'No he's real, all right. Long ago he tried to overthrow God because he wanted to be God. As a result, there was a battle in Heaven. Nick Rebel lost that battle and he and his demons have been sentenced to Hell. That's their miserable, eternal fate. Meanwhile, they're allowed to cause havoc on the train. They hate humans and want to take as many of us to Hell with them as they can. They strongly oppose The Message and continually work at discrediting it. Nick Rebel specialises in mesmerising, enticing, bewitching, seducing, distracting and charming. He probably would like people to think he's just a myth because that would make his work easier.'

'And what is this Communications Centre?'

'Sounds harmless, doesn't it? Actually it's the mass media centre which transmits its anti-Message, anti-God, anti-Book propaganda every day in the train's TV and radio and internet system. You find it in all kinds of programmes – news, current affairs, documentaries, films, music. The Centre has perfected subtle techniques of mind control.'

'Mind control? These people are using mind control techniques, you say?'

'That's right.'

'But I thought you said this train is being influenced by Nick Rebel and his demons?'

'It is, but they operate mainly through the Communications Centre.'

'Hold on, Luke. You're telling me that everyone on the train is being subtly manipulated by people who work in this Communications Centre who themselves are being subtly manipulated by an invisible army of demons?'

Watchman flinched a little at the bluntness of my question.

'In a word, yes.'

I laughed. 'Oh come on, Luke. You don't really believe that do you?

That sounds like a giant conspiracy theory.'

'Yes I do believe it and it's more than a conspiracy theory, Simon.'

'Well it doesn't sound very credible to me. Okay then, you tell me how this mass media centre, aided and abetted by these invisible demons, has managed to delude the whole population of this train.'

'It utilises media forms which are intended to reach the largest audience possible – television, radio, newspapers, magazines, films, books, records. You name it, they use it. The aim of the propaganda is to reduce everyone's ability to think independently and to introduce certain thoughts and ideas into our minds.'

'But there must be some clever people on this train who aren't taken in by it?'

'Well all I can say is, if there are people who are so clever, they seem to be keeping their heads down. I've hardly ever heard people seriously consider the possibility that they might be being deceived. They take it for granted that they can think independently and could never be fooled by anyone.'

'I really ought to know better, Luke. I pride myself on being able to think for myself. But I'm curious. I'd like to see this Communications Centre for myself then I can make up my own mind.'

'That's easy. It's the next carriage along,' Luke said, pointing to the carriage between the Observation Carriage and the locomotive that was pulling the train. 'They have a reception area and you might get to talk to someone and you might not. But if you do get to speak to someone, I doubt that you'll be told the truth about what goes on there. Anyway, I think it would be good for you to go and see it. They have literature in their reception area that is available for the public to look at. You might be able to form an opinion about whether what I am saying about it is true.'

'I might just do that.'

The Invitation

'But there's something a lot more important than the Communications Centre that you should check out and that is The Message. There will be a meeting in one week's time when The Message will be fully explained by one of our best teachers, a man called John Herald. The meeting will be held in the meeting room on the top floor of the next carriage along and is due to start at 2.00pm. There should be a sizable crowd. If you're free, why don't you come along?'

'I don't think so, Luke. No offence. I've found your views about The

Message very interesting but I don't feel that I'm ready to adopt such radical ideas.'

'It could be that old Nick Rebel is subtly influencing your decision, Simon. He will bombard your mind with all kinds of objections to The Message. But I want to set you a challenge, my friend. Whatever is causing you to resist The Message, resist that thing instead. This matter is too important to let anything make up your mind for you. What you've heard about The Message is likely to have been distorted and you, Mr. Simon Seeker, are seeking after the truth, aren't you? Come along and listen to The Message. Then you'll be in possession of the facts. Only then will you be able to judge for yourself.'

'I'll think about it.'

Watchman reached into his pocket and pulled out an A5 sized card.

'I've had some invitation cards printed.'

At the top of the card it read, "Dear" followed by a space to write someone's name in. Watchman wrote, "Simon Seeker" next to it.

'There,' he said, handing it to me. 'I like to personalise the invitations.'

'Thanks.'

'Before you go, Simon, take one last look at the passing world. This Observation Carriage is the ideal place to view it. Observe what you see carefully. Everything you can observe is transitory. It will all pass away eventually. But what you can't see is eternal. Only The Message can tell you the truth about what you can't see. If you do come to the meeting, and if you believe The Message, the world will never look quite the same to you again.'

Watchman and I shook hands and parted. He seemed a nice man who was sincere. But he sure had some strange ideas. It was tempting to dismiss him as a harmless crank yet he did seem to be intelligent and well-informed. I'd never met anyone quite like him before and I didn't know what to make of him. Still, despite his challenge, I had no intention of going to listen to someone talk about The Message. In spite of my search for some meaning in my life, I enjoyed the life I had. The train had much to offer in terms of job opportunities, social life and entertainment. Besides, I had too many other things to do. Too many dreams to pursue.

The Ticket Inspector

I walked down the stairs from the top floor of the Observation Carriage and walked along to the next carriage. I sat in the first seat I came to. The more I thought about Luke Watchman and his talk of The Message, the more intrigued I became. I was sure that he believed it but it sounded odd to me. It was like revisiting religious stories from my childhood, stories that I had abandoned as I grew up. It wasn't that I'd rejected these stories exactly. I was undecided about whether or not God existed but I didn't want to find out in case I had to do something about it. As for his allegation about this Communications Centre and its use of mind control techniques, I found that highly improbable. Still, there was something about Watchman's dogmatic insistence that disturbed me. It kept nagging away at me. I wondered whether there could be some truth to it. I was thinking about whether I should go along to check it out for myself. It was only the next carriage along. I was turning these things over in my mind when I was tapped on the shoulder.

I looked up to see a tall, burly, black man in a grey uniform. He looked to be in his thirties and had short black hair. There was what looked like some sort of ticket machine hanging from his neck but I had never seen a ticket machine like it before. He looked down at me with a blank expression. His voice sounded slightly bored. 'Ticket please.'

I had no ticket. I began to panic. 'Eh, sorry but I don't have a ticket,' I replied apologetically.

'You don't have a ticket?' He sounded surprised. I got the impression that for a passenger not to have a train ticket was a most unusual occurrence and was possibly a serious offence.

'No, sir, I'm afraid I don't.'

'Do you have any identification, sir?' His voice changed to a more formal tone.

I fumbled through my pockets and pulled out the invitation card that Watchman had just given me.

The Ticket Inspector pulled it gently but firmly from my grasp. He looked at the handwritten name at the top of the page.

'Simon Seeker. Is that your name?'

I felt his large brown eyes lock onto me like those of a tiger stalking its prey.

'Eh, yes.'

He typed my name into his machine and carefully scrolled the screen. Perhaps he was checking to see whether I had been in trouble with the police.

'Well, Mr. Simon Seeker, you must have a ticket for the train. Do you know what happened to it?'

'No, sir. I must've lost it or something.'

There was an awkward silence. I wondered what he would do. Lock me up? Beat me up? Throw me off the train?

'Hmm. Okay then I'll have to get you another one, won't I?' he said, his expression softening a little.

'Yes please.' I felt an overwhelming sense of relief.

He lifted up what I took to be his ticket machine to his face as if it was a camera. It turned out that's what it was, among other things.

'Look at the camera please.'

I looked at the camera and smiled, still feeling relieved.

'Don't smile. Just look the way you normally do.'

He took my picture and placed it into a wallet which he had pulled from his pocket. He then handed it to me. 'There you are, sir, one ticket.'

I studied it carefully. It looked more like a passport than a train ticket.

'What's the matter? You look as though you've never seen a train ticket before.'

'What does this number forty mean?' I asked timidly.

He looked at me curiously, as though he couldn't quite believe that I didn't know what the number meant.

'It means that forty is the number of your seat, sir. It is reserved for you. So don't go sitting in another seat. You are in the right carriage but in the wrong seat. You must go along to seat number forty.'

'But why does it give the number forty twice?'

He smiled but quickly changed his expression to a formal expression. He seemed to be having trouble keeping a straight face.

'I don't mean to be rude, sir, but you seem to have dropped into this train from somewhere else. Allow me to explain. The number of your seat aligns with the number of your sleeping berth. As with all seating carriages, the next carriage along is a sleeping carriage. Each seating carriage is followed by a sleeping carriage. The number of each seat ties in with the number of each passenger's berth. Okay? That's where you go when you want some privacy and to sleep, relax, watch TV, etc. Come along and I'll make sure you get safely to your berth, sir.'

Witnessing Watchman's Arrest

I was just about to rise up out of my seat when there was the sound of angry voices which sounded quite near and getting nearer. I remained in my seat and looked in the direction of the sound. It was coming from the direction of the Observation Carriage. I saw three men, two of them in uniform, who looked like railway policemen. They seemed to be escorting a third man further along the train. As they came nearer I saw that the third man was Luke Watchman! He seemed to be under arrest. As they walked along the corridor, Watchman was receiving a considerable amount of verbal abuse from the other passengers.

'Look! There's that preacher guy we've seen on TV. The one who keeps insisting that his religion is the only one that's right.'

'He's a public menace if you ask me.'

'What an idiot!'

'You clown!'

'They should lock him up and throw the key away!'

One particularly irate passenger threw a well-directed punch at Watchman, landing squarely on his nose, which started to bleed. I watched them pass. The Ticket Inspector moved closer to me to let the three men pass him in the corridor. As they passed by, Watchman saw me and gave me a faint smile of recognition. I wondered what crime he had committed. He seemed like a decent enough fellow to me. Deluded perhaps, but harmless. It looked like he might not be attending that lecture next week. As the noise of the commotion subsided, the Ticket Inspector asked, 'Do you know him?'

I guessed he must have suspected by my shocked look that I might have known the arrested man.

'No. No. I don't know him. I might have just spoken to him briefly once, I'm not sure.'

I wondered whether he would remember the invitation card from which he got my name and connect it with Watchman. Apparently he didn't.

'I'm glad to hear it. He's one of those believers. You shouldn't mix with people like that. They're dangerous.'

Believers? What did he mean by believers? And what did he mean by dangerous? I decided not to ask. Whatever else Watchman was, I would not have described him as dangerous, rather as an innocuous eccentric.

The Ticket Inspector repeated his offer to escort me to my berth.

'Okay, come on now. Let's see if we can find your berth, shall we?' He had adopted a faintly condescending tone, as though he was speaking to a young child. But I wasn't in a position to argue.

I followed him obediently to the next carriage.

He paused at the berth numbered forty. 'I could be wrong here but I'm guessing that you don't have your key either?'

'Eh. No, sir I don't.'

'Okay. I'll unlock it for you.' He pulled out a master key, unlocked the door and held it open for me. 'There you are,' he said. 'I'll get a key cut for you and give it to you when I have time.'

'Thank you. Thank you very much.' I was grateful for his patience and kindness.

Explaining the Train

'Just one more thing, Mr. Seeker. This is a very long train. It can take a very long time to go through all the various carriages. Remember, each carriage is followed by its own sleeping carriage. If you go far along the train, you might not be able to return back to your berth in one day. So you will need sleeping accommodation and not all sleeping carriages have vacancies. So if you ever decide to go wandering to a distant part of the train, it would be advisable to book your accommodation in advance. You might already know how the train operates, Mr. Seeker, but in case you don't, or have forgotten, I'll explain it to you. There are a number of specialised carriages, such as those for administrative and legal purposes, hospitals, prisons, shopping centres, gymnasiums and so on. There are really too many too mention. But if you take my advice, Mr. Seeker, you won't go wandering far. And remember to keep your ticket in a safe place.'

'Thanks. I'll bear that in mind.'

It was a relief to close the door behind me. I could only take so much humiliation.

The berth had a fold-up bed, a small desk, a television and a small toilet and shower cubicle. I pulled down the bed and plonked myself down on it. Whew, what a day!

Thoughts about my conversation with Luke Watchman returned. How could such a nice guy be treated with such violence and scorn? What could he possibly have done to deserve such treatment? Sure, he had a low view of the mass media and believed that they were biased against this thing he called The Message. But this society prided itself on allowing freedom of speech. Did the authorities have a problem with Luke Watchman as a person? Or was it The Message itself that they disapproved of? Or was it both?

I decided not to go to the meeting the next week to hear about The Message. I found it interesting but not interesting enough to attend a meeting about it. But Watchman's talk about the Communications Centre did interest me. It bothered me too. It was probably rubbish but I was curious. I decided to go along and check it out as soon as the Ticket Inspector brought my door key. The key arrived sooner than I had expected. It was put through my letterbox. I picked it up and made sure I was able to lock and unlock the door. Then I went along the short distance to the Communications Centre to see it for myself.

The Communications Centre

I walked into the reception area of the Communications Centre. There was a large window behind the reception desk and I could see a large office area lay beyond. It was buzzing with activity. Most people were seated at desks, working on laptop computers, some were on phones, and some were reading newspapers and magazines. Some were walking around briskly with papers in their hands. By comparison, the reception area was tranquil. Some businessmen were sitting around looking somewhat tense, apparently waiting on appointments. Some young people who looked like students were milling around the drinks machine. I walked up to the reception desk where a young, smartly dressed female receptionist with large black-rimmed spectacles was seated.

'Hello. Can I help you?' she said cheerfully with a pleasant smile.

'Eh, well I am interested in the work of the Communications Centre and I just thought I would come along to try to find out more about the valuable work you do here,' I replied awkwardly.

'What's the name of your company?'

'I'm just doing some research as a private individual.'

'Oh, I see. You've chosen a difficult time I'm afraid, sir. We have a major conference going on at the moment and the people I would normally get to speak to you are at the conference.'

I nodded and turned to leave.

'Oh, hold on. I've just thought of someone who might be available to help you.'

She picked up the phone on her desk and a few minutes later, a sixty something man with a bald head and a limp appeared from a side door. He was jacketless with a crumpled white shirt and a grey tie with a yellow stain which was loosened. His general appearance was not impressive.

'Hello, sir. Cyril Weary at your service. What can I do for you?'

'Hello. I'm Simon Seeker. I've been reading about the work you do here and I'm trying to find out more about it. Would you be able to answer a few basic questions for me?'

Weary nodded. 'Okay. Follow me.'

I followed him through the door he had appeared from, along a corridor and into an office. It had a sign on the door. 'Cyril Weary – head journalist.'

'Sit down, Mr. Seeker,' he said pointing at a chair facing his desk. He sat down behind the desk and looked intently at me for what seemed like a minute and a half. He was clearly sizing me up. I found him rather intimidating.

'Now, Mr. Seeker. Tell me why you are here again.'

'I'm trying to find out more about the valuable work you do here.'

Weary looked intently at me again.

'Mr. Seeker, do I look stupid to you?'

'No, no. Of course not,' I said, not knowing what he meant by the question.

'Nobody turns up here on their own to find out more about the work we do. Everybody who owns a radio or a TV set or is on the internet knows what we do. The whole train knows what we do. So tell me why you are really here. The truth please.'

I thought hard for a few seconds about the possible implications of telling him why I came. I regretted having come. But there was no way out now. He looked like a perceptive, no-nonsense kind of guy, so I decided to level with him.

'Well, I've heard a theory that this place is not quite what it seems,' I began warily.

'Really? What do you mean, not quite what it seems?'

I started to reply but the words just wouldn't come out. I simply did not know how to tell this guy what Luke Watchman had told me.

Weary looked at me again with that appraising look. 'Oh come on, Mr. Seeker. Spit it out.'

'I've heard that this place is putting out fake news and using mind control techniques to influence the population of the train. I wondered if there might be some truth to it.'

He laughed out loud. When he stopped laughing, he looked serious.

'Fake news? Mind control techniques? Is that what they're calling it now? You know, Mr. Seeker, you've got some nerve to come here and say something like that.'

We stared at each other for a few seconds without saying anything. I was starting to panic. I tried to think of a reason to terminate our conversation but couldn't think of any.

Summoning some courage, I said, 'Well? What do you have to say about that? Tell me it's all nonsense and I'll be able to sleep soundly in my bed.'

Weary looked pensive. Then he smiled a condescending smile. 'Mr. Seeker I like you.'

'I like you too, Mr. Weary,' I lied.

'You remind me of myself when I was your age. Always looking into things. Never accepting what people say unless you can verify it.'

I began to relax a little. 'I've been working here for a very long time. But I'm retiring in two days' time. That's why I'm not at this high-powered conference.'

He looked around his office as though memories of the past were flooding back to him. He sighed deeply.

Cyril Weary Tells All

'I might as well tell you. It won't do you any good. You won't be able to tell anyone because no-one will believe you. I must emphasise that what I'm about to tell you is confidential. It must go no further than this room. Is that understood?'

'Of course.'

'If you did tell anyone and it came back to me, I'd only deny it anyway.'

He got up and made us both a coffee. As I watched him, I wondered what he was about to tell me. He handed me a coffee and sat down with his.

'Fake news and mind control techniques, you say?'

'Well, is it true, yes or no?'

'You can call it fake news, mind control, coercive persuasion, thought manipulation, re-education, subliminal perception or brainwashing. You can call it whatever you like.'

'Is that an admission?'

'Look. What you have just told me is a conspiracy theory. It's not new. I've heard it before and many others like it. There have never been so many conspiracy theories as there are now and this place – this Communications Centre – is largely responsible for them all. That's why some people are talking about fake news. This place has lost the trust of the people and that's why all these conspiracy theories get started. People believe in conspiracy theories because they suspect that the media – that's us – might be lying to them on behalf of the powers that be.'

'So there is some truth to what I've been told?'

'There is a lot of truth to what you've been told.'

'So who are the powers that be?'

'Don't ask. Let's just call them the ruling elite.'

'Who are they?'

'They are members of the nobility, royalty, intelligentsia and experts of various kinds.'

'The next obvious question is – why are you lying to the people?'

'Why do you think? It's to control them. What else can we do? The masses are not able to handle the truth. They are not equipped to make sensible decisions. So the ruling elite have to make decisions for the masses and we in the mass media publicise those decisions. We use our skills to get the masses to accept them. We don't have to understand them or agree with the decisions. Our role is to support the ruling elite. Most of the time these decisions are for their own good but the masses wouldn't accept that. This means we have to spread misinformation for public consumption in order to keep control. If we don't, we'll be inundated with speculation and insinuation that will risk fostering mass paranoia and will endanger public order.'

'So people like you in the media are servants of the ruling elite? You write and report only what they approve of?'

'Exactly, Mr. Seeker.'

'You make it sound like the ruling elite versus the general population, Mr. Weary.'

'That's exactly what it is.'

'You condemn conspiracy theories but what you're telling me sounds like a conspiracy theory.'

'It's not a conspiracy theory. It's a fact. Some influential people have suspected it over the years but they have been systematically discredited or silenced in any way deemed to be appropriate. The population at large are simply not qualified to decide on important matters. The elite decide those things for the good of the masses then we promote their decisions to the masses. The masses aren't fit to decide their own fate. They are like sheep that need to be led.'

'But surely people are able to decide for themselves what is in their own best interests and what is not?'

'No, Mr. Seeker, they are not. That is a myth.'

'But in a democracy, people pick their own leaders and decide their own fate.'

'In theory, yes. But in practice, they don't really. Governments of all political persuasions are controlled.'

'But isn't it better for the ruling elite that the general population are educated?'

'Only if they are educated in a system approved of by the rulers. Otherwise, it's better that the general population are ignorant to ensure that they can be more easily led. The masses are fit only to be spectators of the action that is taking place around them, not to be participants.'

'But how do you manage to keep the whole population in ignorance?'

'Here in the Communications Centre, we shape public opinion and attitudes and we define what normality is. We use every media outlet available – television, radio, films newspapers, music, video games and the internet.'

'But I thought the function of the mass media is to inform the public?'

'To inform the public, you say? Well that's one way of putting it I suppose. We inform the public about what they should believe. Studies have been conducted into our effectiveness in shaping public opinion and, from these studies, the sciences of public relations and marketing have emerged, which assess and perfect the process of what you might call mind control.'

'Okay. I'm a normal member of the public. Not particularly intelligent but not particularly stupid either. How do you influence me?'

'That's easy. By distracting you. Mankind has an almost unlimited capacity for distractions. We use popular culture to nurture your ignorance by feeding you a diet of mind-numbing, trivial entertainment and publicising stupid, egotistical celebrities for you to imitate. We feed you with ideas about what is normal and acceptable in a civilised society. Then you won't think too deeply or question anything. You will blindly follow the trends. You will walk along the path that the elite have chosen for you.'

'Mr. Weary, you seem to be suggesting that the masses are ruled by a kind of invisible government.'

'I'm not suggesting it, Mr. Seeker. I'm stating it emphatically. The ordinary man has his opinions shaped by people he doesn't know, has never even heard of and who are invisible to him. It has to be this way if society is to function smoothly. The elite are unable to control all these people by force. It has to be done by a subtle form of mind control.'

'But surely the masses have to give their consent to matters which concern them?'

'Their consent? That's a laugh. Public consent is manufactured by the propaganda put out by the elite. The masses are manipulated to accept the elite's agenda.'

'But how can you manipulate all these different kinds of people without them knowing about it?'

'Look, Mr. Seeker. If the ordinary person knew what was being imposed on them, they would protest and riot. When the ruling class wants to introduce a change, especially a change that they know the masses will not like, it is introduced slowly. It is repeated endlessly in literature, in films, in newspapers, in news items and even in music lyrics. After a few years of this, the masses become desensitized to it. The change is then publically introduced and the masses passively accept the change with indifference and apathy.'

'But what about the really clever people? You can't fool them, can you?'

'Of course we can. We con them into thinking they are free and well-educated and independent thinkers but it's us who feed them these lies. They are so sure they could never be manipulated that their vanity does most of the work for us.'

'But what about all those high profile anti-establishment rebels in the fields of literature, acting and music? Surely they don't accept the decisions of the elite?'

'Rebels? They're not rebels. They just look and speak like rebels. That's all part of the grand deception. The mass media manufactures rebel figures to promote the illusion that we live in a free society in which some people are free thinkers. They are not free thinkers at all. They are just promoting marginal views but they are still part of the establishment's agenda.'

'From what you are saying, it's safer for the masses to be in a lazy state of conformity and passive acceptance of the status quo?'

'That's right, Mr. Seeker. It is better for ordinary members of the public to seek to escape the absurdity of reality and lose themselves in a hypnotic state of satisfaction.'

'But what about religion? You haven't banned religion.'

'No we haven't banned religion. We allow all types of religion and people are free to choose whichever religion they want. We are keeping a close eye on one or two of them though.'

'Does this include The Message?'

Weary looked at me with that intense look again. 'The Message? What do you know about The Message?'

'Not much. I've heard of it, that's all.'

'We haven't banned The Message but we are keeping a close eye on the people who preach it.'

'Why is that?'

'Why is that? I'll tell you why. That stuff is dangerous.'

'Dangerous? Why is it dangerous?'

'Because it is critical of everything a civilised society stands for. It is critical of the authorities and what they are trying to do for them. It is even critical of other religions. They teach that the society in the train is in a mess and is getting worse. They believe that some guy called Victor Love who died long ago will come to take over the train and the world. If enough people believed what they teach it could lead to civil disorder. No, we have to make an exception for The Message. People can have any religion except that one.'

'What's the point of all this deception and control of peoples' lives?'

'The point is to keep this train moving along the rails without any problems.'

'So where is this train headed anyway, Mr. Weary?'

'Who can possibly know that? I don't care anyway.'

'At last, something you don't know! So, to put it in a nutshell, you are saying that life has no purpose? It has no meaning? Death is the end?'

'That's right, Mr. Seeker. Life has no purpose. It's a joke. There is no point to it, no meaning, no plan, and no hope. You and I will die. And beyond death, there is nothing.'

Warned about The Message

I thought about what Luke Watchman had told me about the train being influenced by demons who are condemned to Hell and who are determined to take as many of us with them as they can. I thought about Watchman's declaration that there is an alternative for those who believe The Message. But how could I possibly broach the subject of the supernatural with this man sitting opposite me – this man who appeared to be so pragmatic and cynical and unspiritual?

‘Mr. Weary, I have one more thing I would like to ask you but I don’t quite know how to approach it.’

‘Well you haven’t done badly so far in stating your views, Mr. Seeker. Go ahead. I’m listening.’

‘Okay. You asked for it. You’ve been telling me that the whole train is being manipulated by a mysterious invisible government composed of ordinary human beings that you call the ruling elite. Is that true?’

‘Yes.’

‘What would you say if I told you that the ruling elite might be being manipulated themselves by an invisible group of spirit beings who don’t like us?’

‘Spirit beings? What do you mean by spirit beings?’

‘I mean demons, Mr. Weary. Malicious angels called demons under the leadership of Prince Nicholas Rebel.’

‘What would I say? I’d say you were crazy, Mr. Seeker.’

‘But it would be ironic, wouldn’t it? A mysterious, powerful, concealed group of people called the ruling elite who think they are in control but who are actually being controlled by a more mysterious, more powerful, invisible group of demons who are superior to them in every way.’

‘It would be ironic if it were true. But it isn’t.’

‘So you reject the idea of a spirit world composed of bad and good forces that are offering us either Hell or Heaven after we die?’

‘I reject it totally. And I would say that anyone who believes that is in need of psychiatric help.’

‘Fair enough.’

Weary looked at me intently. ‘I would warn you to stay well clear of anyone who tries to tell you about The Message. It’s garbage, pure and simple. And it will get you into trouble with the train authorities.’

I nodded but said nothing.

A brief silence ensued during which we looked at each other. It seemed as though we both knew there was no point in continuing our conversation.

‘Are we done here, Mr. Seeker?’

‘Yes I think we are, Mr. Weary.’

I thanked Cyril Weary for his honesty and left the Communications Centre deep in thought. Weary had just admitted that the whole train was being subjected to mind control techniques. I would never have believed it if I hadn’t heard it with my own ears. Maybe Luke Watchman wasn’t so daft after all.

The Meeting Room

I lay on my bed and thought about Luke Watchman's allegation that the Communications Centre was an elaborate fraud, a facade. Cyril Weary had been quite open in saying that mind control techniques were routinely used there. So Watchman was basically right. Of course, he had gone much further than that with his strange metaphysical explanation. According to him, demons who hate mankind are controlling the human controllers. Not surprisingly, Weary was scornfully dismissive of this view. He also rejected the idea of life having a purpose. Still, the arrest of a seemingly harmless citizen like Watchman made me wonder if something unorthodox, maybe even malevolent, was going on clandestinely. As I thought on this, Watchman's words gained more credence.

Yet the thought of life having no purpose made me feel depressed. It was then I remembered that Watchman had talked about something called The Message which claimed there was some sort of higher purpose to life. A divine purpose. Maybe it was just the mood I was in at that time, but I found that thought rather appealing. Like a glimmer of hope.

Watchman said there would be a meeting the following week at which The Message would be explained. The more I thought about The Message, the more intrigued I became. I thought about Watchman's challenge to me to go ahead and listen to a fellow speaking about The Message. What was his name again? I think it was John Herald. I thought of excuses not to go but, after careful consideration, I decided to go along to the meeting and check it out. Why not? I had nothing to lose.

John Herald Explains The Message

I walked into the large Meeting Room about five minutes before the meeting was due to start. At one end of the room there was a lectern and the room had around two hundred seats, nearly all of which were occupied. There was a quiet buzz of conversation and an air of expectation filled the room. I guessed that the speaker, John Herald, had a reputation that had preceded him. Not everyone respected him however. I passed by a man who said to his friends, 'I wonder what this babbler will say.'

I heard a woman say, 'I think he's just picked ideas and philosophies from various ancient sources and repackaged them into a religion.'

A handsome, red-haired man in his thirties of smart appearance entered the room and heads turned as he walked purposefully to the lectern. He wore a dark blue jacket with a light blue, open-necked dress shirt and carried some papers that looked like his notes. After welcoming everyone with a warm smile and thanking us for attending, he launched resolutely into his presentation.

'We are living in perilous times, my friends. We have been deceived by the powers that be. We have been lulled into a false sense of security. As a result, we are heading for disaster unless we wake up and heed The Message. That is what I want to speak to you about today. It is most important that you pay careful attention to what I am about to say. It will either make complete sense to you or you will find it offensive. There is no in between. I refuse to water it down. What I am going to tell you is the truth.'

His voice was deep and powerful and authoritative. He spoke with an intensity that was compelling.

'I will begin by explaining the situation that you and I – and everyone else on this train – find ourselves in. I will keep it as simple as possible. Despite what you may have been told and come to believe, there really is a God. He is wise and good and He loves us.'

At this point, when Herald had just begun his address, two men stood up and unfurled a banner which read, "Beware of The Message. Don't be taken in by it. It's hate speech. It's dangerous nonsense".

They angrily shouted out a number of accusations against The Message and against Herald. The most frequently repeated accusation was, 'This man is a troublemaker. He is crazy. Don't listen to him!'

Some in the audience shouted, 'What happened to free speech? We've come to hear him for ourselves. Let him say what he's got to say and we'll make up our own minds about it.'

Herald smiled at the protesters and paused while two stewards gently ushered them out of the room. When order was restored, he resumed his presentation.

‘In ancient times, this God delivered His will for us in a document called The Message. It contains His Law and it is for our own good. Those who accept it are accepted by God. Tragically, our forefathers rejected it. They succumbed to the evil influence of Prince Nicholas Rebel and his demons. That decision had a catastrophic effect on our forefathers by bringing death on them. It also caused all their offspring, including you and me, to be born in a corrupt condition. We have inherited their rebellious nature. We are born sinners. Sin just comes naturally to us. Like our forefathers, we are liars and thieves and adulterers and murderers and a lot of other things too. Some of us are more corrupt than others but everyone is born in this corrupt condition and we remain this way throughout our lives. That doesn’t mean we don’t do good things sometimes. But it does mean that we are all rebels at heart and are unable to please God. Even the good things we do are often tainted by selfish motives. As a result, this train is heading for a place that everyone has heard of and few people believe in. A place called Hell. This is what we deserve. Hell is a dark region of eternal affliction and sorrow. It is a region from which there is no return. Don’t think that when you die you will be instantly annihilated and experience nothing. That is not true. You are not just a flesh and blood being, you have inside you something that lives forever. It’s called a soul. Your soul contains the essence of who you are. Your personality. Your thoughts. Your memory. You need to understand that your soul – the real you – will live forever in this horrible place called Hell. You are in great danger! It’s time to wake up! You are being deceived by Prince Rebel, who is actually the god of this train. He and his demons specialise in deceit and they often use human instruments to perpetuate this deceit.’

At this point, there were gasps of shock and cries of derision from some in the audience in almost equal measure. Others sat in a kind of stunned stupor.

‘I don’t like your use of the word sinners when referring to us,’ a young man yelled loudly.

‘Of course you don’t,’ Herald replied calmly and with a faint smile. ‘That’s because you are a sinner. We all are. But keep listening. There’s good news coming up.’

An elderly man shouted, ‘According to you, there’s some kind of life outside the train engaging in a battle between good and evil. Frankly, I think all this talk about a god and this Prince Nicholas Rebel is ridiculous.’

Herald continued undaunted.

‘The fact that there’s life outside the train shouldn’t surprise you. You can see these containers of life-sustaining items on the platforms at our regular service stops. Where do you suppose they come from?'

'And you're suggesting that they come from God, are you?' one young woman shouted in a derisory tone.

'I'm not suggesting it, lady. I'm stating it emphatically.'

'How can you know that?' she shouted back defiantly. 'You can't prove that.'

'Who else but God would freely give us everything we need to sustain life and health?'

His comments caused some members of the audience to murmur and gesture animatedly to others around them. Many let their feelings be known by their loud comments.

'I find your statement that we are born with a corrupt nature deeply offensive. There are a lot of good people on the train,' one middle-aged woman yelled.

'You're telling us that we're all going to Hell forever and ever,' a young lady said. 'I think you're just trying to scare us into accepting The Message. What you're teaching is a fear religion.'

It was clear by this time that John Herald was not only a gifted and engaging speaker, he was also a brave one. He held up a hand to appeal for calm.

'My friends, the information that I am sharing with you today is not something that I have made up. It is contained in The Message and it is different from any other book. Much false information has been disseminated about The Message by people who, for reasons of their own, are biased against it. I am here to tell you the truth about The Message.'

An elderly man in the audience held up a hand to speak. Herald paused and nodded to him to go ahead.

'That is very sad but it does explain some things I've always wondered about. But what can we do about this state of affairs?'

Herald nodded slowly and carried on speaking.

'I'm coming to that. This situation grieved God greatly and, many years ago, He sent His Servant, Victor Love to explain The Message to us. Victor Love lived a perfect life as an example to us of how to obey God's Law. He showed us how to love God and people too. But the train authorities rejected The Message and killed Him. Or, at least they thought they had killed Him. But He is not dead. He suffered greatly to bring us the truth but He is very much alive. His enemies think they defeated Him but what looks like a defeat to them is actually a great victory. It has worked out perfectly in accordance with the plan of God. His suffering has in effect become the payment for all the evil we have done. It enables all who accept Victor Love as their King to be forgiven by God. Victor Love was received up into Heaven and will one day return with an angelic army as King of the whole train – in fact, King of the whole world. The train's journey will cease at that time. He will set up a worldwide kingdom that will last forever and His capital city will be King's City. One day, the End Section of the train will be decoupled and will travel on to King's City. Those who believe will go to the End Section when the time is right. They will know when that time comes. King Victor has promised to meet us there. Everyone who believes The Message and vows allegiance to Victor Love as his King is acceptable to God. This belief – this faith – purifies us in the sight of God and means we will be accounted worthy to enter King's City. When King Victor returns, He will bring with Him the souls of all the believers who have died. All believers – those who have died previously and those still alive at that time – will be given new bodies suitable for eternal life and we will reign with King Victor in His kingdom forever. This is salvation, my friends. King Victor will judge those who have refused to believe and condemn them to Hell along with Prince Nicholas Rebel and his demons.'

When Herald spoke of Victor Love, eternal life and a future judgement, many scoffed.

'I don't believe Victor Love ever existed,' a young man shouted. 'He's just a myth.'

'I do believe he existed but I think he was just an ordinary man,' another young man shouted. 'He was a good teacher with some good ideas but He's dead now. He's not coming back. If He was going to return, He'd have returned by now.'

The mention of Victor Love as a real, historical Person who would return to bring the train's journey to an end and to rule the world incensed many in the audience but others wanted to hear more.

An irate old man growled, 'You believers in Victor Love have formed yourselves into groups and organisations and churches throughout the whole train. You seem to be making this Victor Love fellow out to be a kind of Messiah figure. Who or what is He in your view?'

'Everything that God is, Victor Love is.'

Scornful voices could be clearly heard all around the room as Herald referred to Victor Love in such exalted terms. Others appealed for peace for Herald to continue.

'Everyone is either a believer or an unbeliever according to how they respond to The Message. We have only one lifetime in which to determine our own eternal destination.'

An old man stood up and laughed scornfully. 'You said this Victor Love fellow will make King's City the capital city of the whole Earth! Have you ever been there? It's been battered by many years of fighting over it. It's badly in need of renovation. Some world capital city that would be!'

'It is abandoned and forsaken now but it will be renovated when the King returns. It will be totally transformed and will become the most desirable place on Earth to live.'

At this point, a smartly dressed, middle-aged man asked to make a comment.

'I would like to try to summarise everything you have said today in my own words just to satisfy myself that I've understood you. Is that okay?'

John Herald smiled and nodded. 'Sure, go ahead,' he said.

The man looked around at the audience and began to speak in a loud, cultured voice.

'God created our forefathers, then Prince Nicholas Rebel, or Nick Rebel as I know him, conned them into disobeying God. Their natures were corrupted as a result, so God rejected them. Rebel was then free to deceive them and their descendants as much as he liked and, as a result, this whole train is deceived.'

Some members of the audience began to laugh quietly as the man continued.

'Many generations later, this person that you call Victor Love appeared from somewhere and lived a perfect life so that he could be killed. Or was he really killed? Then God proclaimed that everyone who believes in Victor Love is acceptable to Him and will live forever with Him in Heaven. They will be saved from an eternity in Hell. This Victor Love fellow, who wasn't powerful enough to defeat His enemies when He came the first time, will return one day with an army of angels to this pathetic place called King's City from where He will rule the whole Earth, judge all His enemies and condemn them to Hell. Then Earth will become the new Heaven. Have I got it right, Mr. Herald?'

The appreciative laughs from the audience grew louder. Some applauded the man.

‘I wouldn’t have put it that way myself, sir, but you have summarised the main points reasonably well,’ Herald answered.

‘Then what you have said sounds very strange to my ears, Mr. Herald,’ the man replied. ‘I think all your learning has made you mad.’

‘No I am not mad, my friend. What I have said is true. Every word of it.’

‘I feel sorry for all you believers,’ an elderly man shouted. ‘You’ve put your faith in this Victor Love fellow. You are so sure He’s going to show up again and rule the world that you’ve given up on this present life. You’ve given up today for tomorrow.’

‘Whatever we have given up in this life will be as nothing compared to the reward that King Victor will give us when He returns.’

‘What you are preaching is just another religion,’ one middle-aged man yelled. ‘And I reject all religion.’

‘That’s your right to believe that, sir. But I would have to disagree when you say that what I am preaching is just another religion. I believe it is quite different from any other religion. In fact, I would hesitate to even call The Message a religion at all, at least in the sense that the word is generally understood.’

‘You condemn everyone who disagrees with you,’ another middle-aged man shouted. ‘I agree with what it said on the protesters’ banner. You are using hate speech.’

‘No I am not using hate speech, my friend. I’ll tell you what hate speech is. Hate speech is, if I know someone’s behaviour will cause him to end up in Hell and I tell him he’ll go to Heaven, that’s hate speech. What I’m telling you is love speech.’

The noise from the audience grew louder and some shouted out derisory comments.

Herald shouted above the noise, ‘I believe that the return of King Victor Love is imminent. You must decide whether to believe what I have told you or whether to reject it. Think carefully, my friends. Salvation is being offered to you today. Your eternity is hanging in the balance. And I wouldn’t delay making this decision too long if I were you.’

Herald then brought his presentation to a close with an urgent appeal to believe The Message and vow allegiance to Victor Love as their King.

As people left, many grumbled loudly. Others around me discussed the presentation with some indicating that they would like to listen to Herald again. As I sat thinking about what Herald had said, there was something about it that seemed to ring true. Maybe it was his resolute conviction and his sincerity.

My guilty past flashed before me like the passing countryside. I felt the burden of my guilt grow heavier.

Questioning Herald

After the lecture, I joined four young people who were waiting to ask Herald some questions. We had to wait for ten minutes or so as a large, middle-aged lady was hogging Herald's attention. We started talking about the lecture and about ourselves as we waited. There were two white men, Bertie Rich and Mark Waverer, a mixed race lady called Nicole Enigma and an Asian-looking man called Malik Fearful. They all seemed to be as interested as I was about The Message. Finally, the large lady left and we were able to speak with Herald.

Bertie Rich, said, 'Why don't most people want to believe this Message?'

'Because the truth is a mystery to them. It's as though they have a veil over their eyes. As a result, The Message seems like foolishness to them,' Herald replied.

Malik Fearful said, 'But not everyone has heard The Message. Surely they can't be condemned to Hell if they have never heard The Message?'

'Everyone does not have to hear The Message,' Herald replied with a gentle emphasis.

'But did you not just say that it is only by hearing and heeding The Message that a person can be acceptable to God?' Fearful persisted.

'That is true, but everyone can observe the view from the train. Everyone can see the creation. God's existence should be obvious to everyone just by looking at His marvellous creation. God has revealed Himself to everyone through what He has made. The creation declares His existence and His glory. You might describe the creation as a kind of universal language without words. The creation is a powerful witness that God exists and that is enough to condemn people to Hell. However, the creation is not adequate to save people from Hell. Only The Message can do that but God is not obligated to have everyone who has ever lived hear The Message. In fact, He is not obligated to get The Message to anyone at all. The only thing God is obligated to do, as far as sinners are concerned, is to send sinners to Hell. Those of us who have heard The Message should rejoice that we have heard it and understand that it is only because of the grace of God that we have heard it. Now I believe that God is able to convey The Message to people in other ways too. I believe He can enlighten peoples' minds in a number of ways. But the only way to be sure of salvation is to accept The Message and King Victor Love.'

'You said that God is loving, yet He condemns people to Hell forever. What kind of love is this?' Nicole asked.

'I would say that Hell is what it is because God is who He is. God is loving; but He is also holy and righteous. Hell shows the justice of God against evil that is not repented of. Hell should be the ultimate deterrent against persisting in evil. It should drive us to The Message and King Victor.'

'But I don't understand why most people don't want to believe The Message,' Mark said. 'You say that it's like a veil is over their eyes and it seems like foolishness to them. But it seems clear enough to me.'

'Then thank God for that, Mark. Most people on this train want nothing to do with The Message. They prefer the way of our forefathers.'

'But surely they don't want to end up in Hell?' Mark replied.

'No of course they don't. But they don't believe the train will end up there.'

Bertie looked puzzled. 'But I'm struggling to understand how the majority of people can be so deceived about something that will affect where they spend eternity.'

'Never underestimate Prince Nick Rebel. He deceived our forefathers and is still deceiving most people on the train.'

The look on Bertie's face changed to amazement. 'That is incredible! Most people on the train deceived!'

'It is incredible but true.'

'You have explained that the train and all unbelievers on it will eventually end up in Hell. But we have often seen many dead bodies being unloaded. What happens to them and to all those who die during the journey?' asked Nicole.

'At death the soul is separated from the body. The souls of unbelievers go directly to Hell. They arrive before the train gets there. The souls of believers go directly to Heaven but they will return to King's City with King Victor and the rest of us who are believers will meet them there.'

Intrigued by Nicole Enigma

There was something about Nicole Enigma that held my attention.

Beautiful, mixed race features, around forty, slim and medium height, black hair swept back into a ponytail, wearing jeans and a tee-shirt. The combination of her smooth ebony skin, her blue almond-shaped eyes and the air of confidence she exuded would have made her stand out in any crowd. She reminded me of the kind of people who are used to wielding authority. There was a passionate intensity about her questions. While the rest of us shared something about our lives and backgrounds, she did not. So I concluded that she was secretive and I wondered why. Was she hiding something? That made me more interested in her. Where did she come from? I wondered if she had a husband or a boyfriend, what she did for a living, who her friends were. There was something about her that I found interesting. As I looked at her, certain words came to mind. Confident and calm but also quiet and intense. She had an intriguing aura about her. Mysterious lady. She attracted my interest although I felt she was trying to deflect attention from herself.

Calvary Junction and the End Section

'You mentioned in your lecture that the End Section of the train will be decoupled from the rest of the train and will travel to King's City,' Bertie asked. 'What is this End Section and where will this separation happen?'

'The End Section is the last two carriages of the train and it will be separated from the rest of the train at a place called Calvary Junction. We will then go on to King's City and the glorious rendezvous with King Victor. If you believe in King Victor, prepare to go to the End Section as soon as you possibly can. I believe His return is drawing near. There's no time to lose.'

'But why didn't you urge your audience to go to the End Section?' Nicole asked. 'You told them the End Section would be decoupled one day but you didn't tell them where or when.'

'They didn't ask me where or when. The reason they didn't ask me is because they didn't believe it would ever happen. If they had asked me like you have asked me I would've told them.'

Chosen?

During a lull in our conversation, Herald looked intently at the five of us and said, ‘You know, I think the five of you have been chosen to go to the End Section. I think the interest you are showing indicates that.’

‘Chosen by whom?’ Nicole asked forcefully, with an edge to her voice.

‘By God of course. He draws people to Himself like a magnet.’

‘But don’t I have any say in it? Can’t I decide not to go?’ Nicole demanded.

‘You can resist Him for a while but only for a while. Your corrupt nature will resist. Prince Nick Rebel and his demons will try to stop you. But, if you have been chosen, God’s will for you will prevail. In the end, He will make you want to go.’

‘But why would God choose us to go to the End Section and not any of the other people in the audience?’ Bertie Rich asked. ‘Do you mean we’ve been chosen and they haven’t been chosen?’

Herald looked thoughtful.

‘It’s not easy to explain. Let me put it this way. You do have free will, of course. Everybody does. God knows our hearts and I believe that He chooses those who really want to be chosen.’

‘Does that mean that there are more people who are not chosen than those who are chosen?’ Malik Fearful asked.

‘Yes, those who are chosen are relatively few.’

‘Is there anything else we need to know, John?’ Fearful asked again.

‘No one can know everything there is to know about God, at least not in this lifetime. But there are some general things you should know about Him. He knows everything. He is all powerful. He is everywhere. He is sovereign, that is, He can do whatever He decides to do. He is righteous. He is merciful. He loves us with a possessive love. He will not tolerate us worshipping anything else as God. He will not share His glory with another. He is well aware of our tendency to worship people and things. We must worship Him alone.’

Paul Comforter

‘If I’m right about you and you have really been chosen the next step for you is to speak to a man called Paul Comforter. He has been sent to do this work by the leaders of our group of believers. Paul is a faithful messenger who refreshes the souls of those who have sent him. He also refreshes the souls of all sincere seekers after truth. He has arranged to meet anyone from this meeting who is interested in The Message in one week’s time. That will give you time to think about what you have heard from me today. If you want to gain a deeper insight into the practical implications of accepting The Message, he will be able to help you. He will also encourage you to make a firm commitment to travel to the End Section with him. You will find him sitting on his own. He is a tall, black guy in his forties, slim with black hair and a short neatly-trimmed beard. Comforter has an encyclopaedic knowledge of The Message. He will tell you about it and give you your own copy. Then he will accompany you to the End Section. Tell him I have sent you.'

'When is he going to the End Section?' Mark asked.

'Soon. Very soon.'

'Where can we meet this man Paul Comforter?' Nicole enquired.

'He will be in the Refreshment Carriage from mid-morning one week from today.'

'I'll think very seriously about going along to meet him,' I said.

Bertie Rich said, 'I intend to go. I'd like to hear more about The Message.'

'Same here. I want to talk to him,' Mark Waverer said.

'I think I'll go along too,' Fearful said. 'I don't know if I'll go to the End Section but I want to hear more from Paul Comforter.'

'I won't go now,' said Nicole Enigma. 'I need more time to think about it.'

With that she left abruptly, with just the briefest of nods to the rest of us. With her went my hope of finding out more about her. Strange lady.

'So there are four of us. Bertie Rich, Malik Fearful, Mark Waverer and myself. Will you come with us?' I asked Herald.

'No, I can't come with you. There are others on this train that I must reach with The Message. I hope to catch up with you later at the End Section.'

The Battle Ahead

'Just one more thing,' Herald said, as though he had just thought of something he should have told us earlier. 'If you do decide to meet Paul Comforter and to make a definite commitment to going to the End Section, you need to know that you will have entered into a battle. Not a physical battle, a spiritual battle. And this battle will take two forms. It will be an external battle and an internal battle.'

'What do you mean, John?' I asked.

'If you do decide to follow the true God – the God who inspired The

Message – you will have chosen to reject the god of the train, Prince Nick Rebel. As a result, you will meet external opposition. You will be discriminated against and persecuted by some non-believers. Even by those nearest and dearest to you. You will feel compelled to tell the good news of The Message to anyone who will listen. And you will find, as you do, that most will reject it. They will also turn away from you, even those you considered to be your friends. You will also have to resist clever and destructive heresies from false teachers. But that is not all. You will have effectively become different people. Actions and words and thoughts that defined the way you were – the person you used to be – will then be abhorrent to you. Consequently, you will find yourself in an internal battle between your mind and your flesh. Your mind will be set on obeying God but your flesh will try to get you to revert back to your old ways. You will constantly have to resist the pull of your flesh and obey what your mind is telling you to do. And you will probably find that this internal battle is harder to fight than the external battle. It will not be easy. You will need to develop the habit of regular daily prayer and reading of The Message. And you will find that God will help you.'

Herald looked at each of us anxiously.

'I felt I needed to warn you. The way to the End Section is not easy. Are you still interested in The Message? Do you still want to meet Paul Comforter?'

We thanked him for his honesty and assured him that we still wanted to find out more about The Message from Paul Comforter. We then went our separate ways and agreed to meet in the Refreshment Carriage in one week's time. But I still wasn't sure. It was a massive decision. I didn't know if I was ready to make it.

The Train Police Office

As Bertie Rich, Malik Fearful, Mark Waverer and I left the Meeting Room, we saw two people standing by the door. One of them was Nicole Enigma and the other was a large burly uniformed member of the Train Police. As we approached, Nicole Enigma walked away hurriedly. I wondered why she speaking to him.

'Come with me, gentlemen please,' the policeman said in a deep authoritarian voice that sounded more like a command than a request.

Warned by Sergeant Gordon Hostile

We exchanged wary glances and followed meekly. We had little choice. He led us into an office on the same upstairs level as the Meeting Room in the next carriage along. It had the words "Train Police Office" and "Sergeant Gordon Hostile" on the door. He closed the door behind us and took four chairs from a corner of the room and placed them in front of the desk. He then sat down behind the desk, motioning us to sit on the chairs.

When we were seated, he looked at each of us gravely.

'Well, gentlemen, I must warn you that the Train Police take a dim view of the type of meetings that you have just attended. I know what Mr. Herald said and I have a recording that can be used in court to form the basis of a prosecution. I have also been informed about the discussion the four of you had with Mr. Herald after the meeting. It is because of the interest you have shown in Mr. Herald's lecture that you are here now.'

My immediate thought was, Nicole Enigma! Who else would know about the discussion we had with Herald after his lecture? I wondered how someone so beautiful could be so deceitful.

'Now we are reasonable people in the Train Police. We believe in free speech but we regard these types of meeting as potentially divisive. We have had Mr. Herald and Mr. Watchman under surveillance for some time. Mr. Watchman has recently been arrested for public order offences. In due course, we will deal with Mr. Herald too. But I wanted to warn you that you are in danger of being arrested if you persist in showing an interest in the ideas of people like Mr. Herald.'

'But what's the harm in his ideas, sir?' I asked.

'What's the harm? What's the harm?' Sergeant Hostile slammed his fist on the table in a sudden display of anger that startled us. 'Mr. Herald spoke of this train heading for Hell, as though there is such a place. He spoke of the train being influenced, directly or indirectly, by this fictitious person Prince Nicholas Rebel. He claimed that The Message is divinely inspired and that other religious books are not and that we are all condemned to Hell if we don't believe The Message. He also spoke about somebody called Victor Love who apparently lived and died long ago but Herald claimed he is still alive. He said this guy was sent by God to teach us how to live. He said that someday this guy is going to return with a big army of angels and declare himself King of the world! Then he will condemn everyone to Hell who doesn't submit to him! That is what I call divisive and I will not tolerate it! Do you understand?'

We all nodded. He had made himself perfectly clear.

Interviewed by Nicole Enigma

Sergeant Hostile took a deep breath and appeared to become tense.

'Now someone from a special branch of the Train Police Department called Train Security has asked to speak to you,' he said gravely, as though we were to face a terrible ordeal. He rose and beckoned us to follow him. He led us to the door of an adjoining office and knocked on the door.

A voice from inside said, 'Come in.'

He went inside.

'Here are the people you asked to speak to, Ms. Enigma.'

Ms. Enigma! Train Security! I had wondered about her. Now I was about to find out a lot more about this "Ms. Enigma".

'Show them in, Sergeant Hostile.'

He motioned for us to go in and closed the door behind us. I had the impression he didn't want to spend any more time with Ms. Nicole Enigma than was absolutely necessary for the furtherance of his duties.

It was a small office. Enigma sat behind a desk. She looked up from some papers she had been reading and glanced at each of us impassively. She still looked pretty but she looked different too. Gone was the casual look. She wore a smart black jacket with white buttons and a grey blouse. She looked formidable and ominous. She had feigned interest in The Message only to find out more about it and those who were showing an interest in it. She was a devious, conniving… I began to despise her.

'Bertie Rich, Malik Fearful, Mark Waverer and Simon Seeker,' she said, looking at each of us in turn. 'Let me tell you something. I know as much about this group you are seeking to join as any of you do. More probably. So I know why you are going to meet this man Paul Comforter. It's to help you decide whether or not to go to the End Section. I was at Mr. Herald's meeting too, remember. We at Train Security regard this group as a threat to the security of the train. We have you under constant surveillance. We monitor your movements continually. There is nothing you can do, nowhere you can go, that we don't know about.'

'But, Nicole… eh, Ms. Enigma...' Bertie Rich tried to say something.

'Mr. Rich! Don't interrupt! I know how highly you regard this person called Victor Love. The strength of any believer's commitment to this group is largely determined by how highly you regard Him. If you can demonstrate to me that you have changed your minds about joining this group in the End Section, I will be prepared to call off our surveillance. But I need to be sure you are telling me the truth. So here's what I propose. If you denounce Victor Love as a fraud right here and right now, I will call off our surveillance. I will also remove your names from our list of persons who are of interest to us. What do you say, gentlemen?'

There was a tense silence.

'That would be tantamount to blasphemy,' Waverer responded. 'You can do whatever you like, but I won't deny him or blaspheme his name.'

The rest of us agreed.

'All right, gentlemen. You have made your decision and I will make mine regarding you. I will continue to monitor your every movement. I can't stop you from going on this fool's errand to talk to Mr. Comforter and going on to the End Section but, if you step out of line, I will have you arrested and you will go to prison for a long time. If I ever have cause to speak to you again, you will be in serious trouble. Goodbye, gentlemen.'

We trooped dejectedly out of the office to be confronted by Sergeant Hostile.

'You can go now but you'd better not give me any reason to call you into this office again on this matter. Consider yourselves warned. Now go.'

We did not need to be invited twice to leave his office. We left the office and walked downstairs and congregated on the lower level.

'That sounded pretty threatening,' Fearful said. 'I don't think he was bluffing.'

The rest of us agreed.

'I don't know about you,' I said, 'but I intend to meet this Paul Comforter. I believe what John Herald said and I want to hear more. Comforter will be waiting in the next carriage along – the Refreshment Carriage. I want to hear what he has to say.'

'But you could go to prison,' Fearful replied. 'We could receive very long sentences.'

I looked around to ensure that no one could hear me and then I looked at each man again.

'I know. But if The Message spoken of by Herald is true, then it is more important than freedom. It's more important that life itself. It involves where we will spend eternity. What could be more important than that?'

There was a tense silence.

'I agree with you, Simon,' Bertie Rich said softly. 'I want to hear more. I'll come with you. But we must go separately to avoid suspicion.'

Mark Waverer nodded in agreement. 'Same here. It is dangerous but I just have to hear what this Comforter fellow has to say.'

Malik Fearful Leaves

The three of us looked at Malik Fearful for his response.

He shook his head slowly. 'Sorry. Things are going well for me right now and I don't want to take the risk. It's just too dangerous.'

He wished us well and walked away.

Bertie, Mark and I looked at each other in silence.

Finally, Mark summed up the way we were feeling. 'I'm beginning to get the impression that if we persist in trying to find out about The Message, this will not be the last time we'll be in trouble with the authorities.'

Bertie and I nodded our heads in agreement.

I felt nervous. I had never been in trouble with the authorities before. But my mind was made up.

'I don't know about you guys,' I said quietly, 'but I have to find out what this is all about.'

Bertie and Mark agreed that we had to find out about The Message.

'As Bertie said, we must go separately,' Mark advised. 'It's the next carriage along so we should be able to make sure we are not being followed.'

With that, we left separately and made our way to the Refreshment Carriage.

Stop the train, I want to get off!

Thinking It Over

When we left the office of the Train Police, we went our separate ways for one week to consider what we had heard about The Message from John Herald and to decide whether we were willing to forsake all and proceed to the End Section. I sat alone in my cabin and thought about the developments of the previous week.

First, a stranger called Luke Watchman had told me about something he called The Message, which claimed that there was life outside the train. He seemed very sure about that. He said the train was heading for a destination of eternal gloom and suffering called Hell but, if I believed The Message, I could escape that and be taken instead to a different destination – a place of peace and happiness – called Heaven. He urged me to go and listen to a lecture by a man called John Herald.

Then the Ticket Inspector talked to me as though I was an idiot just because I had lost my ticket and was feeling a bit disoriented at that time. It was while talking to him that I saw Watchman being arrested. Then Cyril Weary in the Communications Centre insisted that everyone on the train was being – for lack of a better term – brainwashed. His opinion was that Watchman and everyone who believed him were stupid. Then I went to listen to Herald's lecture because I wanted to find out more. Herald filled in the details about The Message and he said that if we wanted to escape Hell and go to Heaven instead, we would have to leave everything and journey to the last two carriages on the train. The End Section, he called it. When some of us showed an interest in what he was saying, he said he thought we had been called by God. He pleaded with us to seek counsel with a guy in the Refreshment Carriage called Paul Comforter with a view to making a firm commitment to go to the End Section. I found

Herald very persuasive but many in the audience thought he was mad. Then some of us were escorted to the office of the Train Police and given a good telling off for showing an interest in Herald's lecture. Whew! It had been quite a week! What was I to make of it all?

I found The Message intriguing but the claim that life existed outside the train sounded fantastic. Could such life really exist – God and angels and all that? And was Victor Love still alive and about to take over the world? It took faith to believe that. And even if I did believe it, the total commitment required to respond to it was daunting. I was being asked to make a very big decision. A decision I didn't ask for and one I didn't want to make. I was being required to take a giant leap of faith and leave everything I knew and had worked for to travel to this End Section. I was being asked to let go of things that were familiar and comfortable and to let something unfamiliar take their place. I was being required to surrender my life. I found this scary. Must I really abandon myself to a god I didn't know? And I wasn't even sure there was an End Section anyway. What if I went all the way there only to find it was all a big con? I would feel humiliated. I would have to return and admit I had been conned. And I didn't have long to make up my mind. One week, that was all. One week to decide whether or not to meet up with this Paul Comforter fellow in the Refreshment Carriage. One week to decide whether to turn over control of my life to this group.

Herald said he thought perhaps I had been chosen to go to the End Section. I wanted to believe that such a god existed because that would mean there just might be a reason for this life. But I wasn't sure I did. And even if He did exist, why would He call me anyway? I was just an ordinary guy. I began to think of reasons why I should resist this call, or whatever it was, and forget about The Message.

A Visit from Max Joker and Craig Sharp

While I sat in my cabin considering such things, there was a knock on the door. It was my two oldest and best friends, Max Joker and Craig Sharp. I looked at them with a mixture of delight and amazement. I wondered how they knew where I was living. As I hesitated by the open door, they both brushed past me as though they were used to visiting me in this cabin and sat on the sofa. After some general small talk, I asked them what they thought about The

Message. Both of them said much the same thing. 'Forget all about it, Simon. It's all nonsense.' Maybe they were right. Max and Craig invited me to go with them to a nearby lounge carriage where they sold our favourite beers and played our favourite music. I told them I was tired and needed an early night and they left shortly after.

Contemplating Futility – the Bleak Alternative

I wanted to get away from The Message and be able to get on with my life the way I did before I heard it. I tried to put The Message out of my head and think about other things. I would exercise my free will. I would defer a decision. But I started to feel guilty about that. I had no peace. I found it hard to sleep. In addition to my thoughts about The Message, I couldn't get Cyril Weary's insistence that everyone on the train was being brainwashed out of my head. It filled me with indignation. There was no escape from my thoughts. Every waking hour I was plagued by them. A voice from deep within me cried, 'Stop the train, I want to get off!' But the only way to get off the train was to die. And I wasn't ready for death yet.

Then I asked myself, 'What is the alternative to believing The Message?' I came to the conclusion that the answer was futility. I mean that this physical life by itself is incomprehensible, even unknowable. Life is meaningless unless there is some purpose to it all. It is also fleeting because life is short. Death is our destiny. Human effort and achievements are futile because one day you have to leave everything you've earned to someone who hasn't worked for it. That person will have the benefit of everything I've accumulated. That person might be unworthy of all they have inherited but he or she will get the credit and I will be forgotten.

How can there be any meaning in a secular view of life? And how can there be peace if there's no meaning to life? All my past efforts to find peace had ended in dismal failure. Every time I got what I wanted, it never seemed to satisfy me for long. Every time I didn't get what I wanted, I became miserable. But maybe those things wouldn't have been good for me anyway. Maybe this is part of some grand scheme designed to lead people to the conclusion that peace can't be found apart from God. Maybe this is how He shows His love for us. Maybe He uses futility to lead us to Him. Perhaps God doesn't force anyone to revere Him but He makes it impossible for anyone to have peace unless he or she does revere Him. It was beginning to look like life was futile apart from God. Hearing something of value without responding to it is pretty futile too and The Message claimed to have eternal value. Was it now time for drastic action? Was it time to change my priorities?

I Don't Belong Here Anymore

Suppose God really did exist and suppose He really had chosen me? Was I resisting His call? My friends had both said that The Message was nonsense. But what if God had chosen me and not them? They probably would say it was nonsense, wouldn't they? I started to feel that I no longer belonged where I lived. Something about The Message had begun to change my way of thinking.

After a few days, I became aware of a sense that I was being drawn by a power that I couldn't resist to respond to The Message. It was like an invisible magnet was pulling me to go along to the Refreshment Carriage to meet Paul Comforter. The feeling began to feel urgent and persistent. It began to feel bigger than everything else in my life. It began to feel irresistible. I decided that I had to go and talk to Paul Comforter. What was the harm in that? In the end, the decision was an easy one to make. And what did I have to lose anyway?

The Refreshment Carriage

Refreshed by Paul Comforter

Following our week's break to make a decision on the proposed journey to the End Section, I went along to the Refreshment Carriage. There I saw Bertie Rich and Mark Waverer sitting beside a man fitting John Herald's description of Paul Comforter – a black man in his forties, slim with black hair and a short neatly-trimmed beard. What his description did not include was that Comforter was also very muscular. He looked like he had been an athlete of some kind in his youth.

'Hello. Paul Comforter I presume?' I smiled.

He rose to greet me, extending his hand. He was tall. Over six feet. His warm smile revealed even, perfectly formed white teeth.

'That's me. And you must be Simon Seeker.' His voice was deep but with a gentleness in it.

He had a kind face although his nose looked like it had once been broken. Yet there was a softness in his blue eyes. An inner tranquility seemed to shine through his face.

I took a seat beside them as the others told him that a man called John Herald sent us to ask him to explain more fully about The Message and its implications for the way we have to live.

'We want to know all there is to know about The Message,' Bertie Rich said. 'We need to know what is involved in making a commitment to The Message. John told us that we would be refreshed by what you had to say. He also said that you would escort those of us who want to go to the End Section.'

He nodded thoughtfully. 'It's great to meet the three of you. I'm sure we'll be refreshed together as we talk about The Message.'

The three of us sat opposite him and looked expectantly at him, rather like three people who were about to be interviewed.

He looked at the three of us in turn and smiled reassuringly.

'The most refreshing thing you can do in this life is to make a firm commitment to being a life-long believer in The Message and King Victor Love, whatever it takes. King Victor is the Way. The Way leads to the End Section and on to the eternal kingdom in King's City. This commitment will change your whole outlook on life. The most refreshing things you can hear are those things which pertain to the Way. You will be encouraged and inspired as you learn about King Victor and what He taught. You have believed The Message from John Herald and now you are invited to make a firm commitment. The time has now come for believers to make their way to the End Section. But I need to counsel the three of you first to be sure you are ready to go there.'

Choosing his words carefully, he said, 'The first thing you need to know is that there is only one way to enter King's City and to receive eternal life in the kingdom of King Victor. King Victor is the Truth. There are many deceivers and you must beware of counterfeit messages which teach that there are other ways to King's City.

'The second thing you need to know is that you must seek King's City with all your heart and be willing to sacrifice whatever it takes to get there.'

'What do we need to sacrifice?' Bertie Rich enquired anxiously.

'Everything, Bertie. Absolutely everything. Time, money, goods, even your very life.'

'I have so much in the way of material things and my wealth is growing all the time,' Bertie said. 'And even though it hasn't brought me happiness and peace, it would be so hard to give up my wealth.'

Comforter looked at him anxiously and nodded slowly.

'The third thing you need to know is that you must be willing to obey the Law of God here and now. The Law is the basis of the way of life in King Victor's kingdom. This will mean rejecting your former hopes and habits and lifestyle. You will need to grow in the knowledge and rules of the kingdom. You will not be able to do this perfectly, no one can. But you must be willing to correct errors when you discover them and keep on growing. This will entail a complete change of direction in your life. Frankly, you will have to become like a different person. You will find that your former friends will be friends no longer. Perhaps even family members will reject the new person you have become. As you journey to the End Section, you will meet opposition and some of it could be fierce.'

Comforter looked at us closely, as though looking for a reaction.

There followed a short period of silence as we considered the implications of this change of direction in our lives. It was a life-changing decision for all of us. Decisions didn't come any bigger than this.

'John Herald told us that we'll feel compelled to tell others about The Message,' I said.

'That's true. We must convey The Message to others. It's the most wonderful good news. In fact, it's the only really good news around today. Most people will reject it but a few will accept it. Many of those who reject it will hate you for telling them about it.'

'John Herald warned us that we would be involved in a battle if we decide to go to the End Section. What will this battle be like?' Mark asked.

'The battle will be twofold. A battle from outside yourself involving opposition, such as I have described and also an internal battle as your old nature battles with your new nature.'

Another period of thoughtful silence followed.

'Have you made a decision yet?' Comforter asked gently.

'Yes, I want to go to the End Section and on to King's City,' I replied.

'Are you sure?' Comforter enquired.

'Yes, I am sure. I accept that I need Victor Love and His teaching. I want to live for Him from now on. I am willing to give up everything for Him. I want to go to the End Section.'

He looked at Mark Waverer. 'What about you, Mark?'

'I'm willing to give up the failures and frustrations of today for the glories of tomorrow. I want the salvation that is graciously being offered. Count me in.'

Bertie Rich Leaves Sadly

Comforter then turned to Bertie Rich.

'What about you, Bertie? Are you willing to give up everything to get to the End Section and the glories of King's City?'

There was a long pause during which Bertie looked thoughtfully into the distance. Finally, speaking quietly and sadly, he replied,

'I'm sorry. I'm so sorry but I can't. I just can't leave everything I have and everything I expect to have in the future.'

'Why not? What you will receive in King's City will be far greater than anything you have here and now.'

'You don't understand. With money, I have respect. I have power. I have security. I can have the best things that money can buy. I can have everything this life has to offer. I can have the most beautiful women. And you are asking me to give all that up?'

'I'm asking you to be prepared to give it up, Bertie because that's what God is asking you to be prepared to do. You might not have to give anything up but you have to be willing to give everything up.'

'Why can't I just stay here and use my wealth to help to spread The Message?'

'Sorry, Bertie. It doesn't work like that. You can't dictate the terms of your salvation. It must be a total commitment.'

Bertie looked close to tears. He shook his head, avoiding eye contact with any of us. Then he rose slowly and walked away.

'Are you sure you want to go through with this?'

The stillness that followed was hard to endure. Finally, Paul Comforter broke the silence.

'Let me ask you again, are you sure you want to go through with this?'

Mark and I both assured him that we did.

'Then both of you must accompany me to the End Section of the train. That is where all believers must go. This means we must travel in the opposite direction to this train, not only spiritually but literally. I must warn you, friends that it will not be easy. The way is narrow and difficult.'

'As narrow and difficult as walking along the corridor of a moving train?' Mark replied with a wry smile.

'You could put it that way, but are you prepared to go in one week's time?'

'One week's time? I've just had a week to think about whether I would go and listen to John Herald's lecture. Now I'm being given a week to finish up my affairs and leave!' I said.

'That's right. I'm giving you one week to get ready for the journey. We can't delay it any longer.'

I thought about the sudden drastic change it would mean in my plans. I had already charted out a course for my life. Now all that would have to change. All those plans for my career, a family, a house, friends, hobbies. All of it would have to go out the train window, so to speak.

The decision when it came, came suddenly.

'Okay. I'll go. I'll be ready one week from today.' There was a strange mixture of hesitancy and triumph in my voice. It was as though I had been reborn.

'I'm willing to go too,' Mark said with a broad smile. 'How long will the journey to the End Section take, Paul?'

'It's hard to say, Mark. It depends on the progress we make and that depends on the opposition we face. It could take some months.'

'How much luggage will we need?' I enquired.

'It will be best if we travel as lightly as possible, Simon. I think an average sized backpack should suffice.'

'An average sized backpack! That's what I call travelling light!' I exclaimed.

Receiving Copies of The Message

'Now I must tell you about The Message. It is complete and nothing needs to be added. It converts the soul. It testifies of God to us. And it is reliable. It was not written as a history book, but it contains much history. Among the most conservative lists, there are more than one hundred characters that can be conclusively identified within secular history. The Message was not written as a scientific book, but it does not contain any statements which can be shown to be unscientific. There are no mistakes of any kind in it. It makes even simple people wise. It gives spiritual understanding. Even the most brilliant philosophers cannot do this. The words in The Message are founded on wisdom. They are equal, just and proper. The Message speaks of King Victor Love and it will triumph in the end. The Message makes the heart glad because it is fair and just. The words are spotless, clean and without fault. The Message records the sins of men and women but always in a disapproving way. The words in The Message direct us to King Victor Love by Whom we are cleansed and made acceptable to God. The Message leads us to examine our own hearts and to repent of our faults. These words will last forever. They are true and they are righteous. They are more precious than gold. They are sweeter than honey. There is great reward in obeying these words. The Message contains valuable instruction for all people – especially for believers.'

At this point, Comforter paused and looked intently at us. 'Do you have any questions?' he asked.

A calm stillness followed during which I thought carefully about what Comforter had said. His words seemed exciting to me.

'No I don't. Your words have been so refreshing, as we were told they would be,' I said.

'I can't think of any questions at the moment,' Mark said.

'Wonderful!' Comforter exclaimed. He reached out his hand again and we shook hands for a second time as though to seal the deal.

He reached into a bag on the seat beside him and pulled out two thick books, handing a copy to each of us.

'The Message you heard from John Herald is the same Message as in this book. You will need a copy of The Message. Put it in your backpacks. It contains everything you need to know. It has the rules and the wisdom of King Victor. Make sure you read it and meditate on it every day. You will find The Message to be a protection against fear and discouragement and also a weapon to counter the lies of enemies. As we make our way to the End Section, you will need its wise guidance. It is most important that I accompany you to the End Section. As you are new to this way of life and are not yet familiar with The Book, I will be by your side to help you.'

'Thanks. I will treasure my personal copy of The Message. But why do I need to read it and meditate on it every day?' I asked.

'Because it refreshes the soul. As you read it and think on its inspired words, your nature will gradually be changed to become more like that of King Victor and your soul will be refreshed. Often on the journey, you will become weary. Only The Message has the power to refresh a weary traveller.'

'Then I will indeed read it and meditate on it every day,' I said.

'So will I,' Mark replied.

Wise Companions

'But you have emphasised the importance of accompanying us,' I said. 'Although we are new to this way of life and are not yet familiar with the teachings of The Message, why do you need to come along with us? Are we not able to go on our own? Please don't misunderstand me, I'm glad of your company but why is it so important that we go together?'

'Because every believer is refreshed by the company of another believer. As we are travelling in the opposite direction to the train, and as there is so much opposition to The Message, believers need to be continually refreshed by each other's company.'

Assurance

'As you will appreciate, Paul, I am making a drastic change in my life. There may be times when I will wonder if I have done the right thing. How can I have this assurance that it is right to forsake all to follow The Message?' I asked.

'The first thing to remember, Simon is that you know in your heart that your eyes have been opened and that you have turned from darkness to light. Like the unbelievers on this train, you were afflicted by a spiritual blindness. Now your eyes have been opened.

'The second thing is that you have actually turned from darkness to light. You have made the great decision to act on what you know and to live in darkness no longer but to walk in the light from now on.

'Third, you have now turned from the power of the evil Prince Nick Rebel to the power of God.

'You have taken these three steps, Simon. Now you can be assured that the decision you have taken is right.

'The same goes for you, Mark.'

'I suspect that many believers don't have the assurance that they really are believers,' Mark responded.

'That is true, my friend,' Comforter replied. 'But we do.'

Excitement Rises

'Now that the three of us have been refreshed by our discussion of The Message and all it means, we can now go back to our cabins and prepare for the journey to the End Section. I'm really looking forward to starting the journey,' I said, feeling relief that the decision had been made and excitement at the prospect of the journey ahead. 'It's exciting. Like going on a pilgrimage.'

'Like a pilgrimage, Simon?' Comforter smiled. 'You could put it that way I suppose. Now that we have been refreshed by each other's company, it's time to make preparations for the journey ahead.'

'John Herald told us that the train will separate at a place called Calvary Junction,' I said.

'That is true. At Calvary Junction, the train will stop and the last two carriages will be detached from the rest of the train. I don't want to go into too much detail at this stage, but a second train will then be formed from the two detached carriages. The people in the detached carriages have made their decision that they want to go to King's City. The locomotive at the front of the train will take the main part of the train on to its prescribed destination. The points will then be changed at Calvary Junction and another driver and crew will join us. The separated section comprising the last two carriages will then go on a different route to King's City.'

On making a commitment to The Message, I felt elated. It was like being reborn.

'Remember, we must leave in one week's time. No one knows when the separation of the End Section will take place so it is most important that we get to the End Section as quickly as we can,' Comforter reminded us.

'Now I must stress, if the worst happens and we die en route, we will be taken to Heaven anyway. We will then return with King Victor to King's City. We have made the commitment and our salvation is assured. But it would be so wonderful to meet fellow believers en route. We will meet people on the way who will try to stop us. They will use every argument, every temptation, to get us to change our minds and go back to the way we were. We must resist. We might encounter violence. Whatever the difficulties, whatever the cost, we must continue on to reach our goal of the End Section.'

With that, Mark Waverer and I bade a joyous farewell to Paul Comforter and arranged to meet him in the Refreshment Carriage for the journey in one week's time.

Telling our Families

Home Sweet Home

After making the momentous decision to journey to the End Section in one week's time, Mark and I returned to our respective cabins to prepare for our departure. We needed to pack a few essentials into our small backpacks for the journey. As I was conscientiously deciding what to take for the journey, there was a knock on my cabin door. It was my mother, Annie. I was amazed. How did she know where to find me?

'Ah, Simon. There you are,' she said as she brushed past me into the room. She looked around the room the way she used to inspect my room at home.

'It's been so long since you visited me that I thought you'd forgotten where your dear old mother lives. I decided to come and fetch you and bring you back home. I've heard about this religious idea you've got now. We've got a couple of visitors. You can tell us all about it.'

It was a strange feeling following my elderly mother to her home, not knowing where she lived. I kept thinking of questions I wanted to ask her. I followed her as she purposefully negotiated the corridors of several carriages as though she had been doing it all her life. I had to walk briskly to keep up with her. It reminded me of my childhood. She stopped at the door of her cabin. On entering, I discovered that my younger brother, Alfie lived there also. My older cousin Betty Posh and my younger nephew Albert Bright were visiting.

I felt anxious about telling them what I had come to believe. I didn't feel as though I was a good example of how a believer should behave. They knew me better than anyone. They knew my faults. But they wanted to know and I had to tell them what The Message was all about. The train was bound for Hell, simple as that. I had to warn them. Whether or not they accepted The Message, nothing would ever be the same from now on. If they rejected it, they would need to understand that they would always be my family and I would always love them, but I have a new family now. All believers were my family now, in a spiritual sense.

Mother's Response

After dinner that night, I broke the news to my mother.

'I'll be sorry to see you go, son. I used to worry about you. I used to think you might be taking up with bad company. But in the short time that you've been looking into The Message, I've seen a change in you. You don't swear. You don't get drunk. You're patient and polite. You're more at peace within yourself and you're happier. You've always been searching for something. Maybe now you've found it.'

'Thanks, Mum. So you don't mind me going to the End Section?'

'No I don't mind. I believe there's life outside the train too. I have my own views about the meaning of life. I just don't go along with all aspects of The Message. But if that's what you believe, son and if that's what you want to do, then go with my blessing. When you reach the End Section, I think you'll discover that not everything you've been told is true. Then maybe you'll come back.'

Alfie's Response

The reaction from my brother Alfie was predictably indifferent.

'I'm suspicious about The Message and the kind of people who proclaim it. And tell me this. What good has Victor Love ever done for the people on this train?'

'It's hard to imagine the history of the train if Victor Love had never been born and if He had never done what He did. He was the inspiration behind a lot of literature and music and art. So many people have followed His example and His teaching by doing good for others. But most importantly, if He had not come to the train and delivered His teaching and set us an example of how to live and then suffered such hostility from His enemies, none of us would have any hope of going to Heaven after this present life is over. We are accepted by God on the basis of our acceptance of Victor Love as our King.'

Alfie just sneered but did not reply. He just picked up a music magazine and started reading it.

Auntie Lil Skeptic Delivers Her Verdict

Shortly after dinner, the doorbell rang. It was Auntie Lil Skeptic, my mother's sister. Her reaction to my plan was typical of her sceptical view of all things to do with religion.

'You don't have to go to join a church or any community of believers, Simon. I'm a private believer myself and I've never joined any organisation. I don't feel comfortable with groups of believers. I love Victor Love but I hate His followers. I feel as close to God when I'm looking at creation as when I'm in a formal worship environment. In fact, closer.'

'I agree that you don't have to join a community of believers to be a real believer, Auntie Lil. But The Message doesn't mention lone believers. It speaks of communities of believers. We each have been given abilities and we are to use these abilities to help one another. When you say you love Victor Love but you hate His followers, that's like saying you love your friend but you hate her husband. It's obvious that a relationship like that isn't going to last. Committed believers want to be with other believers. Faith doesn't tend to thrive, or even survive, in isolation.'

'If you ask me, Simon, a lot of believers are hypocrites.'

'There are hypocrites among believers and there are hypocrites among non-believers. It's easy to label a believer when he or she falls short of the standards they profess. But some who call themselves believers are not true believers. They have not submitted their lives to King Victor. Believers are not perfect and we sin sometimes. King Victor Himself has strongly denounced hypocrisy. Hypocrisy is a sin and some of us believers need to be forgiven for that.'

Uncle Tom Sharp Lectures Me

The doorbell rang again and it was Uncle Tom Sharp. Uncle Tom was a successful businessman and enjoyed a fair level of prosperity. It seemed to me that he had always regarded me as someone who would never amount to much, although he was much too tactful to say so. Deep down, I knew that he was superior to me in just about everything I could think of. It wasn't uncommon for him to lecture me about various things. And when he heard that I believed The Message and was about to act on it, the temptation to put me right proved too much for him to resist. When he lectured me, he always called me son.

'You know, son, I've read a lot about history, and most wars have been caused by religion. Think carefully about what you're getting involved in.'

'There's no doubt that religion is often implicated in the history of various wars. I'm sorry to have to disagree with you, Uncle Tom but to say that most wars have been caused by religion is not true. Most wars have been carried out in the pursuit of power and prestige and profit even if leaders have claimed religious motives. Many political leaders through the ages have used religion to manipulate and control people. You say that religion causes war but actually, people have refrained from fighting, and have sought peace instead, because of religious beliefs. The Message demands that believers do not fight and do not seek vengeance because vengeance belongs to God alone. It advocates non-violence and is a force for good.'

'Okay, son. But religion is one of the causes of war. If there was no religion, we would have a greater chance for peace.'

'I suppose religion is one cause of war but many who claim to believe in King Victor are not true believers. Religion is sometimes a factor I admit. But if you dig a bit deeper, you usually find that other motives are involved, like greed and vanity and hatred. The real cause of war is sin in the hearts of men. It's naive to say that, if you were able to remove religion, we would be more likely to have peace. On the contrary, I would say that religion keeps the depravity of man in check.'

Betty Posh Gives Her View

Betty Posh had been listening intently, just nodding or shaking her head from time to time. But with the first break in the conversation, she weighed in with her view.

'Frankly, Simon, I think that religion is just a crutch for people who can't cope with the demands of life.'

'People often make this charge, Betty and, in one way, it's true. Religion gives peace to the soul and this should not be underestimated. It helps us cope with the terror of death by promising us a wonderful afterlife. It brings great comfort to people who are suffering by giving them the hope of this afterlife of peace and happiness. This is especially true of those who are poverty-stricken or who have to live with painful, debilitating illnesses or those who are constantly oppressed. For all believers, it gives a firm foundation to build one's life upon. And what's wrong with a crutch anyway? Is it such a bad thing? Why are you opposed to something that gives people hope?'

'But the problem, Simon is that it's a false hope. Believers have created a god to worship because they have a need for a father figure who can fulfil their every wish. Religion is just an illusion motivated by wish-fulfilment.'

'Maybe your view tells us something about you, Betty. Could it be that you have a need for a father figure not to exist? Could it be that your wish-fulfilment is for there not to be a god and an afterlife and judgement and Hell? You see, not all aspects of religion are consoling, Betty.'

'Well I have to admit, Simon that I hope God doesn't exist.'

'Exactly. You say that believers have created God but The Message states something rather different. It states that mankind would prefer that God didn't exist. Mankind is in rebellion against God and doesn't want Him to exist because that would mean that they have to answer to Him.'

'Look, Simon, although I personally don't believe in any god, I can see that you do. I think your involvement with this group has been good for you. So I think you should go to this place you call the End Section. I hope you find real peace and happiness.'

'Thanks, Betty. I appreciate that.'

Nephew Albert Bright Exhorts Me

My younger nephew Albert Bright couldn't resist a dig at me either.

'I think a lot of these religious groups are just after your money, Simon. They're on the lookout for naive people they can con. They promise prosperity for those who are willing to impoverish themselves, while the leaders flaunt their wealth as examples of how God will prosper you if you are obedient enough. They try to make you feel guilty if you don't give more than you can afford. They'll produce quotes from The Message and twist them out of context to try to convince you. They regularly talk about sacrificial giving. For people who condemn worldliness, these religious leaders sure talk a lot about money.'

'I know some unscrupulous religious leaders do that but that kind of approach doesn't come from The Message. It tells us not to give out of compulsion but to give cheerfully. The Message itself is free but it takes money to proclaim it and those who are proclaiming it should be supported financially. But asking for money is an emotive subject and it must be done sensitively.'

'The people I'm talking about have become very wealthy and they're not particularly financially transparent either. They're secretive about things like how much their leaders are being paid.'

'We must be careful about stereotyping religious groups, Albert. They're not all like that. The love of money is a snare to being a true believer.'

Sad Parting

I tried to persuade all of them to come with me to the End Section, but all declined. It wasn't easy leaving my family. I realised again that living out my faith would not be easy. I would be living by a different standard to the others on the train, even my own family. I wondered if I had fully counted the cost of what my new life would entail. But then I remembered The Message. It was so wonderful and so unlike anything I had ever heard before, that it just had to be true.

The next morning, I went to the Refreshment Carriage for a happy reunion with Comforter and Waverer and I forgot about the sad parting.

Mark Waverer's Sorrow

Comforter was there waiting for us when I arrived. Shortly after, Waverer arrived. We could see that he was visibly distressed.

'What's wrong, friend?' I asked.

'All my relatives strongly advised me not to go.'

'My home was split down the middle on it, Mark. My mother and my cousin Betty were fairly supportive. My younger brother couldn't care less. My Uncle Tom and my Auntie Lil were strongly against it.'

'What made it even worse for me, Simon was that my girlfriend, who I had been going out with for a long time and who I had hoped to marry, also urged me not to go. She was upset that I had chosen religion over her. She said that I had changed and was like a stranger to her. She told me that she even doubted that I ever loved her and thinks that I'm using religion as an excuse to break our relationship. She's hurt and angry at me.'

'That must be so hard to take,' Comforter replied sadly. 'Like Simon's home, my home was evenly divided on the idea. But I had no girlfriend so I had no problems in that way.'

'Me neither,' I said, 'but I would've found it hard to break off that kind of steady relationship.'

We commiserated with Waverer as best we could and then set off on our journey.

The Quiet Carriage

Paul Comforter led the way as we journeyed from the Refreshment Carriage to the End Section and the first carriage we entered was the Quiet Carriage. The atmosphere was calm and dignified. As it is a designated area for those who wish to carry out work on the train or to read or just to enjoy some peace, this particular carriage appeared to be occupied almost exclusively by scientists, philosophers and academics. It seemed to me as though they were exchanging the latest theories of various branches of science and philosophy. The seats were arranged in groups of six with three seats facing each other across a central table.

Comforter was walking rather quickly and Mark Waverer and I struggled to keep up with him. As we passed one particular group of seats occupied by three men, I tripped over someone's carelessly outstretched leg and fell heavily, hurting my right wrist. As Comforter looked back and hesitated, the person whose leg had tripped me up helped me to my feet.

'Are you all right?' he enquired.

'Eh, yes I think so but my wrist hurts.'

'You look a bit shaken,' he responded. 'Come and sit down for a while.'

'Yes come and sit down,' one of his two friends said. 'We are becoming rather bored by each other's company.'

I looked at Comforter like a schoolboy looking at his teacher for permission to do something. He appeared reluctant to sit down. It seemed to me that he did not welcome any delay in our progress to the End Section. However, he said nothing but shrugged his shoulders and sat down. Waverer and I joined him, with the three of us sitting opposite the three of them.

'Allow me to introduce ourselves,' said the man who tripped me up. 'My name is Eric Pride – Professor Eric Pride to be precise – and these are my friends Doctor Charles Fool and Lady Deepti Vain. I am a philosopher, Dr. Fool is a scientist and Lady Deepti is an academic who was honoured for her work as a government advisor on education.'

We nodded at each person in turn as they were introduced. I noticed that they all appeared to be around the same age – about mid-fifties. They were all quite formally dressed. Both men wore ties.

I started to take more notice of their appearance. Professor Pride was a tall brawny man. Even when sitting down, his height was obvious. He was probably well over six feet. And he had long legs, as I found to my cost. He had grey wavy hair and was distinguished looking with a grey pinstripe suit.

Doctor Fool was fairly plump and bald with a ruddy complexion and wore a dark suit. He had black, thick-rimmed glasses with rectangular frames and looked like he had a jovial disposition.

Lady Deepti was of Indian appearance, slimly built with long black hair which had turned grey at the sides. She had two gold rings on each hand and a gold necklace and she wore a dark blue trouser suit. She looked rather worried.

'And who might you three young gentlemen be?' she asked.

'My name is Simon Seeker,' I replied, 'and these are my friends, Paul Comforter and Mark Waverer.'

'Might I enquire where you are going in such a hurry?' she replied.

'We are believers in The Message and in Victor Love and so we are bound for the End Section,' I explained.

Judging by the reaction of the three of them, one would've thought I'd just said something offensive. The three of them looked scornful.

'Victor Love! Victor Love! We don't mention that name in this carriage. We deal in facts in the Quiet Carriage not fantasy,' Professor Pride scoffed.

'Well actually, Eric, we do sometimes mention his name but only as a swearword,' laughed Doctor Fool.

That remark caused considerable merriment among the three of them.

'Don't tell me you really believe that Victor Love is still alive and will one day return to rule the world? You look like intelligent men. You haven't been duped by The Message too have you?' Professor Pride said with a derisory laugh.

Before we could respond, Dr. Fool asked in a patronising tone, 'Why do you want to go to a dilapidated place like King's City anyway?'

Again, we had no time to reply before Lady Deepti spoke.

'Surely you know that God is just an ancient myth with no basis in fact?'

'I don't believe it is a myth,' I said. 'A man called John Herald explained The Message to us and we believe that it is quite different from any other book.

We believe it to have been divinely inspired. Herald told us that those who believe The Message will go to Heaven when they die. He said that it is now time for believers to go to King's City, where we will be met by the returning Victor Love who will at that time be taking over as King of the world. We believe what Herald said is true. It answers many of the questions that we have had about life. Herald then sent Mark and I to Paul Comforter here and Paul has kindly been instructing us in The Message.'

Doctor Fool's Discourse

'The Message is divinely inspired, you say?' Fool responded with a condescending smirk on his face. 'My dear friends, science has shown conclusively that there is no God. Life consists of nothing more than organic chemistry. Life evolved entirely by chance from a simple single-celled organism which arose from non-living matter. You must discard any idea that it was created by God or that it is in any way mysterious or special.'

'The Message says that God created all life,' Comforter responded.

'The Message! The Message!' the doctor thundered. 'I do not accept that The Message is a reliable source of information.'

'On that we will have to disagree,' Mark replied, adding, 'I fear you are misinformed, sir with regard to single-celled organisms. I've read quite a bit about them and I can tell you there is no such thing as a simple cell. Cells are amazingly complicated and highly organised structures. So much so that a cell has been likened to a factory. And it can do what no factory can do. It can reproduce itself.'

'But since we are here,' Fool persisted, 'it must have happened by chance without the intervention of any supernatural agent.'

'I perceive that science to you is fundamentally a game with one rule,' Mark replied.

'Okay,' Doctor Fool said, somewhat patronisingly, 'tell me what the one rule is.'

'It is simply to explain the origin of life without invoking the supernatural,' Mark replied.

'That is true,' Comforter interjected. 'The Message speaks condemningly of people who did not like to retain God in their knowledge.'

Ignoring Comforter's comment, Fool said, 'My studies in the field of science have led me to believe that the concept of a god is outdated in this modern world.'

I responded with some indignation, 'I too have read a lot about biology. Let me tell you a little more about cells. The existence of a cell requires not only materials but organisation. Organisation like that cannot just evolve. An intelligent Being had to do the organising. And, in addition to that, the cell is coded with information.'

'What do you mean?' Fool said.

I leaned across the table, fixing my gaze on Fool, and said in a quiet voice, 'I mean that this thing called DNA in living things stores information. It has an inbuilt coding system. Each of us has a unique "DNA profile" which is derived from body cells like saliva or blood or hair. This is why DNA is now an important means of detecting crimes and determining parentage. What I would ask you, sir is simply this, where did this information come from? Information cannot just evolve by itself. Somebody had to put it there. The only way this could have possibly happened is if it was guided by an intelligent Creator God.'

'But The Message tells us specifically that God did not use evolution as His tool,' Comforter added hastily.

'It seems to me that it takes more faith to believe in evolution as an unguided process than it does to believe in God,' I said. This comment caused Mark to laugh loudly and nod his head in agreement.

'I can see that we will not reach agreement on this,' Fool responded.

'You have that right, sir,' I replied.

Professor Pride's Reasoning

At this point, Professor Pride intervened. 'I cannot accept your reasoning for the existence of God based on biology alone,' he said to me. 'It seems to me that philosophers down through the years have shown, by a process of logic, that there is no God.'

'Okay, then let us consider the design argument for the existence of God,' Mark replied. 'You philosophers like to reason. So let's reason together. The design argument reasons that God must exist on the basis of apparent design in the universe. The traditional form of the argument is the "Watchmaker" analogy. It postulates that a watch is a complex thing which has obviously been designed. It reasons that, as the Earth with all its wonderful varieties of life forms is much more complex than a watch, it must have been designed too.'

'Of course I have heard of the Watchmaker analogy,' Pride replied. 'I have also heard of a response to it which raises a number of points. For example, the analogy between things which mankind has designed, such as a watch and the wonders of the natural world is too unclear to be able to conclude that the world is the handiwork of a Designer. The argument states that, even if it could be proved that the natural world is the product of a Designer, the mind of that Designer would need as much explanation as the natural world. It also says that, even if we do accept the existence of God, that wouldn't tell us anything about that god. For example, it wouldn't tell us whether there is life after death or whether God answers prayer.'

'I would not say that any of these points are convincing,' Comforter said.

'Neither would I,' I replied.

'None of those points have convinced me either,' Mark said. 'But there is a more modern form of the design argument proposed by a philosopher. This argument states that the existence of the universe is a remarkable fact that cries out for explanation but science can't explain why the universe exists. It notes that the universe conforms to the laws of nature but that science can't account for why these laws exist.'

The professor leaned forward in his chair and, with a dismissive wave of his hand, declared, 'But the defence of the design argument you have just quoted has been criticised by still another philosopher who questioned how a disembodied being like God can act on the material universe. He reasons that the organising ability of God needs some explanation.'

'I can see that you are not convinced by what I've said,' Mark replied.

'So let us now move in to a still more modern version of the design argument – the Anthropic Principle. Like previous versions of the argument, the Anthropic Principle is based on scientific findings that this Earth appears to have been specially designed to support life. There are a number of examples of "fine tuning" which point to a Designer creating the exact conditions necessary for life to exist on Earth. Some examples: the distance between Earth and the sun, the rotation of the Earth, the Earth's magnetic field and the hydrological cycle. It seems to me that the current evidence from various branches of science is pointing towards design and that as a result, the case for an intelligent Designer is compelling.'

‘I agree,’ I said. ‘Besides, surely, everything must come from something. There must have been a “First Cause” that created the universe and I believe that First Cause is God.’

Pride was beginning to look somewhat deflated by this point. He looked at the ceiling for a few moments as though looking for divine inspiration. He shrugged his shoulders and sighed.

‘There is an element of subjective reasoning involved here. Two people can look at the same things and come to very different conclusions. With regard to the design argument, maybe all that can be said in summary is that the handiwork of a divine Designer is in the eye of some beholders and not others.’

‘Well I know what I believe,’ Mark said.

‘And you know what I believe,’ said Comforter.

Lady Deepti Vain Intervenes

At this point, a lull in the conversation ensued. Lady Deepti Vain took her opportunity.

‘I’ve been listening with interest to your arguments for the existence of God using the biological and design arguments,’ she said. ‘I remain unconvinced partly because it seems to me that you are relying too much on The Message. In my experience, it is never good to rely on just one source of information. Besides, how can you be certain that God inspired it?’

‘Because it contains many detailed prophecies which have come true, because historians have never been able to demonstrate that it contains historical inaccuracies and because science has never been able to disprove it,’ said Comforter with great passion. ‘The Message is comprised of various documents which were written by many different authors over a long period of time, yet there are no contradictions in the original text, and there are only a relatively few minor copyist errors in the version we have today.’

Lady Deepti seemed taken aback by the force of Comforter’s reasoning. After a short silence she said, ‘How do you know the various documents in The Message are reliable? After all, none of these documents are actually original, are they?’

Comforter responded with enthusiasm like a man who was warming to his subject. ‘It is true that the original documents are gone, but we have thousands of manuscripts which are dated at only around 25 to 50 years from the date of those original documents. All these manuscripts help ensure the accuracy of The Message.'

'Okay. Let's say that the manuscripts are genuine and reliable. But that doesn't mean that the content of the manuscripts is actually true. What is written in them could be an attempt to deceive.'

'Again what you say is true,' Comforter responded. 'But the writers of these documents are often shown in a bad light. They are shown to be men who were slow to understand what was being said to them, men who were afraid, men who lacked faith. Why would they portray themselves like this if it was an attempt at a hoax? And some of these writers died for their faith. No one would die for something they knew to be untrue. Finally, why does The Message repeatedly emphasise that the way of life that it advocates is difficult? If it was a hoax, wouldn't The Message try to make it sound easy and attractive? Listen, my friend. One thing is clear. The men who wrote these manuscripts were sincere.'

Lady Deepti was beginning to look uneasy. 'But, Mr. Comforter, there were many documents about purporting to explain the way of God in the first few centuries after the events it describes. Some of these documents contradict one another. Who decided which documents would be included in The Message and which documents should be rejected? I think it was a group of powerful men who decided these things and why should I accept their decision?'

'Lady Deepti, there was no conspiracy by a group of powerful men to decide which documents should be included in The Message and which should be rejected. In fact, the recognition of these documents was a natural process. It was not a matter of regulation. These documents were widely acknowledged as inspired practically as soon as they were written. Subsequent ecclesiastical rulings did not confer on them any authority they did not already possess. They did no more than recognise their previously established divine inspiration.'

Lady Deepti was not going to concede any point without a fight. 'But what about these so-called "lost books"?' she continued. 'There are a number of these books or documents. Some theologians claim they shed additional light on The Message and that they should have been included.'

Comforter looked a little bemused as he replied. 'It is true that a number of other books appeared a few centuries after The Message was completed, but they were rejected by the body of believers by common consent. The reason they were rejected was simply that they failed the test of orthodoxy, by which was meant conformity with the general teaching of The Message. Everything in

The Message is inspired by God and is meant to be included. There are no missing documents in The Message. None whatsoever. It is complete.'

Lady Deepti shook her head and waved her forefinger disapprovingly at this answer. 'But the suggestion is often made that these other books depict the Victor Love as He really is. It is my belief that the references to Victor Love in The Message are the product of later traditions and that these other books which were rejected are actually the original and accurate accounts of what Victor Love really said and did. I think the real Victor Love is to be found in the rejected sources.'

'I do not believe that any serious scholar of The Message regards these rejected documents as shedding light on the real Victor Love. In addition, many scholars believe these documents were written much later than the documents referring to Victor Love which are contained in The Message. They are of some interest but there is little reason to think they provide us with any reliable information about the real Victor Love. Frankly, these documents that you are referring to are Gnostic religious writings.'

'But why do you disparage Gnosticism?' Lady Deepti retorted.

Comforter paused briefly and thought about the new subject that had just been introduced. 'Gnosticism was a religious view that was prominent during an earlier age. Some believe that it has never really died out and still exists in various forms today. Gnosticism was a diverse movement and there is no real consensus on the meaning of the gnostic texts.'

'Permit me to review what Gnosticism is,' Lady Deepti volunteered.

'The word, Gnosticism means, "insight" and "enlightenment". Gnostics believed that knowledge pertaining to the divine mysteries was of fundamental importance and they thought it was necessary to obtain this knowledge in order to enter the highest spiritual realm and attain salvation. To the Gnostic, this knowledge was a secret wisdom for the elite. It was not for the masses. The Message, as you call it, was regarded by Gnostics as, at best, the basic boundary of Gnosticism, and at worst, a corruption of Gnosticism. Gnosticism teaches that there is a pantheon of divine beings. Many Gnostics claimed to be believers of The Message and consequently, Gnosticism was considered to be a dangerous heresy in the first two centuries of the proclamation of The Message.'

'There is no need for you to elaborate further about Gnosticism. From the point of view of believers of The Message, Gnosticism is a corruption of The Message,' Comforter replied. 'The teachings of the "Gnostic Victor Love" contradict the teachings of the Victor Love of The Message. The Victor Love of the Gnostic documents speaks of the need for enlightenment, not sin and repentance like the Victor Love of The Message.'

'It appears as though we will not reach any agreement,' Lady Deepti said with a weary sigh.

Miss Agnes Godhater Arrives

Just then a short, slim, bespectacled lady came to our table and put her forefinger to her lips. 'Shush! Will you people please keep the noise down? This is supposed to be a quiet carriage.'

The others at the table knew her. 'This is Miss Agnes Godhater and she is a librarian,' Dr. Fool said.

'Good old Miss Godhater, ever the librarian,' Professor Pride smiled.

Comforter, Waverer and I apologised and said we were just leaving anyway.

At that point, Pride seemed to remember the incident that brought about the conversation. He asked me, 'How is your wrist? Does it still hurt?'

I moved my wrist slightly with just a little discomfort. 'It's much better now, thank you,' I replied.

Comforter then turned to Mark and me and said, 'In that case, we really ought to be on our way.'

We bade farewell to Professor Eric Pride, Doctor Charles Fool and Lady Deepti Vain and walked towards the end of the Quiet Carriage. We were followed by Miss Godhater who overtook us just before we left the carriage. She turned to face us so that we could walk no further. Her stern expression warned us that she was somewhat irritated with us.

'I heard your conversation with those three people. Tell me this. Why do you think The Message is any different from any other book of that kind? In my library, there are many religious books. I know them all. Their followers claim that these books are holy and inspired too. So why do you say that The Message is unique?'

Again Comforter took the lead in defending The Message.

'I do not wish to appear arrogant, Miss Godhater and I mean no offence to any who believe other books are holy and inspired. I am aware of some of these books but I must confess that I have not read any of them from cover to cover. I have only read parts of them. However, in regard to your direct question, I would say this. I believe that The Message is unique for several reasons.

‘Number one, it is scientifically accurate. For example, the statement is made that infers that the Earth is round. How did the human author who wrote those words know that when the scientists of his day did not know it? I believe it was because God inspired him.

‘Number two, it is historically accurate. Many historical details are contained in The Message and it almost seems to be inviting people to prove it wrong. But it has not been found to be historically inaccurate. On the contrary, archeologists and scholars are always finding evidence – whether it’s the existence of countries or people – which corroborates the historical accuracy of The Message. As you will know, Miss Godhater, errors are to be found in other books which give many historical details. Why are there no errors in this one? I say it is due to divine inspiration.

‘Number three, it reads as one book despite being composed of many individual books, having been written by many authors over a very long period of time. Can any serious student fail to be impressed by this immense body of evidence which cries out for a single, divine source of inspiration?

‘Number four, and this is my final point, The Message contains prophecies which have been fulfilled in historical events. For example, there are many detailed prophecies which concern the life of Victor Love and every last one of them happened as prophesied. For these reasons and others, Miss Godhater, I believe The Message was inspired by God.’

Miss Godhater shook her head firmly.

‘And I believe that religion, especially your religion, is just a psychological crutch.’

I objected to our beliefs being described in this way.

‘It is possible to describe our religion in psychological terms because there are many benefits but that would not negate its validity.’

As she turned to go back to the carriage, she almost spat out her reply. ‘I can see there is no point in arguing with you three. You are just bigots. And you three have been taken in by lies.’

We then left the Quiet Carriage. I remarked to Comforter and Waverer, ‘I’m amazed, really amazed that such clever people are atheists and agnostics and do not believe that there is a God.’

‘The answer is really quite simple,’ Comforter replied. ‘People like them simply do not like to retain God in their knowledge so they will not entertain the idea that there may be a god. They are puffed up with pride. They suppress the truth. Professing themselves to be wise, they have become fools. I think that such people know somewhere deep down in the secret recesses of their hearts that there really is a god. In fact, Simon, I wonder if there are really any genuine atheists at all or whether there are only fools and rebels.'

'But they are so much cleverer than I am.'

'The Message usually appeals to those who are weak and foolish by comparison with the mighty and noble of this world. And you and I are in that category. We humbly accepted the fact that we are helpless and in need of King Victor.'

'In that case, I'm glad to be weak and foolish,' I laughed.

Mark Waverer Leaves

As we turned to leave the Quiet Carriage, Mark stopped and stood slowly shaking his head from side to side.

'What's the matter, Mark?' Paul asked.

'I'm sorry but I can't go any further,' he said sadly.

'But why not?' Paul said gently.

'It's just that... It's just that... I didn't think it would be this difficult. I need more time to think about this. I don't think I'm ready to go.'

'You've not been put off by what the people in the carriage have been saying, have you?' Paul enquired.

'Not really. It's just everything we've experienced since we left the Meeting Room.'

I looked on with dismay, not knowing what to say.

'I did tell you in the Refreshment Carriage that the journey would be difficult, Mark.'

'I know you did, Paul. It's been... more difficult than I anticipated. I think I need to go back and think some more about The Message. I'm sorry to let you down.'

'Don't be sorry about letting us down. Go back and think carefully about it and pray about it too, Mark.'

With that, he shook our hands, avoiding eye contact. He wished us well and walked back in the direction we had come from. I went to follow him but Paul put a gentle restraining hand on my arm.

'Let him go, Simon. Mark is a sensitive soul. It appears that some of the things he's heard and experienced have hit him hard. It may be that all he needs is some more time to think and to pray. I wouldn't be surprised if we saw him again.'

I nodded.

'Come on, Simon Seeker. Let's go.'

Sadly but determinedly, we left the Quiet Carriage. It had been anything but quiet.

The Women's Carriage

Early one morning, as we approached the Women's Carriage, Comforter advised that we don't stop there but proceed as swiftly as possible through it.

'Why is that, Paul? What do you have against women?'

'Nothing I assure you. I have the highest regard for the opposite sex. But we'll meet enough problems on our journey. We don't need to invite anymore.'

For those passing through the Women's Carriage, the corridor did not go through the middle of the carriage as it did in the other carriages. Just before the entrance to the carriage, the corridor turned sharply to the left and went along the outside. Presumably the intention was so that the women in the carriage would not be disturbed by unwelcome attention.

Meeting Marie Jolly

Where the corridor turned to the left, it widened considerably for a few metres. At that point, we found our way blocked by a large rolled up carpet and a young lady standing beside it.

'Ah, at last! A couple of able-bodied men at last! Can you two gentlemen please carry this carpet upstairs for me?' she cried in some distress. 'It's very heavy.'

We readily agreed and Paul took one end of the carpet and I took the other and we cautiously carried it up the stairs. The lady was tall, possibly in her early thirties, with a curvaceous figure, shoulder length black hair and green eyes. She was heavily made up with bright red lipstick and eyelashes enhanced by mascara. She had a broad smile and a cheerful demeanour. Ringlets of tawny brown hair toppled over her shoulders. She explained that she was in charge of general maintenance in the Women's Carriage and that her task at present was to redesign the layout of the women's upstairs lounge.

Her clothes suggested that she was not planning to do any heavy lifting herself. She wore a smart grey trouser suit, a white blouse and high heels. We carried the carpet up to the lounge and rolled it out as she directed us. She then asked us in an apologetic tone to carry up a large table from downstairs. After the table, we were asked to carry up a dozen chairs, then a music centre with a couple of heavy speakers, then a crockery set, then a cutlery set. We were becoming quite tired and were relieved to hear her say that was all she required. Her offer of a cup of tea was warmly welcomed. We sat in the upstairs lounge and had tea and biscuits with her and introduced ourselves. Her name was Marie Jolly. She asked what we did for a living. Paul told her that he was a locksmith who also did some carpentry work and that I was an electrical engineer.

'Would it be nosey of me to enquire how you came to be living in the Women's Carriage, Marie?' I enquired.

'No, not at all, Simon. I was divorced a couple of years ago and my ex-husband cleaned me out. He took everything and I found myself without anywhere to live. A friend of mine was living here and she suggested I join her. So here I am.'

'I'm sorry to hear that, Marie,' I said.

'Oh I've gotten over all that now. I'm starting all over and quite enjoying my freedom and my new lifestyle.' She sounded like she was enjoying her new life.

'Where are you two guys going anyway?'

'We're heading for the End Section,' I replied.

'The End Section? So you are believers in The Message, are you?' she asked without a hint of prejudice.

'Yes we are. Do you know anything about The Message?'

'No not really. But I've heard that accepting it takes away your freedom.'

'We all have responsibilities and commitments. Is anybody ever completely free?' Paul asked.

'That's true. But I want to have as much freedom as possible.'

'Freedom is good, Marie, but it shouldn't be a license to be selfish. True liberty is not doing whatever we want. It's having the power to do what's right.'

'But, Paul, you believers have all these rules to obey. That's not freedom to me.'

'It's true that rules and regulations can enslave people. But the rules and regulations that God gives are for our own good. They produce peace and happiness and, believe it or not, they also produce freedom.'

'Freedom from what, Paul?'

'Freedom from fear.'

'Fear of what?'

'Fear of rejection. Fear of loneliness. Fear of death. Fear of a future judgement.'

'But I'm enjoying my present lifestyle. If I became a believer, would I have to give it up?'

'That depends on what your present lifestyle is, Marie. When someone becomes a believer, it's a new beginning. In a sense, it's like being born all over again. We hate what we once loved and we love what we once hated. So we stop doing things that we have come to understand are wrong, not only because The Message tells us they're wrong, but because we don't want to do them anymore. We want to live our lives in a way that pleases God and He gives us the strength to be able to do that.'

'Hmm. I'm not sure that God would want me to become a believer.'

'Why do you say that?' Paul enquired.

'There are two issues in my life. My divorce is one of them. Can someone like me who is divorced make a fresh start in God's eyes?'

'God ordained the institution of marriage in the beginning. Marriage is sacred to God. It is meant to be for life and He hates divorce.'

'But are there any circumstances in which He would allow divorce?'

'Yes, under certain conditions. If one partner commits fornication or adultery, then divorce is allowed. Or if one partner is not a believer and leaves the marriage, then divorce is also permitted. Divorce might also be possible where a believer was divorced before he or she became a believer. But although divorce is permitted, it's not compulsory. I believe that in most cases, divorce can be avoided with counselling.'

'Let me get this right, Paul. In those three conditions, is the injured party allowed to remarry?'

'Yes I believe so but you would need to seek counselling from an authorised believer.'

'You've made me feel better, Paul. One of those conditions applies to me. I've always thought that you black men are compassionate.'

'I'll take that as a compliment. Now that we've got your divorce out of the way, what's the other issue?'

Marie looked uncomfortable.

'It's personal. I don't want to discuss it. I don't think a man would understand anyway, not even you, Paul.'

'That's okay, Marie, God loves you and He is willing to forgive any sin once you repent of it. Now tell me, are you willing to listen to The Message?'

'No, not yet. I might have to change something in my life. Couldn't I just accept God on my deathbed?'

'You could if you knew the day and the circumstances in which you are going to die. But you might not die in bed. And even if you did, you might not be mentally capable of making such a big decision. The best time to accept God is right now, Marie.'

Marie Jolly appeared to be showing an interest in The Message. But our conversation was interrupted by the door being flung open and the sound of footsteps on the floor as a young lady walked towards us.

Irene Sweet Enters

'Ah, Irene there you are. These two gentlemen have done the heavy work for us. Gentlemen, this is a fellow resident of the Women's Carriage, Irene Sweet.'

Irene Sweet had black hair which was swept back and held in place by a dark blue hair band. She wore faded jeans, a tee-shirt and light blue trainers. She was dressed for work alright. She looked about the same age as Marie – early thirties. Her black eyelashes fluttered above her brown, walnut-shaped eyes, giving the impression of someone who was lacking in confidence. This might have been due to the presence of strangers, especially male strangers. Still, she had a sweet, demure smile. She was very pretty. Irene told us the story behind her presence in the Women's Carriage. She had been deserted by her husband and, like Marie, her circumstances were such that she was forced to find alternative accommodation. She confided that, as Marie was working full-time and she was not working at present, she often felt lonely.

'Loneliness is hard to deal with,' I said. 'I've often felt lonely myself. The problem is, wherever you go, the loneliness goes with you.'

'How do you deal with it, Simon?' Irene asked.

Before I answered, I looked at Marie. I didn't want to exclude her or to monopolise the conversation. But she had indicated that she often felt lonely too.

‘Firstly, I had to admit that I was lonely. That wasn’t easy because my vanity prevented me from admitting it for a long time. Then I did what everyone does. I looked for someone who would make my loneliness go away. I tried meeting new people by entering different social circles. I tried getting involved in a cause. Nothing really worked very well. That could have been more to do with me and my problems than the other people. I tried analysing the causes of my loneliness. I concluded that certain factors in my childhood had made me a private person. I had a few friends but I felt somewhat disconnected from them in my opinions and tastes. Then a broken romantic relationship made the loneliness worse. As I wrestled with my loneliness, I had to accept that there were some things that I couldn’t change. I recognised too that there are other things that I could change and that I needed to change. So I set about changing those things. During this process, I discovered that there’s a difference in being on your own and being lonely and that being on your own can be a positive thing.’

‘How can being on your own ever be a positive thing, Simon?’ Irene asked rather derisively.

‘You can do things like reading and writing and studying courses and thinking. Thinking about life. Thinking about God.’

‘Thinking about God?’ You believe in God, do you?’

‘Yes, Irene, I believe in God. And I think there’s a spiritual vacuum in all of us.’

‘What do you mean by a spiritual vacuum, Simon?’

‘I mean everyone has a kind of spiritual loneliness until they get in touch with God. Since I became a believer, I only feel lonely occasionally but most of the time, I’m happy and fulfilled. And on those occasions when I do feel lonely, I remind myself that loneliness isn’t a sin.’

‘Actually, Simon, I believe in God too. But I don’t think I could go through that painful process of self-examination that you put yourself through.’

‘You believe in God? Wonderful! Then, Irene, I think you should begin by asking God to give you courage.’

‘What do I need courage for?’

‘Most lonely people need courage to reach out to other people and to overcome the fear of rejection.’

‘You’ve given me a lot to think about, Simon. Although I believe in God, I’ve never made a definite commitment like you have. I’ve thought about joining a community of believers but I never have.’

'Why not?'

'Well, to tell you the truth, Simon, as my husband has been gone such a long time, I have to assume that he won't be coming back. So I consider myself separated, soon to be divorced. I'd like to be married again but I've heard that there are a lot more women than men among believers. Is that true? I mean, if I did join a group of believers, would there be any single men my age?'

Comforter took over the conversation with Irene at this point as he was more experienced in the faith than me.

'Yes, in most communities of believers that would be true,' Comforter admitted.

'Why is that, Paul?' Irene asked.

'There are a number of theories about this, Irene. One theory is that the teachings emphasise qualities that are regarded as somehow less masculine. Qualities like repentance, service, submission, holiness and humility. Another theory is that the masculine ego balks at admitting they need to be forgiven. Still another theory is that men don't usually have believers as role models in their lives so going to a worship service is not considered a particularly masculine thing to do. Others would blame the type of worship music that's often played. Some have even claimed that the decor in worship areas offends masculine sensitivities. Things like flower arrangements, pastel colours and frilly curtains. But none of these theories adequately explains the gender gap. I think the basic reason that men don't become believers is that they have a different religion. And that religion is masculinity. Men like to do manly things and to be seen to be doing them. Things like work and hobbies. Attending a worship service is considered to be something that women and children do. The men that do attend often do so just to please their womenfolk.'

'Can this situation ever be changed?'

'Yes I believe it can. The teachings need to stress that becoming a believer means a lifetime of adventure and risk-taking. It means rebelling against the norms of society. That would appeal to many men.'

Irene nodded slowly but said nothing.

'Look, folks, why are we standing around here talking about religion when there's a lot of work to be done?' Marie said. 'It's great having you two guys around and I need to make use of you while you're here.'

'We'd be happy to help. What do you want us to do?' I replied.

'Paul, you did say you're a locksmith. I have a few doors downstairs in the women's cabins on my list of things to be done. I've had reports of some of them not locking properly and others not closing properly. Would you mind taking a look at them?'

'But I don't have any tools with me,' Paul protested weakly.

'Don't worry. I have tools,' Marie announced gleefully. 'Irene, will you get the list of scheduled work from my desk downstairs and show Paul the cabin doors that need to be repaired?'

Irene agreed and led Paul downstairs.

Meeting Marie Jolly's Friend

When they had gone, Marie turned to me and said, 'Simon, I have something to show you. Follow me.'

She led me into a corridor off the lounge and then into a large room at the end of the corridor. She closed the door behind us and, pointing to a double couch, she said, 'Take a seat.' I sat down and looked at her, wondering why she had brought me there.

She must have seen my puzzled look for she laughed and said, 'I just wanted to show you one of our guest rooms. These rooms are for visitors to the Women's Carriage who need to stay overnight. This is the largest and most private room. You and Paul are welcome to stay here for as long as it takes to finish the work I have for you.'

It was well furnished, with a dressing table, a two-seater settee, a couple of chairs, and two single beds.

'But are male visitors allowed to stay here?' I asked, hoping the answer was no.

'Yes, Simon. Even male visitors.'

'I'll mention it to Paul and see how he feels. But I should tell you that he is focussed on reaching the End Section as soon as possible.'

'Try to talk him into it. It's good to have men around. They come in handy at times,' she said with a sweet smile.

'Would you like a coffee?'

'Sure.'

She made the coffee and sat on the two-seater settee opposite me. I was suddenly aware of the sexual tension that often descends when a man and a woman are alone together. The presence of the beds added to the tension. Was she making an advance? We talked about life in general and our backgrounds.

We were getting on reasonably well when our conversation was abruptly interrupted by her mobile phone. Marie pulled it from her hip pocket.

'Hello, Vanida dear. I'm in the large guestroom. Come round and have a coffee.'

That invitation to her friend to join us indicated rather forcefully to me that she had not been making an advance in my direction after all. I wondered what Vanida would be like. I didn't have long to wait to find out. Within a couple of minutes, the doorbell rang and Marie got up to answer it. A young woman entered the room and looked startled to see me. She looked like she was of Thai descent with her short, straight black hair, small nose and wide cheekbones.

'Oh, this is Simon Seeker. Simon, this is my friend Vanida Wary.'

Both women embraced. It was a lengthy, affectionate embrace. It was followed by equally lengthy eye contact between both women.

Vanida looked slightly younger than Marie, possibly in her early twenties. She was casually dressed in jeans and a blue tee-shirt. She smiled briefly when we were introduced but her demeanour indicated to me that she felt tense. Maybe it was my presence that had unsettled her.

Vanida sat on the settee beside Marie, their knees touching. Marie grasped Vanida's hand.

Now it was my turn to feel uneasy. Trying to appear relaxed, I asked Vanida what she did for a living.

She said she worked part-time in the restaurant of the Women's Carriage and that she was happy in the Women's Carriage, especially after meeting Marie. After listening to her for a few minutes, I formed the impression that her personality was quite different to that of Marie. She seemed caring and submissive. She spoke softly with some kind of accent, but I didn't recognise it.

'Do you remember that I told Paul there were two reasons why I thought God wouldn't want me to become a believer?' Marie interjected.

'Yes. I think you mentioned your divorce being one reason.'

'Well, the other reason is my friendship with Vanida. We are living as a couple you see and we are very happy together.'

'Oh, I see.'

'You disapprove?' Vanida asked, studying my face.

'Why ask me if I disapprove, Vanida? My opinion on these things doesn't matter a hill of beans. It's what The Message says that matters. Nothing else.'

'Are you going to tell us what The Message says?' Vanida persisted.

I paused, trying to think what to say. I hated having to answer the question.

'Eh, well to tell you the truth, believers have become quite divided on this issue in recent times.'

'But what is your view?' Vanida persevered, keeping up the pressure.

'Well, to tell you the truth, I'm still trying to make my mind up about that. Ask Paul. He knows more about The Message than I do.'

'You know what. I think Marie was right in saying that God wouldn't want her or me, and people like us, to become believers.'

'One thing I do know, Vanida is that God wants everyone to become believers but He has certain standards that we all have to accept.'

An uneasy silence followed.

'Let's get back to the lounge, Simon,' Marie said. 'I have some electrical work for you to do.'

It was with some relief that I bade goodbye to Vanida. I guessed that the feeling was mutual. I followed Marie back to the lounge.

She showed me some electrical work that needed to be done – a couple of loose power sockets on the wall, some plugs that needed to be fitted, and some light bulbs that needed to be changed. She provided me with a few tools. So I set about doing the work and tried to forget about her amorous suggestion.

Soon, Paul and Irene returned, looking for some locks and woodscrews.

'Look, it's nearly lunchtime. Why don't you guys stay for lunch?' Marie suggested jovially.

'Are men allowed to eat here?' I asked.

'Yes, men are allowed in the upstairs dining area but not in the general seating area. The dining area is just along the corridor.'

So we both gratefully accepted the invitation.

Lucinda Charm Appears

As we were directed to a table in the dining area, we both felt self-conscious as we were the only men and there must have been around thirty women. Some of them didn't look too pleased to see two men in their dining area. A few of the women entered the dining area holding hands. We were seated with Marie and Irene when we were joined by another lady.

'This is our friend Lucinda. We always eat together,' Irene explained.

Lucinda was thin and pale with prominent cheekbones. She looked about my age, early to mid-forties. She wore black linen trousers and a red sweater.

She looked surprised to see us, presumably because we were men in an environment reserved for females.

She nodded at each of us with the merest hint of a smile as we were introduced. Her name was Lucinda Charm. There was an intensity in her blue eyes that I found quite alluring. There was something nebulous, almost ethereal, about her that held my attention. She didn't smile much. I was interested in why she was living in the Women's Carriage. She said that she had broken up with her boyfriend and that she blamed the breakup on bouts of depression that she was prone to. When she learned that we were believers on our way to the End Section, she asked how we felt about depression.

I was amazed at how such a beautiful young woman could suffer from low self-esteem.

'It's good that you're able to talk about your depression, Lucinda,' I began gently. 'Often, those who are suffering from depression don't want to admit it. Due to the stigma that is often attached to depression, people can become rather good at hiding their depression. They might not even know themselves what their problem is because the symptoms can sometimes seem to be contradictory. Do you know what brought your depression on?'

'I had a difficult childhood. I felt I wasn't wanted. I found it difficult to hold down a job. My self-esteem plummeted. When I reached my teenage years, I turned to drugs to shut out the reality of my pathetic life. Sometimes I find it hard to get out of bed. Other times, I find it hard to breathe. I have felt suicidal.'

'I'm so sorry to hear that, Lucinda.'

'Do you think that people who commit suicide go to Hell, Simon?'

Paul took over at this point.

'This is a difficult topic, Lucinda,' he said. 'Not all believers are in agreement about it but I will give you my personal view. God gives us life and He is the only one who should decide when a person's life is to end. Suicide is rejecting God's gift of life. That is serious. Those who commit suicide don't tend to consider the effect it will have on their loved ones who are left behind. The effect can be devastating. Suicide is a sin but it's not the greatest sin and it's not an unforgiveable sin. Some would point out that when a person commits suicide, they usually have no time to repent before they die. I would answer that by saying that many, if not most of us, will die with some unconfessed sin or sins in our lives. I believe that when a person becomes a believer, that person's salvation is assured. I don't believe that any sin, including suicide, can cause us to be rejected.'

'That's a comforting thought, Paul.'

'Depression is not a choice. It's not a character defect. And it's not a sin. There might be a number of causes. It's important to seek psychiatric or medical treatment.'

'I've tried all that.'

'It's possible there's a spiritual element to your depression.'

'What do you mean?'

'There are spiritual forces around who are hostile to humans. Just because we can't see them doesn't mean they're not real. It's possible that they would try to exacerbate your problem.'

'It's funny you should say that, Paul. For a while, I used to play with Ouija boards with a few friends just for a laugh. But we stopped when it started to get scary. Still, I find the occult fascinating. You know, witchcraft, mediums, demons and all that.'

'Messing around with Ouija boards or anything to do with the occult is very dangerous, Lucinda. These spiritual forces can use things like that to influence us and prejudice us against God.'

Lucinda frowned at Paul's admonition. But she didn't look convinced.

'Where can I get help with my depression, Paul?'

'There are no easy answers to the problem of depression. Even some believers struggle with it at times. But if you were to turn to God, you would find much comfort and possibly complete healing. In any community of believers, you are likely to find a safe haven where you will not be judged.'

'But I've heard that the religion of believers is patriarchal and that women are treated as second-class members.'

'Yes I've heard that too,' Marie chimed in.

'Unfortunately, there have been instances where this has happened but it was never condoned by King Victor Love,' Paul stressed. 'We value all humans equally. Women are valued just as highly as men and always have been. This is in stark contrast to the way other religions have treated women and still do. Women make up the majority in most communities of believers and I think that speaks for itself. Women occupy leadership roles too in many communities.'

The three women agreed that the role of women sounded much better among believers than in many other organisations.

When lunch was ended, Marie again brought up the amount of work that needed to be done.

'Are you guys in a hurry to get to the End Section? I would really appreciate it if you could stick around for another day or two to help me in finishing the work. We are due to complete the lounge in two days. Why don't you stay in one of our guest rooms for a night or two? You can share our best room. We keep it for special guests. I mean, would an extra day or two matter to you?'

Paul was reluctant to stay overnight. I deferred to his wishes in that regard. However, Marie kept urging us to stay, so that we eventually gave in and agreed to stay for two nights.

'Wonderful!' Marie exclaimed. 'As you were looking for locks and woodscrews, Paul, am I right in assuming there are more doors to attend to?'

'Yes. I'm only about half finished.'

'Fine. So you can carry on and finish the doors. Then I have some other work for you to do. Simon, I have some more electrical work to show you that needs doing and some other things that I need to get your advice on.'

Alone with Irene Sweet

'Simon, can you come down to my cabin in about an hour's time please?' Irene asked. 'I need you to look at some electrical appliances in my room. I'm worried about whether they are safe or not.'

'Sure, Irene. I'd be happy to.'

Paul and I went about our assigned tasks diligently and, after one hour, I went to Irene's cabin and knocked on the door.

Irene came to the door looking voluptuous. Gone was the tee-shirt and old jeans. She wore a short mauve dress held up by two thin straps. It emphasised her curvaceous figure. Her black hair was no longer held up by a hair band. It dangled on her bare shoulders.

'Come in,' she smiled. Her smile no longer seemed so demure. More flirtatious. Red lipstick accentuated her full lips.

Her legs were no longer hidden in old jeans. They were gloriously displayed, especially when she sat opposite me. Her black eyelashes still fluttered but now in a way that seemed seductive.

On entering her cabin, the smell of perfume was strong, almost overpowering. A romantic song played. The lyrics were erotic.

'What did you want me to look at? You know; the electrical appliances?'

'Oh, never mind that now. There'll be time enough for that later. Tell me about yourself, Simon.'

My face began to feel flushed. My voice sounded strained and breathless as I started to tell her about my background and my hobbies for about ten minutes. Then I ran out of things to say. We sat looking at each other in silence. She looked ravishing. She was irresistible. I felt myself succumbing to this gorgeous creature opposite me. Was she thinking what I was thinking she was thinking? The sound of the doorbell interrupted the silence. Ding dong! Ding dong! It was the most irritating doorbell sound I had ever heard.

'I'd better see who that is.'

She rose and opened the door. It was Paul coming to see if a lock on one of her doors needed fixing.

'No, you must have the wrong cabin number. You'd better come in anyway.'

Paul smiled to see me. 'Did you get the work done, Simon?'

I felt a little flushed. 'I think everything's in order now,' I replied, not knowing what to say.

'Good. I'm sure Marie has given you plenty of work to do, Simon. Let's get to it.'

I left with Paul, feeling a mixture of emotions. Did he interrupt us deliberately? What would have happened if Paul hadn't showed up when he did? I would never know now. Was I sorry he turned up? Yes. Was I proud of my weak resistance? No.

As I was finishing work for the day, Marie came up to me and handed me a note. It was an invitation from Lucinda to go with her that evening to the lounge bar in the next carriage along. I was flattered. I couldn't understand why she had asked me to take her out but I wanted to go. I didn't want to tell Comforter as I was sure he wouldn't approve. As we were sharing a cabin, it would be difficult to explain my absence that evening. I decided to tell him that I wanted to go along to the lounge bar in the next carriage for a quiet drink and to read any magazines or newspapers that were lying around. I knew it was unlikely he would want to come along as he didn't care for alcohol or lounge bars. I felt guilty about that but I did it anyway.

An Evening with Lucinda Charm

I met Lucinda in the upstairs lounge that was being renovated. She smiled broadly to see me. Perhaps she thought I wouldn't turn up. She wore a smart grey trouser suit with a mauve blouse. Her make-up accentuated her strange appeal. She looked prettier when she smiled.

We walked along to the lounge bar in the next carriage and spoke of our families and our education. On reaching the lounge bar, we ordered drinks, a whisky and lemonade for me and a vodka and orange for her. We found a quiet corner and sat down. I felt guilty because I felt that I shouldn't be in this situation with a lady who was an unbeliever and who did not appear to be interested in becoming a believer. I felt like a hypocrite. But I pushed any thoughts of guilt aside and focussed on this beautiful creature beside me.

'I wanted to speak to you on your own because you seemed to be sympathetic about my depression.'

'Well I've had some bouts of depression too.'

'Your friend Paul is a nice guy but he's a bit of a know-all. He sure talks a lot too. And I don't think he knows much about depression.'

I smiled, not knowing quite what to say. She had just insulted my best friend.

'Do you miss your boyfriend?'

'I miss the togetherness. I need someone to talk to, someone to lean on, someone to... well, you know, someone to be with.'

The time flew by as we spoke of music, politics, hobbies and depression. I ordered another round of drinks, then another, then another. We got along well together. I was interested in her and she seemed genuinely interested in me. We talked about almost everything except the main thing in my life – The Message and its implications for mankind. It came briefly to mind several times during the evening and each time I felt guilty. It was the guilt which prevented me from mentioning it to her and she didn't bring the subject up. It was as though she wanted to ignore it. We were both quite tipsy as we left the lounge bar.

'It would be nice to do this again, Simon.'

'Yes it would, Lucinda.'

'How about the same time tomorrow?'

'Fine. I'll look forward to that.'

I walked her to her cabin and we kissed by her door. Then we kissed again, then again. I pulled her more tightly towards me. She gently pushed me back.

'Good night, Simon. See you tomorrow.'

'Goodnight, Lucinda.'

It was late when I got back to the guest room but Comforter was still up. His eyes followed me as I walked across the room. I avoided his eyes. I felt guilty.

'How was the lounge bar?'

'Oh, it was okay. You know, just a normal lounge bar.'

'Who did you go with?'

'What makes you think I went with anyone?'

'The perfume for one thing. The lipstick on your cheek for another.'

'Okay. I went with Lucinda.'

'It's none of my business, Simon but that girl has problems that need to be sorted out.'

I felt resentful at Comforter's intrusive line of questioning.

'You're right. It is none of your business, Paul.'

A long, tense silence followed.

'What problems do you think she has anyway?'

'Well, she has bouts of depression. And she dabbles with demonism.'

'Well one reason I went out with her was to try and help her with her depression.'

'How can you help her with that? She needs professional counselling. And did you help her with her fascination with demonism too?'

Hurried Departure

On that tense note, we retired for the night. I felt excited at Lucinda's interest in me but guilty at the same time. Early the next morning, Comforter was up and about. The noise he was making woke me up.

'Come on, Simon, get up. Get your things together. We're leaving.'

His voice contained a brusqueness that I'd never heard before from him.

'Leaving? What do you mean we're leaving? We said we'd stay another night to help them with their work.'

'There's been a change of plan. We're leaving now. Right now.'

'But I can't leave right now. I'm in love with Lucinda.'

'You're in love? How can you dare to fall in love when the world as we know it is coming to an end?'

Comforter was angry and he was urgent.

'But we can't just leave without saying goodbye,' I protested.

'I've left a note saying that we needed to leave in a hurry. Now move!'

I was reluctant to leave. Comforter grabbed my arm forcibly and pulled me towards the open door. It was a reminder to me, if I needed one, that he was bigger and stronger than me. Following on behind me, he pushed me through the door and closed it behind us. As we walked along a corridor to the end of the Women's Carriage, Comforter followed behind me, pushing me forward when he thought I was slowing down.

'Move, Seeker move!' he shouted several times.

I was feeling sullen. I resented Comforter making decisions like that for me. The long, resentful silence between us lasted for several hours. As we left the Women's Carriage, Comforter pointed to some empty seats and we sat down. He looked at me with that softness in his blue eyes that I had first noticed about him and had come to appreciate.

'I had to do that, Simon,' he said gently. 'You were being sucked into something that would've diverted you from your life's calling to go to the End Section. I could see that you were being tempted. The Message tells us to flee fornication and that's what we've done. We've told those women about The Message and if any of them are interested they can follow it up.'

I sighed deeply. He was wiser and more disciplined than I was.

'I suppose you're right.'

Still, I wrestled with the memory of the Women's Carriage. And it took me a long time before I could fully forgive Comforter for the way he handled it.

The First Class Carriage

After Paul Comforter and I had passed through a couple of full and noisy carriages with various trip hazards in the corridor, we came to the First Class Carriage. The atmosphere was noticeably different from that of the other carriages. It was genteel and sophisticated. The passengers looked prosperous, even aristocratic. The carriage was more spacious than the other carriages and had large reclining seats with extended leg room. There were complimentary refreshments at a vending machine and newspapers and screens with news and travel information. On entering it, we felt somewhat intimidated but we tried not to look out of place. We got our drinks from the vending machine and walked along the corridor looking for empty seats. We soon discovered that there were not many empty seats.

Meeting Erica Envy and Marcus Strife

A sudden movement of the train made me spill some coffee on the pale-green skirt of an attractive red-headed lady who looked about forty years of age. She was reading a book. Sitting beside her was a man of about the same age who was sleeping. She looked up at me with understandable irritation.

She seemed to study my face as though trying to determine something about me. Then she looked briefly at Paul.

'I'm so sorry,' I said. 'We were looking for seats when...'

She waved away my apology.

'You're welcome to sit here,' she said, nodding at the vacant seats opposite them.

As we gratefully settled into our seats, she said, 'I hope you like some conversation as you travel. I know I do. Anyway, I'm bored with this book.'

We were in the process of introducing ourselves when the man beside her woke up. He had longish black hair which just about covered his ears and wore a grey dress shirt with a purple tie which had been loosened.

'I'm Erica Envy and my sleepy friend here is Marcus Strife. We're both politicians. We're in the same party so we don't argue much with each other. Not about politics anyway.'

It didn't take long for the inquisitive Ms. Envy to ask about us and where we were going.

I explained as briefly as I could that we were on our way to the End Section en route to King's City.

'Oh believers, eh?' she replied. 'Tell me this. Don't all religions lead to God?'

'No, I don't believe they do,' I responded.

Ms. Envy looked a little irritated at my emphatic disagreement. 'But most of the great religions have a lot of moral standards in common. Doesn't that indicate that they're all serving the same god?'

At this point, I put my coffee on the table lest I spill it again.

'The idea of all religions leading to the same god is an attractive idea to many people. After all, disagreements between religious groups have led to arguments and persecutions and even wars and we would all like to see such things stop. It is true that the teachings of The Message are not unique in terms of their morality. Other religions have some form of the Golden Rule – treat others as you want them to treat you and all that. It's easy to see why many people believe as you do that all religions are basically the same. In my view, the main difference between them and us is the way we regard King Victor Love. To us, He was more than just a man and we feel that there is plenty of evidence to support that claim.'

'You have made a good point there. But it seems to me that all you people of faith can learn about tolerance and compromise from us politicians. Over the years, Geoffrey and I have had to compromise with all kinds of things – divorce, abortion, homosexuality, same sex marriage, transgender people and so on.'

'Tolerance is important. All faiths should exercise tolerance towards those of other faiths and towards all who hold different opinions. However, in basic matters of faith, no compromise is possible.'

'But why not?'

'The fact is there are major differences in what the different religions teach. If they all lead to the same god, how do you explain the fact that they disagree in their ideas of what God is like? Some believe God is a personal Being but others believe He is impersonal. Which is it? If you were to ask worshippers within the various religions whether all religions are the same, I think you will find that they will vehemently deny it. So how can there be any compromise?'

'Okay, I hear what you are saying. But apart from the various ideas about the one you call King Victor Love, are there any other basic differences between what you believe and what other religions believe?'

At this point, Paul intervened. 'I would say that a basic difference is that we believe that human beings can do nothing to save ourselves. Other religions say, "do this or do that". We say everything that needed to be done to reconcile man to God has already been done by King Victor. Our religion is focussed on a person – King Victor Love. All we have to do is believe and obey.'

'I don't think it matters what you believe as long as you are sincere.'

'But, Erica, a person can be sincere but wrong.'

'Hmm. What do you say, Marcus?' Ms. Envy asked her quiet friend.

The look on Marcus's face became stern. 'What about those in other religions? If they live in accordance with whatever truth they have, if they do their best with whatever truth they understand, surely you would not say that God will condemn them to Hell?'

'False religions don't lead to God, Marcus. There is only one Way to gain eternal life. Besides, no one ever has lived in accordance with the truth they have,' Paul responded.

'In my opinion, you two are brainwashed. And I don't believe in God anyway. I think all religion is nonsense.'

Ms. Envy looked embarrassed by the forthrightness of her friend's reasoning. 'Come on, Marcus. We have a meeting with the Secular Society to attend.'

With the briefest of acknowledgements, Erica Envy and Marcus Strife were gone.

Paul looked philosophical. 'The Message says that where there is envy and strife, there is confusion and every evil work. Those two look like they could cause us trouble. I'm glad they've gone.'

I nodded silently.

Meeting Frank Malice

As we continued walking through the First Class Carriage, we increased our pace as we wanted to leave it as soon as we could. We had nearly reached the halfway point when someone called out to us in a loud voice, 'Hey there! I say!'

We looked around to see a burly, bald man in his sixties beckoning us over to where he was seated. He was wearing an open-necked grey dress shirt and his discarded jacket and tie were hanging from a clothes hook by the window where he sat.

'Do either of you know anything about The Message?' he called out. 'I am working through a crossword puzzle and it contains a quote from The Message. It has four letters.'

'What is the quote?' Comforter asked.

The man replied, 'If anyone says, "I love God" and hates his brother, he is a something. The word has four letters.'

'The word you are looking for, sir is liar,' responded Comforter.

'Liar?' Liar?' the man repeated. 'Are you sure?'

'Yes I am sure,' replied Comforter confidently.

'Let me see. Four letters across. Liar. Yes it fits. I take it you know The Message rather well?' the man said.

'I don't want you to think I am boasting, but yes, I think I do know it rather well,' Comforter replied.

'That is a most interesting coincidence,' the man said. 'I have recently been thinking a lot about a question that is related to the word, liar and, in my profession, it is actually a very important question.'

I looked quizzically at Comforter and asked him, 'Do we have time to help this man?'

'We must always be prepared to give an answer to everyone who asks you to give a reason for the hope that you have,' Comforter replied.

So we both sat down and introduced ourselves. 'Pleased to meet you, Paul and Simon. My name is Frank Malice and I am the Editor of *Gossip Times*.'

'*Gossip Times*!' I said. 'That must be the most popular newspaper on the train!'

'It is certainly the most popular,' he assured us. 'It has the largest readership by far.'

Then Comforter asked Mister Malice what his question was.

'My question is simply this,' he said, looking at each of us in turn. 'What is truth?'

'What is truth?' Comforter repeated his question thoughtfully. 'You have asked a profound question indeed, sir. It is a question that has reverberated down through the ages. I will try to explain in simple terms.'

'Please do,' responded Malice.

'Many people today are cynical about truth. Some deny the concept of truth. Others view it as a community consensus,' Comforter began. 'Firstly, let me say that it is possible to know the truth and the truth sets us free from error and lies. Truth flows from the mind of God and is consistent with His character. Consequently, God is the Author of truth and He is the Judge of what is true and what is not true. As The Message was inspired by God, every word in it is eternal truth. The Way of The Message is the Way of Truth. Another way of putting it is to say that truth is that which corresponds to reality. King Victor Love came to the train long ago to testify to the truth.'

Malice bristled at this. 'Look, Paul. You seem to be an educated man. You must know that there are a number of worldviews and philosophies that challenge your concept of truth,' he said. 'For example, I am attracted by the philosophy of relativism which says that all truth is relative and that there is no such thing as absolute truth.'

'When you say that all truth is relative, is your statement a relative truth or an absolute truth?' I enquired. 'If it's a relative statement, then the statement is meaningless because no one can know where and when it applies. If truth really is relative, why can't Paul and I, who believe in absolute truth, be correct too?

'But if your statement is an absolute statement, then you are admitting that there is such a thing as absolute truth. And if there really is no such thing as absolute truth, then why should we believe your statement that there is no such thing as absolute truth? Isn't that rather akin to you inviting us not to believe you?'

Malice sighed deeply as he thought about the implications of our words.

'I suppose I am a sceptic at heart,' he replied.

'If you are indeed a sceptic,' I said, 'then you must be sceptical of everything that claims to be truth.'

'Yes I am sceptical of everything that claims to be the truth,' he said.

'Does that mean you're sceptical of your own scepticism?' I teased.

Malice chose not to reply to my question.

'Of course, there is another popular worldview and that is pluralism,' he said. 'It says that all claims of truth are equally valid.'

'But that is just not possible, my friend,' I protested. 'If I was to claim that the Earth is balanced on the back of a giant turtle and Paul here was to say that the Earth is round and suspended in space, how could both our claims be equally valid? If you chose to believe one claim and to deny that the other claim is true, then you have denied the basic tenet of pluralism.'

'Now you are just being silly.' Malice spat out the words as though he had just eaten something distasteful.

'I don't think so,' I said. 'Pluralism seems to me to fail to appreciate the difference between truth and opinion.'

'And your view of absolute truth seems arrogant to me,' Malice replied.

'Is it arrogant for my friend Paul, who is a locksmith, to say that only one key will open a particular lock?' I enquired. 'And would you say that a teacher of arithmetic was arrogant if he said that two plus two equals four?'

'But your view of absolute truth is offensive and divisive because it excludes people who hold a different opinion,' Malice retorted.

'You seem to misunderstand that truth, by its very nature, excludes its opposite,' I said. 'Besides, absolute truth is vital in various areas of life because there can be serious consequences for being wrong. For example, if a doctor gives you the wrong medication, it could kill you.'

After a long pause, Malice said, 'I might be able to agree that there is such a thing as absolute truth but only in the field of science not in religious concepts.'

'I would like to make a comment here,' Comforter interjected. 'When you claim that only science can make statements that are absolute truth, you are actually making a statement that cannot be tested by science.

'Besides, science is unable to say where the laws of science came from because it presupposes them.'

'I don't think I am ever going to reach agreement on what truth is with you two,' Malice sighed.

'You have made a true statement there, my friend,' I replied. Comforter nodded in agreement. On that discordant note, we took our leave of Frank Malice.

The Waiter

Paul and I sat silently looking out the window at the countryside flashing past. I was thinking about the people we had met and wondering what lay ahead. Probably Paul was thinking similar thoughts.

‘Excuse me, gentlemen, would you care for some refreshments?’

We looked up to see a smiling young man with brown curly hair wearing a white waiter’s jacket and pushing a trolley along the aisle.

‘What do you have?’ I asked.

‘Tea, coffee, a variety of soft drinks, crisps and nuts. They are all complimentary.’

‘What about those bottles of beer and spirits and the sandwiches and croissants?’ I said, pointing to them on the trolley.

‘Oh, those you have to pay for, sir,’ he answered, his tone apologetic but still smiling. ‘It’s like anything in life, if it’s of more value, you have to pay for it. Nothing of real value is ever free.’

‘That sounds rather cynical coming from a young man like you,’ I said. ‘Do you really believe that?’

‘Yes, sir, I really do. I’m not aware of anything valuable that’s free.’

This seemed like an invitation to me to share The Message with this young waiter. ‘I know one thing that is of great value and it’s totally free. In fact, you couldn’t pay for it even if you tried.’

His smile faded and was replaced by a puzzled look. ‘Really? And what might that be, sir?’

‘It’s The Message that tells us that we can live forever if we believe it.’

‘And what do I have to believe, sir?’

‘You have to believe that God exists, that He is holy and that He knows and loves you and that He sent His servant Victor Love to proclaim the truth. If you believe this, you can live forever with Him in happiness and glory in His kingdom. That is the basis of The Message. It’s a priceless promise and it’s totally free.’

‘But everything I have learned from my youth has taught me that if something is free, it can’t be worth anything. Surely everything has a price of some kind, even The Message, as you call it?’

‘You are an astute young man indeed,’ I replied. ‘While it’s true that you can’t pay for it because it is priceless, yet there is a price.’

‘Isn’t that a contradiction? You say it is priceless yet it has a price. I’m not sure I understand you.’

‘It’s priceless because no one could ever pay for eternal life in happiness and glory. How could they? It’s a free gift. It has to be free. But, in order to receive this free gift, you have to give everything you have, everything you are, to Victor Love as your King. You have to surrender your life so completely to

Him so that it is no longer you who live, but He is living in you and directing your thoughts and actions.'

'That is a very high price, sir.'

'Yes, but it's also a very high prize.'

'I have never heard anything like that before. I need time to think about it.'

'Here, I have something for you,' I said reaching into my bag. I pulled out a short booklet which explained the essentials of The Message.

'But I can't pay for it. I have no money on me.'

'That's okay. It's free.'

He took it and flicked through its pages cautiously. 'Thanks. It does look very interesting.'

He started to push his trolley again and his smile returned. 'I will read it, sir. I promise.'

Meeting Daiki Boaster

There followed another period of introspective silence between Paul and I. During such periods when we were not engaged in conversation ourselves, one tends to become more aware of other peoples' conversations. A slim, prosperous-looking and formally dressed young man of Japanese appearance had been on his mobile phone almost since we arrived in the carriage. I had heard bits of his conversation. It was something about stocks and shares. It didn't really bother me. Still, I was glad when he finally put his phone down. The silence was pleasant. To my surprise, he came over to us.

'I thought I should come over to apologise.'

'Apologise?' I said. 'What about?'

'Well, I've been on my mobile phone almost since you two arrived and some of the conversation must have sounded quite loud and heated.'

'There is no need to apologise,' I said. 'But it's nice of you anyway. Judging by the parts of your conversation that I heard, you seem to be interested in stocks and shares?'

'Yes I am. Very interested. It's my job to be interested. I'm a banker. But let me buy you a coffee. It will be good for me to speak to someone face to face after that long phone conversation.'

He returned with three coffees and sat down, introducing himself as Daiki Boaster. According to him, he was upwardly mobile and was earning a great deal of money. He spoke at some length about his career, his achievements and his aspirations. He then seemed to become aware that he had not asked about us. It seemed that he did out of politeness rather than genuine interest.

As we explained our backgrounds and our intention to get to the End Section en route to King's City, his interest seemed to perk up.

'I heard a preacher say once that The Message promises wealth to those who believe. Is that true?'

'No, it is not true,' Paul answered firmly. 'Some believers are poor. The Message does not promise wealth or health or success or fame. What it does promise is eternal life. That is one thing that money can't buy.'

'What do I have to do to get eternal life?' Daiki asked, seeming to become earnest.

'You have to acknowledge that you are poor in a spiritual sense – that is, you are a helpless sinner who is in dire need of forgiveness. You have to be willing to turn away from those sins and accept Victor Love as your King now and forever,' Paul replied.

'But isn't my success and my wealth a sign that I already enjoy God's favour?'

'No, wealth and success are not necessarily signs of God's favour. Nor is poverty a sign of God's disfavour.'

'If I did become a believer,' Daiki said slowly, 'and I'm not saying I ever would, but if I did, what would I have to do with all the money and materials things I have accrued?'

'You need to humbly acknowledge that your wealth is a gift from God and that He has entrusted it to you. He gave you the talent that you now enjoy. He gave you the power to get wealth. So you will need to use your wealth in His service.'

'You don't mean I have to give it all away?'

'Not necessarily. But you have to be willing to give it all away. You need to put your wealth at God's disposal.'

'At God's disposal? What does that mean in practice?'

'It means sharing your wealth generously with the poor. It also means supporting His work on this train.'

'But I've gotten used to being prosperous. I'm not sure I could live without it. Besides, having wealth and material goods seems so reliable and reassuring and permanent. Maybe I'll feel differently when I'm old. I might feel like becoming a believer then.'

'Riches are uncertain, my friend. They can sprout wings and fly away. In a spiritual sense, wealth is dangerous because it can deceive you into thinking that you don't need God. You are serving your wealth instead of serving God. This can lead you into all sorts of temptations. You can't serve two masters. Put your hope in God, not in your wealth. In this way, you will be laying up treasure in Heaven,' Paul advised. 'No one will be able to steal it from you there.'

Daiki shook his head sadly. 'Don't ask me to do that because I can't.'

'Daiki look at me,' Paul said earnestly. 'What good would it be if you were able to obtain the whole world but lose your own soul in Hell?'

Daiki said nothing in reply but looked troubled.

'A man's life doesn't consist in the things he possesses,' Paul continued. 'You can't serve both God and money. It has to be one or the other. If you decide to channel all your energies into serving money, then money has become your god.'

'I don't believe The Message and I don't believe in the god you are talking about. So I suppose money is my god, but what's wrong with that, Paul?'

'What's wrong with it, Daiki is that it's idolatry for one thing. And for another thing, the love of money is a root of all kinds of evil. It promises much but delivers only ruin and destruction in the end.'

'But I love money and the things it can buy. Money is power and, to me, power is satisfaction.'

'It's not money itself that's the problem, Daiki; it's the love of money. Money tends to make people proud. It just isn't wise to put your trust in wealth. Where you put your wealth indicates what is in your heart.'

'But what else do I have to aim for in this life if not amassing more money?'

'You should aim to serve God, Daiki. You shouldn't worry about the things that money can buy – what you will wear or eat or drink. You should seek what God is offering first and then He will provide everything you need.'

With that, Daiki held up his hand as though to say, 'This conversation is over.' He then arose and bade us goodbye.

As we watched Daiki leave, Paul said, 'It is hard for those who have wealth to accept The Message.'

Arrest!

We were about to leave the First Class Carriage ourselves when we were approached by Nicole Enigma with a couple of uniformed policemen in tow. Erica Envy and Marcus Strife were right behind them. Had they complained about us?

'Didn't I warn you that if you stepped out of line, you'd be in trouble?' Enigma said sternly.

'But we haven't stepped out of line, Ms. Enigma,' I protested. 'How have we stepped out of line?'

'We've been watching you from the time you left the Refreshment Carriage. You've been pushing your ideas about The Message everywhere you've gone. You just won't shut up about it will you?'

She gestured to the two policemen and they led us away with our hands handcuffed behind our backs. I looked behind to see Nicole Enigma exchange some words with Erica Envy and Marcus Strife. I was sure they had made a complaint about us. As for Nicole Enigma, the sight of her threw us into a panic. We had become exceedingly frightened of her.

The Courtroom

Nicole Enigma led the way as Paul Comforter and I walked in handcuffs, escorted by two policemen, up the nearest stairway and along a corridor to a door with the word, 'Courtroom' on it.

'We have the Courtroom and a judge and a jury all ready and waiting for you,' one of the policemen said with a sneer.

I assumed from this that they had been following us and had arranged that both the courtroom and the judge and the jury would be free to hear our case. As the courtroom was immediately upstairs, they had undoubtedly picked the most convenient location to arrest us.

Nicole Enigma led us into the Courtroom, with the two policemen and Erica Envy and Marcus Strife following behind. The Courtroom was moderately sized with a Judge's Bench at the far end, a Witness Stand and Public Gallery on one side and seating for the jury on the other side. A desk for the Court Reporter was positioned in front of the Judge's Bench. Paul and I were led to seating in the front row next to a female Defence Attorney. Also seated in the front row, but at the opposite side, was the Prosecuting Attorney.

Twelve people sat in the area reserved for the jury. There was a public gallery which was three-quarters full, mostly with elderly men and women. A stern-faced elderly man with a white judge's wig sat at the Judge's Bench. His name was Judge Geoffrey Unjust. A bespectacled young lady sat at the Court Reporter's desk and there was a jury of six men and six women with ages ranging from early twenties to late seventies.

It seemed that everything was ready for our case to be heard. Just before our trial was due to start, our Defence Attorney introduced herself as Mrs. Alice Chaos, an attractive lady who looked to be in her forties. She wore a grey pinstripe trouser suit with a purple blouse. An expensive looking pearl necklace hung loosely around her neck. She seemed to be somewhat disorganised as she arranged her paperwork. She pointed to the balding, bespectacled fifty-something man sitting in the front row opposite us and said, 'That's the Prosecuting Attorney. His name is Rupert Foe. He is very experienced and is one of the most talented people in the legal profession. We have our work cut out here, gentlemen.'

I groaned inwardly. I had a horrible feeling that we had the wrong attorney. She leaned over towards us and said in a quiet, urgent voice,

'I'm going to claim that neither of you are really believers – that it's all been a misunderstanding. I will argue that there is no proof that either of you are believers. I will ask the court to dismiss the case against you for lack of evidence.'

Paul and I were stunned. Before either of us could reply, the Courtroom Clerk announced the start of the trial. We were both told to take our place in the Witness Stand. We were asked to swear that we would tell, 'The truth, the whole truth and nothing but the truth.'

We declined to swear for reasons of conscience but we each affirmed that we would tell only the truth.

The charge against us was read out by the Clerk.

'The two men in the dock are charged with being members of a dangerous cult, sometimes known as the Believers, which teaches the following: this train is heading for Hell and is being influenced by some character revelling in the name of Prince Nicholas Rebel. The Message is divinely inspired and other religious books are not. Everyone who does not believe The Message is deceived and will end up in Hell. A hero of some kind called Victor Love, who died long ago, is not dead but will return to Earth with an army to take over the world and set up His kingdom, with King's City as His capital city. He will then condemn all those who never believed in Him to Hell.'

Several members of the jury laughed.

'Silence in the court,' Judge Unjust bellowed.

The Defence Attorney

Mrs. Chaos was invited to speak first to make the case for our defence. Addressing the members of the jury, she said,

'The case for the defence will be very brief. The charge against both the accused is based on a simple misunderstanding. All the accused have done is to show a mild interest in this cult. They attended a meeting and asked a few questions, that's all. They subsequently became involved in some conversations during which they put forward the ideas of the cult. However, there is no evidence that either of them is actually a member of the cult. It is one thing to express views sympathetic to an organisation. It is quite another to be a member of it. I challenge my right honourable friend Mr. Rupert Foe to produce evidence to the contrary. If he is unable to do so, then the case against the accused should be dropped and they should be released immediately.'

Mrs. Chaos then sat down with a confident smile at Mr. Foe.

The Prosecuting Attorney

The Prosecuting Attorney was then invited to make the case for the prosecution. Springing eagerly to his feet, Rupert Foe proceeded to make the case against us.

'I intend to show conclusively, despite the claim by Mrs. Chaos to the contrary, that both the accused are indeed members of this cult. By questioning the accused, I will produce three types of evidence – circumstantial evidence, the testimony of witnesses and motive.

'Firstly, the circumstantial evidence. There has been a marked change in the conduct of both accused since they joined this cult. They have begun to do charitable works like helping at homeless centres and food banks. They used to swear, use profanity, watch adult-rated films and enjoy risque jokes. But they no longer do any of these things. This change has been noted by those who have had only a passing acquaintance with both men, as well as by their friends. But the jury must be able to hear from their own lips why they have started to help others less fortunate than themselves.'

Addressing Paul and I, he asked, 'Will you please explain to the jury why your conduct has changed since you joined this cult?'

Paul and I exchanged glances, and Paul nodded at me as if to say, 'Let me handle this.' He took his place in the Witness Stand and began his reply.

'Nothing we can do in the physical realm – and that people can see – can qualify us for King Victor's kingdom. All the religions of the train teach their adherents to do this or that and you will reap your reward in the afterlife. But the true religion teaches that you don't have to do anything to be rewarded in the afterlife because all that is necessary has already been done by Victor Love when He came to the train many years ago. You could say that He purchased our ticket to King's City when He came the first time for those who believe in Him and accept Him as their King. But after we become believers, we try to live as Victor Love lived when He came here. Believers begin to obey the laws of the kingdom, not only in the letter but also in the spirit. Good works will be a noticeable feature of our lives. But I must emphasise, we don't do these good works to be saved, we do them because we are already saved. When a person becomes a believer, even though we are not perfect, that person begins to display something of the character of Victor Love Himself. The Message says believers should be the salt of the Earth, so believers should certainly make a positive impact on those around us.'

As Paul returned to his seat, Rupert Foe smiled and looking towards the jury he said, 'You have heard it for yourselves. They do not deny that they are members of this cult. It is precisely because they are members that their conduct has changed. Now we will consider the testimony of witnesses.'

He called three witnesses who had known Paul before he became a believer to describe the changes for the better that they had noticed in Paul's life since he became a believer. Three witnesses were then called to confirm the changes for the better in my life. The six witnesses comprised family members, neighbours and work colleagues. Reference was also made to written testimonies of strangers who did not know either of us personally but who had seen us around the community or the workplace. All six witnesses commented on the little things they had noticed us doing – being polite and considerate of others, and so on. All six observed that Paul and I were now different from most people. The written testimonies which were read out concurred with this view. After the testimony of the witnesses, Rupert Foe said to the jury, 'Now that you have heard the testimony of witnesses, we will consider the motives of these two men in changing their behaviour.'

Turning to Paul and I, he asked, 'Please explain to the jury your motives for changing your behaviour.'

Again Paul motioned to me that he would answer the question and he returned to the Witness Stand.

'Motives behind actions will always be questioned and it is an area that only God can know. The Message tells believers to love others and this should be the motive for the good works that we do to others – even to our enemies. The actions of believers should come from a pure heart, not to put on an outward show to impress others.'

Rupert Foe turned to the jury and announced, 'Well, members of the jury, you have heard the evidence. These men do not deny that they are members of this cult. In fact, they openly admit it.'

Judge Geoffrey Unjust said, 'I'm no expert in dealing with religious cults but I would have thought that believers can be identified simply by the doctrines they adhere to.'

He then asked Paul and I if either of us would like to comment on the evidence presented to the court. I took the Judge's comment as an opportunity to reply.

'There is more to being a believer than just adhering to a particular set of doctrines, Your Honour. After all, some believers hold to orthodox doctrines while others accept doctrines which many consider to be heretical. And only God is able to determine who is right and who is wrong.'

'But surely you must agree that the evidence that one is a believer would simply be if that person adheres to the list of rules of that particular cult?' Judge Unjust said ruefully.

'No that is not the case, Your Honour,' I replied. 'A believer cannot prove that he is a believer by obeying a list of rules or by his standard of morality or by what he does or does not do. Otherwise, if that were true, believers would be living lives dominated by rules. That would be legalism and all true believers must resist anything that smacks of legalism. There is more to being a believer than external evidence about their moral conduct. Such conduct springs from the motive of a believer and motive is something that cannot be seen. Many unbelievers have high moral standards and do good works. No, all the external evidence that could be used to convict us of being believers can be reduced to one word – love. In addition to loving others, believers are to love fellow believers and this is how others will know we really are believers.'

'Ah, that word love,' the Judge said. 'And how would you define love, Mr. Seeker?'

'Love is a much misunderstood and misused word, Your Honour. I'll tell you what love is. Love is patient and kind. It doesn't envy or boast. It isn't proud or rude or self-seeking or easily angered. It doesn't keep a record of wrongs or delight in evil. Love rejoices with the truth and protects and trusts and hopes and perseveres. Love never fails. That's what love really is. And no matter how much good we do for others, if we don't have love then we are nothing.'

'You've given me something to think about, Mr. Seeker. Much more of this conversation and I might become a believer myself,' Judge Unjust replied.

‘I wish you would, Your Honour.’

Judge Unjust then brought proceedings to an end and the court was adjourned while the jury considered their verdict. After about half an hour, the jury returned and took their seats. Paul and I braced ourselves for the inevitable.

‘Have you reached a verdict?’ Judge Unjust asked them.

‘Yes, Your Honour,’ the foreman of the jury replied.

‘What is your verdict?’

‘Guilty as charged.’

Paul Comforter and I were then sentenced to two years’ imprisonment. We were then led off to the prison by the two policemen. It was conveniently located on the top floor of the next carriage.

The Prison Carriage

Although Paul Comforter and I had been determined not to deny our faith in the Courtroom – and had even welcomed the opportunity to explain something of The Message – it was with considerable apprehension that we entered the Prison Carriage. On the short journey from the Courtroom to the Prison Carriage, our four man escort could be heard complaining that our two year sentence was much too lenient.

The Induction Process

A steel security door was opened by a young policeman of formidable appearance with a stern expression. We were ushered into the sparsely furnished reception area. Welcoming it was not. To us, it was an alien, threatening environment. An older man sat behind a desk and he asked us a number of questions in a bored, unsympathetic manner. The induction process had begun. I assumed he disliked his job and was looking forward to his retirement.

Did we take drugs? Did we have a drinking problem? Were we on medication? Did we want to see a doctor or nurse? Did we want to see our solicitor? Did we want any of our relatives informed of where we were? Would we like to see a personnel officer? The answer to all the questions was no.

We were searched by the young policeman who had opened the door. Our fingerprints and photograph were taken. We were each given a prison uniform, ordered to take a bath in an adjacent bathroom and to put on the uniform afterwards. The older man at the desk made a list of the clothes we were wearing and the few possessions we had on us. Our personal copies of The Message were confiscated by the young policeman, our protests being dismissed with a wave of his hand. The prison uniform had a number on it. I was prisoner number 76483.

The induction process made it clear to us that the Prison Governor ran the prison his way. He made the rules. The whole prison experience would be harsh. That meant that we would have to carry out six hours of work every day, five days a week. This work could entail making furniture or clothes or gardening or engineering, or working in the prison's laundry or kitchen. Work could also include studying a course to gain new skills. All reading material would have to be approved. We would be allowed one hour outside in an exercise area every day, and our diet would be monotonous, with the same food on the same day every week. We would be allowed two visits each month. The hardship we were to endure would be made even harsher if we ever dared to break the rules. On the other hand, our lives would be made easier if we were well-behaved and undertook further education. This more relaxed regime included easier work tasks, better food, better furnishings and facilities in the cell, more visitors, any books you wanted, unrestricted flow of letters in and out, etc. There would be no work at weekends and prisoners were free to do whatever they wanted to do within reason. Our hour outside would be in an exercise area of the carriage with an open roof but with higher walls to prevent attempts to escape. During this time, we would be permitted to mingle with other prisoners.

For more serious behavioural issues, a system of solitary confinement was available to the authorities. This meant being isolated for up to twenty-four hours a day with no human contact for periods of time which could range from a few days to an indeterminate period of time. We were told in no uncertain terms that the purpose of solitary confinement was to break the prisoners' wills and that it had caused some to go mad.

The induction process was an ordeal by itself.

Another Interview by Nicole Enigma

When the induction process was complete, we were ushered into a nearby office, where we were instructed to sit down on two chairs. Nicole Enigma entered the room and stood looking down at us. She slowly shook her head.

'My offer to help you still stands. I can recommend to the Judge that your sentence be reduced to six months. But you must reject the teaching of The Message and blaspheme the name of Victor Love. That's the only way I can be sure that you have disassociated yourselves from this cult.'

Comforter and I declined. 'We will never speak evil of King Victor's name,' Comforter declared.

Enigma shrugged her shoulders. 'So be it,' she said and left the room.

The Cell

We were then taken past dozens of cells with bars on the doors. Some prisoners looked inquisitively at these two new arrivals as though trying to figure out what our crime was. We were shown to the cell which we assumed was to be our home for the next two years. Paul and I were allowed to share a cell. It was around eight metres by six metres with white painted walls. It had two single beds, two seats and a toilet in the corner. The beds each had a pillow, a mattress, and a thin blanket. There was no natural light and the only illumination was by a single lamp in the centre of the ceiling. There was no television, no radio and no clock. There was no way for us to know how much time had passed or even if it was day or night. There was a bookshelf with no books on it. In that kind of environment, a person could forget their own name given enough time. The austere appearance of the prison gave rise to the impression that the authorities believed that prison should be as unpleasant an experience as possible to deter people from committing crimes. Some hatred seemed to have been included in the design. It seemed to be designed to be disorienting. It appeared that punishment and retribution had been favoured rather than rehabilitation and a new start. Paul and I sat down, sighed and looked at each other but said nothing for the first few minutes of our confinement. Finally, I blurted out, 'I don't know how I'm ever going to cope with two years in this place.'

'You'll be fine and so will I,' Paul said reassuringly. 'We've got each other.'

The next day we were sent to an assessor who would assess each of us to determine a suitable work plan for each of us. The assessor was a small, bald man of about forty with a large moustache. The assessment consisted mainly of him asking us about our abilities, work experience and hobbies. When we learned that we could study a self-improvement course and that a course on theology was included, we enthusiastically requested that we be permitted to study this course. He seemed to have some sympathy for our situation and, he said he would have to get permission from the authorities for us to enrol on the theology course. We had an anxious wait for three days before we were called to his office again, when we were informed that permission had been granted. Apparently, the authorities felt that such a course might correct some theological errors that we had. The assessor also informed us that, if we were willing to put in extra hours of study, the course could be completed within our prison term of two years. We assured him that we hoped to complete the course within two years. We asked if our copies of The Message could be returned to us as it would be helpful in our studies and he agreed to this request. The only provision he made was that we would have to submit our studies and the results of our coursework and exams to him at monthly intervals. At last Paul and I had something to feel positive about in our prison experience. Our course began the following week and we studied the course material in our cell. The time flew by even at weekends because we continued our studies at weekends.

The God Gang

Our walks in the exercise area were a welcome diversion and we were able to see the other prisoners and to speak to a few of them. Word had gotten round among the prisoners about the reason for our incarceration and a friendly, talkative old fellow pointed out five other prisoners who had been imprisoned on the same charge as Paul and I, namely, for believing what it said in The Message. We received this information with considerable enthusiasm and within the next few days, we had met all of them. We discovered that they had all become believers due to the teaching of John Herald and had been on their way to the End Section when they were arrested. They had all been sentenced to two years imprisonment like Paul and I. Each of them had been offered an early release by Nicole Enigma if they would blaspheme King Victor's name. All had declined. A couple of them had served around eighteen months and were anticipating their release. They informed us that Luke Watchman and John Herald had also been arrested and charged with the serious offence of inciting rebellion against the authorities. As a result, they had been sentenced to ten years imprisonment in a high security section of the prison, where they were not permitted to mingle with the other prisoners or with each other. We were horrified at the charge and the savagely long sentence. The seven of us met together during our hourly exercise walks in midweek and also at weekends. The other prisoners called us "the God gang" but, aside from some cynical remarks, there wasn't any hostility towards us. We agreed that we should try to get to know as many of our fellow prisoners as possible. We felt the need to share our beliefs with them. However, we did spend most of our exercise hour locked in conversation with each other because we found the mutual comfort and encouragement we received was so beneficial. The names of our fellow "God gang" believers, in order of age, were Manchu Humble, Arthur Gentle, Hammad Peace, Walter Mercy and Rohan Patience. Each of us were enthralled and inspired to exchange our accounts of how and why we became believers and the insight we received by reading The Message. After a few months, we had become firm friends and we planned to meet up at the End Section when we were released. Thus, in that most austere of environments, the sweetest of friendships were born.

Meeting Antony Undiscerning

It was during one of our weekend walks in the exercise area that we met a fellow prisoner, a middle-aged former politician who had been imprisoned for perjury and perverting the course of justice. He had been a millionaire but, as he was unable to cover the legal costs of his trial, he had been declared bankrupt. After being found guilty, his wife had divorced him. His name was Antony Undiscerning. He used to be Sir Antony but his knighthood was withdrawn after his trial. Here was a man who had lost everything that he ever prized in life. While in prison, and afflicted by guilt and shame, he had begun to think seriously about life. He wondered whether there really was a god and, if so, whether that god had a purpose for his life. He was studying the same theology course as Paul and I so this provided us with a convenient opportunity to tell him about The Message. When he discovered that we were believers, Undiscerning asked us a question which had been bothering him for some time.

'I have been reading parts of The Message and I too have come to believe that there is a god who created everything there is. But I'm puzzled about something. You believers say that God is good and all-powerful, don't you?'

'Yes we do,' I replied.

'I have been reading a lot while I've been in here, especially books on history. These books have reminded me again and again that throughout the ages there has been and still is so much evil on this train. So here is my question. If God exists and if He is good and all-powerful, then why do we have so much evil on the train?'

As a new believer, I did not feel competent to give a satisfactory answer to such an important question. I looked at Comforter, hoping that he would be able to provide Undiscerning with an answer that would satisfy him.

'You have asked a hard question, Antony,' Comforter began slowly and thoughtfully. 'A whole branch of theology is devoted to this very question. It is called Theodicy and it is an attempt to resolve what has been called the Trilemma.'

'What is the Trilemma?' Undiscerning asked.

'The Trilemma refers to three statements. God is all powerful. God is loving. Evil exists,' Comforter answered. 'The reasoning is that, if God is all powerful, He must be able to abolish evil. But, since evil exists, God either does not want to abolish evil or He is not a loving God. On the other hand, if He is a loving God, He must want to abolish evil. But, since evil exists, He must not be powerful enough to abolish it. The conclusion then is that God may be all powerful or He may be loving but, since evil exists, He cannot be both. The reasoning then concludes that God's existence is incompatible with the existence of evil.'

'That is a fair summary,' Undiscerning replied. 'Can you explain it?'

Comforter took a deep breath and launched into an explanation.

'Evil can be said to fall into two categories – natural evil and moral evil. Natural evil refers to natural disasters like earthquakes and hurricanes, famines, etc. Moral evil is the result of human wickedness, such as murder, theft and the deliberate infliction of suffering on another. There have been a number of theories put forward to answer this question down through the ages but the traditional believers' answer is that evil – both natural and moral – was not caused by God. It was caused by the free will which God permitted angels to have. Some of these angels, under the leadership of Prince Nicholas Rebel, rebelled against God and they, in turn, have influenced mankind. The reasoning is that the all-powerful and loving God permitted this to happen because the existence of natural and moral evil is necessary in order to achieve a greater good – the development of godly character in human beings so that they are fit to dwell with Him forever. Believers tend to have the view that not even an omnipotent and omniscient god can create godly character instantaneously but it requires time and mankind must be free to choose between good and evil in order to develop this kind of character.'

‘This seems to me like an adventure in individual freedom which is fraught with risks,’ Undiscerning interjected. ‘I still don’t see why a god who is both all-powerful and loving could not create a hedonist paradise for humans to dwell in if He loves us so much. Surely God could come up with another, kinder way to instil His kind of character within His children?’

‘You have referred to humans as the children of God and I believe the father and child analogy to be instructive,’ Comforter replied. ‘Surely a loving father above all else would want his children to become the best human beings they are capable of becoming? He would want his children to develop the capacity for love and such characteristics as honesty, humility, selflessness, compassion, and humour. In order to achieve this, I believe that this would mean his children would have to become acquainted, at least to some degree, with such things as tragedy, pain, deprivation and emotional turmoil. I do not believe that such a father would treat comfort and pleasure as the main criteria in bringing up his children.’

‘You have answered well, Paul. Thanks for taking the time to explain it so thoroughly to me. It’s been very helpful,’ Undiscerning responded.

We met and talked with Antony Undiscerning often during our two year incarceration and he appeared well on the way to becoming a believer.

Meeting Sam Cynic

Another man we spoke to often in the exercise area was a middle-aged, serial housebreaker called Sam Cynic. He had a small scar on his right cheek and an irritating habit of spitting. Sam had spent around one quarter of his life in prison. He had no time for any religion. He disliked believers in particular. Knowing that we were believers, he asked us on our first meeting, ‘What do you have to say about all the believers who are hypocrites?’

As he was looking at me when he said this, I took it upon myself to reply.

‘Your allegation that there are some hypocrites among believers is correct. But all of us are hypocritical at times, including you, Sam. We sometimes do things that we condemn others for doing. We often announce our intention to do something in front of others but later, in private, we fail to do it. Your question should be, “Why are we all hypocrites?”‘

‘But I’m not a hypocrite, Seeker. Not like you two. I don’t claim to believe in any religion nor any standard of morality.’

‘Sam, we are all inherently aware of a standard of morality that is higher than we are able to live by. That’s why you are accusing believers of being hypocrites. Our nature is basically corrupt. All of us were born this way, including you and I. That’s why we need King Victor. That’s why we preach The Message. Sin, if it’s not repented of, will take us to Hell unless we come to Him to be saved from the consequence of our sins. The Message doesn’t say that when a person becomes a believer, that person becomes perfect instantly. We believe that the only perfect person was King Victor. What The Message does say is that true believers will gradually improve after they accept Victor Love as their King. There are people who claim to be believers but are not. Anyone can claim to be a believer but that doesn’t mean that person really is a believer. A true believer is one who gradually becomes like King Victor.’

‘So you are telling me that everyone who doesn’t believe what you believe will end up in Hell?’

‘You’ve put it very bluntly, Sam,’ Paul interjected. ‘It is not our position to say who goes to Hell. All I can tell you is that no one will get to Heaven unless they accept King Victor. He is the only way in.’

Meeting Delroy Wrath

A few minutes earlier, a tall, burly acquaintance of Sam’s had wandered over to the edge of the exercise area where we were talking and listened for a few minutes. He was bald, black and was built like a weightlifter. I found his appearance intimidating. Sam introduced him as Delroy Wrath and said he was in for extortion. I was hoping he wouldn’t say anything but he did.

‘Well, if this Victor Love guy really is the only way to get to Heaven, what about all those who have never heard of Him? According to you, we are all predestined for Hell,’ Wrath said in a deep, husky voice. ‘They should at least be warned that they’d better learn about Victor Love otherwise they’ll end up in Hell. When I approach someone and offer to protect them for a certain price, I always warn them what will happen to them if they don’t pay. I tell them, “If you pay me the money, you and your family and your premises will be safe. If you don’t, you will lose everything you have and you will get beaten up and you might even die”. And it works. They nearly always pay up. The ones that are reluctant to pay at first soon agree to pay when I and a couple of my pals pay them a visit and rough them up a bit. But, according to you, God doesn't work like that.'

'Delroy, you have asked a tough question,' Paul answered guardedly. 'People are not condemned and sentenced to Hell based upon whether or not they have heard of King Victor Love. God's judgement is always just. People are condemned to Hell because they are sinners who have rejected what God has already revealed to them in the physical creation and in their conscience. Everyone should understand that there is a god. No one has any excuse. So we are all guilty whether we have heard of King Victor or not. But I believe that if people seek God then He will find a way to get The Message to them.'

'I still don't think it's fair. People should get a verbal warning,' Wrath complained. 'I warn people in person before I punish them for not heeding my warning. God, if He exists, should do the same.'

'Delroy, the only thing I will say to your question is that, if you are so concerned about the fate of those who have never heard of King Victor, then the worst thing you could do is to reject Him as your King,' Paul replied.

Delroy shook his head and led Sam away by the arm. As they left, Wrath said, 'I think both of you are deluded, dangerously deluded. I can see why they locked you up. What I can't understand is why you only got two years. You should be locked up for life. You two are more of a danger to society than I am. And the same goes for the rest of your "God gang".'

With that, Sam Cynic and Delroy Wrath walked away. I wasn't sorry to see them go.

'I think we've upset them,' Paul observed warily.

We met up with Sam and Delroy frequently in the exercise area. To our surprise, they sought us out and wanted to argue about The Message. We patiently explained The Message to them each time but each time they argued against it, sometimes with raised voices. On one occasion, Delroy grabbed me by the lapels and pinned me against a wall for telling him that he was a sinner who needed to repent and accept King Victor as his King. He threatened to kill me but was narrowly restrained by Sam.

'Why don't those two characters just avoid us if they hate The Message so much?' I asked Paul one day.

'I'm beginning to think they are protesting rather too much, Simon. The more vehemently they disagree, the more I'm inclined to doubt them.'

'You don't mean you think they are beginning to believe The Message, do you?'

'I don't know. But you can't always tell what is going on in someone's heart by what they say. And we should never judge by appearances either.'

Talking to Harold Horrid

Comforter and I frequently saw a sad looking young man with an unruly mane of long, dark brown hair walking around the exercise yard on his own. We never saw him speak to any of the other prisoners. We became curious about him and decided that we would try to engage him in conversation. One day, we arrived early for our get-together with the "God gang" with the intention of speaking to him. When we saw him, we both made a beeline for him.

'Hello there. You don't look very happy, young man,' I said brightly.

He looked at us defensively. 'I'm not.'

'Do you want to talk about it?' I persisted.

'I know who you are,' he said sullenly. 'You're in that "God gang". I've seen you talking together.'

'You're welcome to join us, if you want.'

'I've heard about The Message and about this Victor Love guy who's supposed to be able to make us acceptable to God. I'm beyond His forgiveness. I'm just too evil. I'm incapable of redemption.'

'Nobody's too evil to be redeemed, friend,' Comforter replied gently. 'You may be a great sinner but there is a great King waiting for you to come to Him and be forgiven. He is able to save even the worst of sinners.'

'You don't understand. I know you mean well but all your talk of forgiveness is just theoretical mumbo-jumbo. My lawyer and social worker blamed my upbringing for the way I've turned out. I'm a career criminal. But I'm the one to blame. No one else. The reality is that I'm just evil and aggressive and nasty. I've done awful things that even disgust me. I'm a liar. I hate any kind of authority. I'm a drunkard and I'm into any kind of dope I can lay my hands on. Nobody can help me, not even your King Victor.'

'Well it sounds like you are showing some remorse. I think maybe your conscience is bothering you. That's a positive thing for a start,' Comforter replied.

'Don't patronise me.'

'I'm not patronising you,' Comforter continued. 'Every one of us is capable of committing the most atrocious acts. That's because we are all born with a heart that's deceitful and desperately wicked. We can't even know the depravity of our own hearts. Given a certain set of circumstances, there's no level to which any of us wouldn't sink. We believers are far from perfect. Talk to any of the "God gang" and they will say the same. The only difference between us and you is that we have accepted King Victor as our King and asked for forgiveness and we know we have been forgiven. You've confessed your faults to us but we can't forgive you. Confess your faults to God. Only He can forgive you and He will if you ask Him sincerely. If you do, you'll feel like a great weight has been lifted off your shoulders.'

He fixed his eyes on us with an intensity that was almost fierce.

'Come and join us for a short discussion, friend,' I said. 'You'll learn about how The Message can help you.'

He just stood there looking at us with a surly expression without saying anything.

'Come on,' Comforter said, gently tugging his arm. 'We'd all be delighted if you would join us.'

Hesitantly and without saying anything, he came with us to meet the rest of the "God gang".

It turned out his name was Harold Horrid and he paid close attention as we spoke of how The Message is an invitation to all to make a fresh start in life. We gave him a copy of The Message which he gladly accepted. He started to attend our daily meetings and began to make progress in his understanding of The Message. The membership of the "God gang" had become eight.

Assaulted!

After a few weeks, the seven of us had become aware of some hostility which had begun to develop against us on the part of some other prisoners. This may have been because we were believers or it could have been that they thought we were being cliquish by meeting together so much. Or it could have been a combination of the two. The hostility started with name-calling and some jostling. At first, we tried to ignore it. Then we decided that we should not make our friendship quite so obvious and that the "God gang" should meet only for an hour at weekends. This restriction on the number of our meetings made us anticipate each meeting all the more. We tried harder to befriend the main protagonists. However, despite our precautions, the hostility increased.

This persecution drew us even closer together as friends.

One day, we held our usual "God gang" get-together, but this time without the pleasure of Harold Horrid's company as he felt unwell that day. We didn't notice that we had been surrounded by around thirty inmates, some armed with knives. Then, with terrifying suddenness, they rushed upon us with loud, hateful curses and fierce violence. 'We hate the "God gang". We hate all you believers. So you think we're bound for Hell, do you? Think you are better than us, do you?'

Our cries for help were drowned by their derisory shouts of hatred. Where were the guards? We tried to fend our attackers off. We tried to protect each other. But we were hopelessly outnumbered. Why did they hate us so much? Punches rained down on us. How did they get the knives in there? Knives were mercilessly thrust into flesh and bone. Again and again and again. Our screams of agony were greeted by the raucous laughter and scornful taunts of our assailants. I saw our dear friends fall one by one. Manchu, Arthur, Hammad, Walter and Rohan. They seemed to be badly hurt. Blood flowed from their multiple wounds. Why was God allowing this? How could they survive this? The horror of the scene rendered me speechless. Then, only Paul and I were still standing but about to fall under the ferocity of the attack. I had no more strength left to fight them off. Suddenly, I was aware of a large black man pushing our attackers aside. It was Delroy Wrath.

'Leave them alone. They're friends of mine,' he growled. He was accompanied by Sam Cynic.

'Go on. Push off the lot of you,' Sam shouted at our attackers. Our attackers fell silent, then backed away.

Delroy put one of my arms over his broad shoulders and half-carried and half-dragged me away. I looked round and saw Paul had collapsed on the ground. 'Paul, Paul,' I said in a weak, strange voice that I didn't recognise as my own. It was then that I felt surrounded by a warm, welcoming darkness and I remember no more.

The Hospital Carriage

The next thing I was aware of was waking up in a hospital. My first priority was to assess my physical condition. I had a heart monitor and an intravenous drip attached to me. The thought of the attack came to my mind with appalling suddenness and I closed my eyes to try to somehow block out the appalling reality of what had happened. I looked down at my arms which had been placed on top of the bed covers. There were deep cuts on each arm. I tried moving one arm, then another. It was painful but at least I could move them a little. My legs felt numb but I could move each of them slightly. Cautiously, I tried breathing deeply. My heart and lungs appeared to still be working.

I looked around the room and saw a bleak sparsely furnished space that reminded me of the prison cell I had so recently vacated. Mass-produced prints of pleasant country scenes adorned each wall and I could see the rear end of my chart which was fixed to the end of my bed. The walls and ceiling were cream-coloured. There was an uncarpeted wooden floor. In a corner was a chair with frayed tartan upholstery.

Located by the door were dispensers for soap, hand sanitizer and rubber gloves.

There were six beds. I had a bed by the window. The other five beds were occupied but the patients were sleeping. Dejectedly, I stared up at the ceiling and wished I could get out of there. But clearly, leaving was not an option.

A pleasant young nurse entered the room. 'Ah, Mr. Seeker, you're back with us.'

'Will I be okay?'

'You have multiple chest and abdominal stab wounds and there was some internal bleeding. One stab wound narrowly missed your lung and another was close to puncturing your intestines, but your vital organs are okay. You've had a close shave, Mr. Seeker and your recovery may take some time but you should make a full recovery.'

I felt so relieved I could have kissed her. Instead, I just smiled broadly. 'That's a relief.'

'You will be offered counselling to help reduce your risk of developing post-traumatic stress disorder.'

'Okay.'

She busied herself adjusting my pillows and blankets.

'What about my friends?'

She stopped and looked intently at me as though trying to decide if I was ready for bad news.

'I'm afraid your friends are all dead apart from Mr. Comforter and his condition is a good deal better than yours.'

It was the news I'd dreaded. All those wonderful, innocent believers, dead! Manchu, Arthur, Hammad, Walter and Rohan! All of them! They had all become very dear to me. Still, I was greatly comforted by my belief that their souls were now in Heaven.

'Mr. Comforter is well on the way to making a full recovery,' she said, in an apparent attempt to cheer me up.

'Where is he?'

'He's not far away. Don't worry about him just now. We'll arrange for the two of you to get together just as soon as you are well enough.

'Oh, by the way, Harold Horrid was asking for you. He is very concerned about both of you.'

'That's good of him.'

'I understand that he had been ill on the day of the attack and wasn't able to attend your meeting on that day. He's fully recovered from his illness.'

Consoling Cedric Grief

There was an old man in the next bed. He looked in his mid-seventies but he could have been older. After a few hours, we started talking. Every few minutes, he would let out a gasp of pain. He was clearly suffering a great deal despite the efforts of the hospital staff to alleviate his suffering. But he wanted to talk. When I asked him what was wrong with him, he told me that he had inherited a severe asthmatic condition. At times he found it difficult to breathe and carried an inhaler at all times. When the asthma got really bad, he had to be admitted to hospital.

‘That must be very difficult to live with, Cedric.’

‘It is. And now I have a bad back too. I could scream with the pain sometimes. Just the luck of the draw I suppose, eh?’

When he learned that I was a believer, he asked,

‘If there really is a God, why doesn’t He heal sick people when they pray that He will heal them? Why does He let them suffer when He could stop their suffering? I mean, look at all these poor people here. If I was God, I would stop all this suffering.’

‘You’ve asked a good question, Cedric,’ I replied. ‘It must be one of the most asked questions ever.’

‘Do you have a good answer?’

‘I have an answer. You will have to judge whether or not it’s a good answer.’

‘Go ahead, Simon. I’m listening.’

‘Obviously not everyone who prays to God for healing is healed. It might be that God has other plans for those who pray to Him for healing. It might not suit His plan to heal a particular person when they pray to Him for healing.’

‘But surely He should heal believers?’

‘Not necessarily, Cedric. A believer may have faith and still not be healed. It doesn’t mean that God doesn’t love them anymore. God might use someone’s illness to accomplish His will in a way that we can’t see or understand. If it was always God’s will to heal believers and for them to always enjoy good health, then believers would never die. That doesn’t seem logical at this time.’

‘I admire your faith, Simon.’

‘Are you a parent, Cedric?’

‘Yes, I have two children but they’re grown up now.’

‘When your children were young and they asked you for something, did you always give it to them right when they asked?’

‘No, of course not. Sometimes I would give it to them later. Sometimes I wouldn’t give it to them at all because I felt that it wouldn’t be good for them to have it.’

‘Then don’t you think that maybe God, as our Father, might do the same to us when we ask Him to heal us?’

‘I suppose so.’

‘You see, Cedric, God doesn’t always respond to our pleas the way we would want Him to. He allows us to endure circumstances that we’d rather He didn't. But that's His right. He doesn't tell us what He's going to do or not going to do. I think that when believers suffer there's always a reason. God is working out something in our lives. We need to have faith and accept His sovereignty and let God be God.'

'It takes faith to believe that, Simon.'

'Yes it does, Cedric but that faith helps us to accept suffering cheerfully.'

Cedric and I had a number of similar conversations during my time in the hospital but I was not able to convince him that God is good and loving and permits people, even believers, to suffer for a reason.

Discussions with Florence Nice

As the days passed I learned that the nurse was called Florence Nice and that she had an interest in things spiritual. We had some interesting conversations and became on first name terms. She was a very fine young woman with a sincere desire to help people in need. She was always cheerful and encouraging. I learned of how she regularly went out of her way to help others. I concluded that she was a genuinely good person. Florence knew the story of how I had ended up in hospital and we had regular discussions about The Message.

'Didn't you say, Simon that no one will be allowed to enter King's City unless they accept Victor Love as their King?'

I agreed that that was my understanding.

'But I don't think that's fair. I think most people live lives that are generally pretty good and sincere. Even if we make some mistakes from time to time, most of us are not all that bad. Okay, some of us might need some punishment, but to send us to Hell forever seems disproportionate to me. If God is loving, surely He wouldn't turn away people who are sincere and try to live good lives?'

'That's a common view, Florence. Most religions and philosophies teach that. But that view contains some assumptions. First, it assumes that most people are generally good. That's not true. I don't know what you consider a good person to be but no one is good enough to earn his or her way into Heaven just by being good. No one, Florence. Human nature is not basically good. It is basically bad. And it only takes just one disobedient act in an otherwise relatively good life to disqualify us from Heaven. Second, that view assumes that Hell is only for a comparatively few people who are really bad. But God is holy and morally perfect. And we're tainted by a fallen nature and we're all in rebellion against God by nature. So we're all really bad in His sight. Even the best of us falls short of God's perfect standard. It's true that God is loving but He is also holy and just. This means that He can't tolerate anyone who is even remotely sinful in His presence. He can't just brush aside our sins as though they had never happened. He would be a bad Judge if He did that. Because God loves us, He is willing to forgive all who vow allegiance to Victor Love as their King.'

'You paint a dismal picture, Simon.'

'But it's only dismal if you leave King Victor out of the picture, Florence. He is the only one who has ever met God's perfect standard. So our eternal destiny doesn't depend on our goodness, it depends on His goodness being transferred to our account. God does that when we accept King Victor and not until then. Without Him, we are all lost. But anyone can accept Him and be saved. Such a wonderful destiny as to be in King's City forever in glory and joy is the ultimate happy ending. It can't be earned by us doing a few good things in this brief human life. It can only be attained by the grace of God. But the good news is that it is available to all who will humble themselves and admit they are sinners who need to accept Victor Love as their King.'

'So I have to admit I'm a sinner and accept Victor Love or I won't be allowed into King's City?'

'That's the way I understand it, Florence.'

'But I'm always helping others, Simon. That's why I became a nurse. I want to help others. Surely God will make some allowance for the good things I've done?'

'As good as you are, Florence, you are not good enough to get to King's City by your own merit. As for God making some allowance for the good things you've done, even if you don't accept His servant Victor Love, I couldn't say with certainty. It's my belief that any allowance that could be made for your good works would only be to lessen your punishment in Hell.'

'But believers do good things for others too. Where do their good works come into this?'

'Believers don't do good works in order to be saved. We are already saved by God's mercy. We do good works because we are saved and because we want to bring glory to God and to reflect His character.'

'Do you expect God to reward you for your good works?'

'Yes we do expect to be rewarded but we don't do good works for that reason.'

'So you're telling me that I need to repent of my sins and rely totally on God's mercy to be saved?'

'Exactly. Salvation is not by works, it is given by the grace of God to those who believe and have faith.'

'But if I did repent and accept Victor Love as my King, how can I know that I will be admitted to King's City?'

'You'll know, Florence.'

'I'll have to think deeply about this, Simon.'

A number of similar conversations with Florence Nice led me to believe that she was nearing a decision to believe The Message and to accept King Victor.

Reunited with Paul Comforter

My convalescence proceeded better than the doctors and nurses expected and in a few days, the monitoring devices were removed from my body and I felt well enough to get out of bed. Within hours, Florence entered my room and announced with a smile, 'Simon, you have a visitor.'

Then the smiling figure of Paul Comforter appeared from behind her. I was sitting in a chair looking out of the window when he walked towards me and grasped both my shoulders gently. What a joy it was to see him again! Tears filled my eyes.

'Hello, Simon. I was worried about you. How are you now?'

'Much better thanks, Paul. And to see you is such a big tonic.'

Florence left the room and Paul and I had the privacy we both desired to encourage each other after the terrible attack in the prison. Perhaps even worse than the nightmarish memory was the dreaded thought of having to go back there to finish our sentence. It wouldn't be safe for us to return there. As far as we knew, there were no other believers in that prison.

Mark Waverer Returns

One day as Paul and I were sitting in an adjacent lounge of the hospital engaged in deep conversation about the trials that were the lot of the believer in this life, we didn't notice the young man who walked quietly up to us and stood looking down at us. As we looked up, we saw the beaming smile of Mark Waverer. What a joy it was in the midst of our suffering to see a beloved fellow believer! He sat down beside us and began to apologise for leaving us back at the Quiet Carriage.

'I was going through a difficult time. Things just got on top of me. I should've talked to you both before I took the decision. As I read carefully through The Book, and especially The Message, and thought everything through, I soon realised that I'd made a big mistake. This society really has nothing to offer in comparison with the glorious prospect of Heaven.'

'No need to apologise, Mark,' Paul said gently. 'We all have our own set of circumstances and problems to sort out. It's great to see you again.'

'It's a great encouragement to see you again, Mark,' I added.

'When I heard about your trial and unjust imprisonment and that terrible attack, I had to come to see you both right away. I heard about the deaths of some fellow believers in the attack and I'm appalled by the news. But I'm so relieved to know that you're both okay.'

'Will you go to the End Section now?' Paul asked.

'Yes I will. Now I know that I fully believe The Message. I wasn't sure before but I am sure now. I'm ready to give everything for King Victor, even my life.'

'That's great news, Mark. I'm sorry we're not able to join you on the way to the End Section. We'll have to finish the rest of our sentence first,' I said.

'That's a pity. I would've enjoyed your company. Okay. I'd better be on my way. I hope to see you there soon.'

Mark left and Paul and I were much encouraged by his visit and his return to acceptance of King Victor.

Given Compassionate Discharge

Paul and I spent many hours each day in the hospital's lounge and one day as we were sitting there, Florence approached us with two letters in her hand and handed one to each of us. We quickly opened our letters and read the contents. The letter we each had was announcing that, in view of our injuries, we were being given a compassionate discharge from prison effective immediately. We each let out a spontaneous cry of unbridled joy.

'We won't have to go back to that horrible prison, Simon.'

'Great news, isn't it, Paul?'

'There's just one condition, Simon.'

'A condition? What's that, Paul?'

'We have to have a counselling session before we are released.'

'Well that doesn't sound too bad.'

Ms Susan Sensible (Counsellor)

The following day I was shown to an office door with the name Ms. Susan Sensible on it. There were some initials after the name which I didn't understand, followed by a word I did understand, or thought I did at least – "Counsellor". I rang the bell at the side of the door and a pretty young woman opened it. She had long black hair, a mauve-coloured blouse and a grey, pleated skirt.

'You must be Simon Seeker,' she said with a cheery smile as she motioned for me to enter and to sit at a chair opposite her desk.

She sat looking at a file – presumably mine – and I sat looking around her office. It was pleasantly furnished with pretty paintings of flowers on the walls. They looked a little amateurish and I wondered if she had painted them herself. On the wall behind her was a large framed certificate and on her desk was a picture of an elderly couple, whom I assumed were her parents.

'I understand from your file that you are a member of the religious cult that believes The Message, Mr. Seeker.'

'I wouldn't say we were a cult, Ms. Sensible but I do believe that The Message was inspired by God and I do believe it.'

'Hmm. I see. You are the type of person who looks for meaning in life, is that correct?'

'I was looking for meaning in life and now I've found what I was looking for.'

'Well let me tell you straight away, Mr. Seeker that I do not believe in any god nor do I believe that life has any meaning.'

'Tell me, Ms. Sensible, do you accept that there are things in this world that you don't understand?'

'Yes, Mr. Seeker, I do accept that there are things in this world that I don't understand. But I can live with that. I don't feel the need to invent nonsensical theories to explain these things. I don't need to answer questions like, why are we here? Why is there something instead of nothing? What's the meaning of life? What happens after we die? I don't think it's possible to know these things. We must be sensible about these things.'

'So how would you describe your worldview?'

'My worldview? I suppose I'm a free thinker because I tend to reject authority where matters of belief are concerned. I consider these things to be personal.'

'Does that include religious beliefs?'

'I don't have any religious beliefs. I try to live a good life without any religious beliefs.'

'What are your moral values based on if not on religious beliefs?'

'They are based on reason, on respect for others' rights and on values that are generally shared. I don't need any god to tell me what's right and wrong. I think our laws and our public institutions should not be based on any one religion or philosophy so that people who have a different religion, or no religion at all, are not disadvantaged in any way by the system. So I suppose I could be called a humanist or a rationalist or a sceptic.'

'What about God, Ms. Sensible? Do you believe there is a God?'

'Maybe there is a god, maybe there isn't, Mr. Seeker. I don't know and I don't care. It seems to me that the evidence is inconclusive and so I would say that the only sensible thing to do is to reserve judgment. In terms of the existence of God, I suppose you would call me an agnostic or an atheist. I'm not sure which.'

'There is a difference, Ms. Sensible. An agnostic is someone who concedes that the existence of God is a definite possibility but who believes that such knowledge is unknown and probably unknowable. So an agnostic is not committed to believing in the existence of God or the nonexistence of God. Their view is that they don't know whether there is a god or not. An atheist does not believe in God at all, period. Which are you, an agnostic or an atheist?'

'Well, in view of the lack of proof about the existence of God, and the lack of proof about the nonexistence of God, I suppose I am an agnostic.'

'It depends on what you call proof. But I would say that the creation provides compelling evidence for the existence of God.'

'What do you mean?'

'Look at the world around us. It's so intricate and detailed and beautiful.

Did it really all just come into existence by itself? That doesn't seem reasonable to me. So I would call the creation compelling evidence.'

'I'm not convinced, Mr. Seeker. I believe the human mind is big enough to ask big questions but not big enough to understand the answers. They are mysteries, Mr. Seeker and I can live with mysteries. It doesn't bother me. We must be sensible, Mr. Seeker.'

'Some agnostics believe in a soul or an afterlife. What about you?'

'I don't believe in either.'

'Fair enough.'

'Now let's get down to business. I see my task as helping you to feel more in tune with our society, which of course, is primarily secular in nature. I see all people as being basically good and able to make necessary changes in attitude when the need to do so is shown to them. Your problem at the moment is you don't see the need to change your attitude to society. I'm here to help you overcome your problems and become a happy and well balanced and sensible person.'

'I've already had a similar conversation with Florence Nice the nurse. I'll tell you what I told her. I don't agree that people are basically good. The Message tells me the exact opposite – that people are basically bad and opposed to the will of God.'

'But we have research that supports our view that people are basically good.'

'Then your research is wrong. And by the way, I am happy and well balanced and sensible already. I don't need your help.'

'Mr. Seeker, your problem is that you imagine there's a spiritual dimension to your life when there is no such thing. You have been deluded into thinking that you are inherently bad and need the help of a god to forgive you and to help you through life. That is not true. We agnostics rely on our reasoning and research to solve the problems life sometimes throws at us. We don't need to rely on some imaginary god.'

'Ms. Sensible, I would say that you are hiding behind layers of self-sufficiency. You need God, you just haven't realised it yet.'

'Mr. Seeker, I think we need to end this session now. I don't think we are getting anywhere nor do I think another counselling session would help. I've done my best but I don't think I can help you. I will write up my report and send it to the authorities.'

With that, Ms. Sensible rose and showed me to the door.

I met up with Paul Comforter after leaving the counsellor's office. He had just had his obligatory session, with similar results.

'Now we can get going again on our way to the End Section, Simon.'

'I'm ready right now, Paul. Let's get going. We've wasted enough time with the trial and imprisonment.'

With that, we fetched our clothes which had been sent from the adjacent prison and joyfully set out once again for the End Section.

The Dining Carriage

On leaving the Hospital Carriage, and still in high spirits at regaining our precious freedom, Paul Comforter and I reached the Dining Carriage and had just entered it when someone called out to us in a loud voice, 'Hey there! Hey there! Hello!'

We looked around to see a plump, bald man in his fifties beckoning us over to where he was seated.

'I hate eating alone,' he said. 'Won't you please join me for lunch?'

He was wearing a white, short-sleeved shirt. His tie and a dark blue jacket were hanging from a peg by the window where he sat.

'Thanks, but we ought to keep going,' said Comforter. 'Anyway, I'm not hungry.'

'Your friend looks hungry to me,' said the stranger. He looked at me and said, 'Does he always speak for you? What is he, your spokesman or something? Come on, sit down and have lunch with me.' He was almost pleading for our company.

'Well I am feeling quite peckish,' I replied, looking apologetically at Comforter.

Comforter shrugged. 'Okay,' he said.

Dining with Gary Greed

We both sat down opposite the man and introduced ourselves.

'I'm Gary Greed,' he said enthusiastically. 'I'm a chef and I love my job because I love food. Food is my passion.'

Greed summoned the waiter over and asked for three menus. When the menus arrived, Comforter and I studied it then ordered a main course.

Greed looked at us with a puzzled look. 'Aren't you having a starter?'

We both declined the starter course.

'Please yourselves. I'm starving.' He ordered soup for the starter and he continued to speak to us while he supped it up. We joined him for the main course but he continued to speak between mouthfuls.

'You know, everybody loves to eat. That's one thing we all have in common. It's a favourite topic of conversation. We all have our favourite foods. They're often related to the culture we've come from and sometimes memories from our childhood.'

'I'm sure you have to know a lot about all kinds of food,' I said, trying to look interested.

'Oh yes indeed. There's a lot you have to know to become a chef. Things like diet, nutrition, salt content, weights and measures, understanding and comparing prices, dealing with suppliers, being able to read nutrition information on labels, and so on. All of it is very important.'

Suddenly, he looked at us appraisingly as though he had just remembered something. 'Judging by the purposeful way you two fellows were striding along, you looked as though you were on some important mission.'

'We are going to the End Section,' I volunteered.

'The End Section?' he said incredulously. 'Isn't that where those nutty religious folk go?'

This led to a conversation about The Message and Greed managed to listen without much interruption, mainly because he was eating as we were telling him about it.

'I've heard that you believers disapprove of gluttony. Is that true?'

'Yes we do,' Paul replied.

'Why? What's wrong with gluttony? I'm a glutton. I admit it. I happen to like my food. What's wrong with liking your food?'

'Well I suppose one reason is that it indicates that food has become rather too important to us. We are to honour God with our bodies. That means avoiding obesity and putting on too much weight because it will damage our health eventually.'

'Weight is a touchy subject with me as you can probably see. But I've seen some believers who are nearly as fat as me.'

'I've seen some overweight believers too, Gary,' I added. 'I think that some believers regard gluttony as an acceptable habit but are often quick to condemn drinking too much or smoking. But it isn't right for believers to gorge themselves on food.'

'You're right, Simon,' Paul said. 'If we are unable to control our eating habits, then we will probably not be able to control our appetite for other things like anger, revenge, gossip or lust. We shouldn't let our appetites control us.'

With his mouth full of food, Gary was unable to reply but vigorously shook his head in disagreement. It was interesting to meet someone who was enthusiastic about his job and was knowledgeable about it but his sole topic of conversation was food. It was becoming rather tedious and having to wait for Gary to finish his latest mouthful before he could speak didn't help. We started to look for a way to end our conversation. After a particularly lengthy question from Paul about modern methods of food production, we decided that, rather than wait for what would undoubtedly have been a long and detailed reply that we would thank him for the meal and say a quick goodbye. We left Gary Greed as he was tucking into his second dessert. We found two empty seats some distance away.

Karim Ambition Advises

After a few minutes, a slim, bald man of Asian appearance plonked himself down beside us.

'Hi, guys. Mind if I sit here? Before we could reply, he said, 'My name is Karim Ambition.' 'I'm in advertising. Here's my card.'

As he handed me his card, I noticed that he bit his nails rather badly.

'Managing Director of *Wily Advertising*. I've heard of them,' I said.

'You've heard of them! I should think so. They're just the largest advertising company on the whole train.'

We had an interesting conversation during which he did most of the talking as he regaled us with some fascinating stories of his experiences in the advertising business. As he spoke, he continually tapped his left foot on the floor. I assumed this was a nervous habit he had developed.

Suddenly he paused and looked at Paul and then me, as though he had just realised that he was doing all the talking. 'But what about you two guys? What are your stories?'

Paul and I exchanged glances as though trying to decide which one of us should answer.

'I used to be in advertising myself but on a much smaller scale to you. My friend Simon here used to be an engineer.'

Before Paul could continue, Karim Ambition interjected. 'What do you mean, you used to be?'

'I was just about to say,' Paul continued. 'We have left our former lives and set out for the End Section.'

'The End Section? You must believe in The Message then or whatever you call it. Now that is interesting. As an advertising man, I find that very, very interesting. Can I ask you what attracted you to it?'

'I think it was the simplicity and bluntness of The Message that attracted me,' I volunteered. 'The Message states that every person is inherently evil and rebellious against God and we will all end up in Hell if we don't believe The Message and accept Victor Love as our King.'

'It also has the ring of truth,' Comforter responded thoughtfully. 'I mean, it's not a popular message with most people. So why would anyone promote it unless they really believed it to be true?'

'But The Message sure is confrontational, guys. This is why I asked you what attracted you to it. The Message is basically saying that we are all lousy sinners who are bound for an eternity in Hell unless we believe in this Victor Love guy. No wonder only a few people ever respond positively to it. What are your membership statistics like? Are your numbers growing?'

'Yes the numbers are growing,' Comforter replied. 'Not spectacularly but we are growing.'

'You should start to emphasise the more positive aspects of The Message.'

'Such as?' I asked.

'Look, I'm an advertising man. I know what attracts people. You could emphasise that God is loving and drop the bit about Him getting angry at sin and judging people. I think you would find that many more people would become believers. You are both intelligent men. You must know what I'm trying to say here.'

'But, Karim, that would be a distortion of The Message,' Paul protested. 'Besides, we have to be honest with people. They should know the whole Message, not just part of it. The part about God being angry at sin and judging people is an important part of The Message.'

'Guys, you know as well as I do that there's enough bad news going around this train already and people have enough problems without you believers adding to their problems by making them feel guilty about their sins.'

'But they should feel guilty about their sins,' I replied. 'Their sins have a bad effect on them and those around them in this life. But even worse than that, their sins will ultimately lead them to Hell.'

'Hell? That's much too blunt. Are you trying to put people off? Apart from breaking the main principles of advertising, I find that approach to be unloving, Simon.'

'It's not unloving, Karim. Since their sins will lead them to Hell, the most unloving thing would be not to tell them.'

'Look, Simon, I'm trying to help you here. You want to attract as many people as you can don't you?'

'Of course we do.'

'Exactly. Then tell people what is likely to attract them, not something that will put them off.'

'What else do you suggest?' Comforter asked.

'I've heard that this loving god of yours blesses those who obey Him, is that true?'

'Yes He certainly does.'

'And those blessings could include health and wealth, could they not?'

'They could do, but...'

'Then tell them that. Give them something positive to cling to, not all this negative stuff about sin and judgement.'

'But that would be another distortion of The Message,' Comforter said. 'Although God is loving and He can bless people with health and wealth, He doesn't promise these kinds of blessings. You might receive those kinds of blessings and you might not. The blessings that all believers certainly receive are spiritual in nature. Things like joy, reassurance, and peace.'

'But can't you just imply that health and wealth come as part of the package? You don't have to say specifically that people will become healthy and wealthy; you just sort of imply it. That would give them hope. What's wrong with that?'

'What's wrong with it is that it would be a false hope. We are not promised health and wealth. What we are promised is blessings and trials of various kinds in this life and eternal life in the next,' Paul replied.

'But don't you want to make The Message more attractive to more people?'

'The Message can't be made attractive in the way you suggest because it is something that divides people because it confronts people with their sins and it demands belief or rejection. Some well-meaning believers try to do as you suggest and make The Message sound more attractive to unbelievers but it simply cannot be done without compromising it. You cannot give unbelievers what they want and still be giving them the truth. The reason is that the hearts of unbelievers are wicked and don't want to be confronted with their sins.'

'But you guys make it sound like unbelievers are not welcome in the company of believers. It's like you're saying that you don't care whether they become believers or not.'

'We do care, Karim. We want unbelievers to join us but we won't give them false hope. We don't court popularity. We tell it to people straight. We refuse to water The Message down. The Message exhorts everyone to accept it but it also contains a warning about what will happen if you don't.'

'Hmm. Well, Paul, I'm surprised you left such an interesting and lucrative job in advertising to go on… sorry no offence, but to go on a wild goose chase to the End Section.'

'We don't believe it is a wild goose chase, Karim. We believe it's the path to King's City, the Heaven on Earth.'

'I don't seem to be able to convince you two, do I?'

'No, Karim you don't,' I replied. 'Anyway, I think that Paul and I need to be on our way.'

With that, we rose and bade farewell to Karim Ambition.

As we walked away, Ambition called out to us, 'Good luck in proclaiming The Message. You're going to need it; The Message is just a load of nonsense. Only a few brainwashed losers like you will ever believe that. And you can tell that to those poor people in the End Section.'

We both grimaced, wondering how many others in the carriage had heard his derogatory remarks.

Jean Worrier Asks For Advice

We had gone only a short distance when a young woman in a light blue tracksuit and a maroon tee-shirt tapped me on the arm as I walked past her seat. 'Excuse me but I couldn't help hearing that man who called out to you as you were walking away. If I understood what he said, you are both believers in The Message?'

'Yes we are,' I replied.

'Then you might be able to help me. I would like to ask your advice. Won't you please sit down?'

Comforter and I exchanged glances and he nodded briefly in acquiescence and we sat down beside the young woman. She had long black hair that was held up by a band. She was slim but muscular with a pleasant smile.

We introduced ourselves and she told us her name was Jean Worrier. When she was sure she had our attention, she began to speak in a low voice, as though she wanted to make sure that no one else heard.

'I'm a professional tennis player in my late-twenties and I'm earning a lot of money. Without going into too many details, let's just say that I have a very good standard of living. I have everything that I've ever wanted from this life. But I'm not trained in anything else. I sacrificed much of my education to practice my tennis. Now I'm beginning to be concerned about what I'll do when I stop playing tennis. I want security in later life. I get advice from all kinds of people about how to invest my money for the future and they all sound remarkably similar. But I know that you people who believe The Message have a completely different outlook to life and things like investments and security. It's important to me to take all points of view into consideration. I would like to hear your advice on the best investments to give me security in my old age.'

'Jean, you don't know for sure whether you will live to old age. No one does,' I replied. 'Security is something we all need yet there are so many people suffering from insecurity. Your feeling of insecurity can be a good thing if it drives you towards the only One who can give you real security. There are many false sources of security in this life. The best security, Jean, indeed the only real security, is to turn to God and believe The Message He has sent. Trust God to protect you and provide for you. Let Him be your security, your fortress.'

'But, Simon, I have control over my life at the moment. I make decisions that I feel are in my own best interests. I might well make some wrong decisions but at least they are my decisions.'

'Be prepared to give up that control in order to trust God.'

'You are asking me to give up control over my life to trust in a god that I can't see to give me the security I crave. Control over my life is the only hope I have to provide me with security.'

'I would say that you shouldn't focus on giving up control over your life. Focus instead on making God your security. When God is your security, you don't need to insist on control.'

Worrier looked puzzled. 'But, Simon, how can God be a better investment than the usual things that people like me invest their money in, like stocks and shares and houses and paintings?'

'Let me be very clear, Jean. I'm not saying you should not invest in these kinds of things – in fact I think maybe you should. You need to be a wise steward of all you have. But you should appreciate that the values of these things you have mentioned is based on confidence, that's all. In fact, the value of money itself is also based on confidence. That confidence can be lost due to a number of things, like war or a glut of something like oil suddenly coming onto the market. And when that confidence is lost, the value of investments of all types can plummet.'

'But that's being very pessimistic, isn't it?'

'I would say it's being very realistic. My advice to you is to invest some of your money but to use a generous proportion of it to do good to others who are in need. Then you will find you will be blessed now in this life and, even more importantly, you will inherit eternal life in Heaven.'

At that point, we rose to leave. 'I like the sound of your advice, Simon. It makes sense to me. I intend to look into The Message and try to apply it in my life.'

'I hope you do, Jean. It really is your best investment.'

Challenged by Alex Smug

Once again we had not gone far before our next encounter. We saw this man in his forties sitting on his own. As our eyes met, he smiled at us.

'Hello. I've been watching you walk along the aisle and I thought to myself, "Those two fellows look familiar. Now where have I seen them before?" Then it struck me. I saw an article in the newspaper about your arrest and the reason you were arrested.'

'That was a painful episode,' I replied.

'Yes I'm sure it was. I actually have a professional interest in your case and a question I'd like to ask you. Won't you sit down?'

So we sat down beside him. He had just finished his meal and was relaxing over a cup of tea.

'Would you like something to drink?'

We both declined.

'What's your question?' Paul enquired.

‘I am a psychiatrist by profession. My name is Alex Smug. I help people who have all sorts of personality disorders. We group these disorders into different sections. One section includes the odd, the eccentric, and the bizarre. Another section involves the erratic and dramatic. And still another section consists of the fearful and anxious.’

‘That’s interesting, Alex but what does it have to do with us?’ I asked.

‘Well you see, one of those personality disorders is a narcissistic personality disorder. This is a mental disorder in which people have an inflated sense of their own importance, an overwhelming desire to be admired. But the impression of confidence is a mask. It covers up a fragile self-esteem that reacts indignantly to the slightest criticism. Along with the confident exterior, there is a general lack of empathy for others.’

‘Go on,’ I said cautiously, wondering where all this was leading.

‘Well, gentlemen. It’s this god of yours that interests me. I’ve read a little bit about Him. Why does He want to be worshipped and praised all the time? In a human being, we psychiatrists would probably call that a narcissistic personality disorder. So tell me, why does the god you worship want to be worshipped?’

‘Your comments are interesting, Alex but you misunderstand the type of being that our god is,’ Paul replied. ‘Let me try to explain. Our god doesn’t need praise from anybody. He doesn’t need anybody’s help for anything. He is completely independent.’

‘Fair enough, Paul. But why does He demand worship and praise?’

‘Because He is God. He is perfect in every way. He is wise and good and powerful. He created everything that is, including you and I and He deserves to be treated with respect. You ask why He demands worship and praise. I would say there are two main reasons. Firstly, it is right and proper that we worship and praise Him as His creatures. He deserves it. But we worship Him, not only because He commands it and deserves it, but because we want to. Any father would be disappointed and maybe even angry if his children were to take him for granted and ignore him. The relationship would be strained. In a way, it’s like that with our heavenly Father. Anyway, it’s natural for mankind in general to praise whatever we value. This whole train resounds with praise. People praise their spouses, their children, their favourite football team, their hobby, the countryside, a wonderful building, and so on. We become advocates for whatever we love and we sometimes invite others to join us in our praise. So it is with believers. We praise and worship God and we invite others to join us.

Secondly, it is good for us to worship God and to praise Him. It's the destiny of all believers to worship Him in Heaven. Those who don't want to worship Him won't be there. They will be in Hell.'

'But, not only does He demand to be worshipped, He also plainly depicts Himself as a jealous god and then He condemns us for being jealous! Explain that to me.'

'Alex, it's a different use of the word jealousy. The jealousy God condemns in humans is the jealousy that is caused by us wanting something that somebody else has. What God is jealous of is when someone gives to another something that rightfully belongs to Him, that is, the praise and worship that belongs to Him and to Him alone.'

'So you are saying there are two types of jealousy, one is okay and the other is not okay?'

'That's right. For example, if you fancied another man's wife that would mean that you were jealous of him because he has a woman that you would like for yourself. That kind of jealousy is wrong because the woman does not belong to you. On the other hand, if you saw another man flirting with your wife, you would be right to be jealous because she belongs to you and you belong to her. That kind of jealousy is right because you are protective of what belongs to you. God is not jealous because He wants or needs something that somebody else has. He is jealous when people do not give Him the praise and worship that belongs only to Him.'

'Okay. I understand the difference but I still think that both of you have been deluded. You are nice guys and I like you both, but I don't like the god you worship or His Message. Now I don't mean any offence, but in speaking to you, I can't help characterising both of you as a particular personality type. It seems to me that you are both suffering from a dependent personality disorder.'

'All right, Alex. Go ahead and explain,' I smiled.

'A dependent personality disorder is characterised by a lack of self-confidence and a dependency on others. This type of person has surrendered his personal responsibility for making his own decisions and given this responsibility over to one or more other people. He submits himself to others and trusts them to look after him. In your case, you have surrendered your lives to this god of yours and, no doubt, to leaders in your organisation.'

'There is some truth in what you say, Alex. I don't deny that I have surrendered my life to God. I seek His will for my life. I try to make decisions based on the principles He has revealed.'

'There you are then. You have just admitted that I'm right about you.'

'Alex, I'm not sure I have just admitted that. But you have asked us why our god requires worship and praise and we have answered it. Now I would like to ask you a question,' Comforter said.

Smug looked a little taken aback. 'Sure, go ahead.'

'Why don't you join us in surrendering your life to God?'

'Are you kidding? I don't hand over control of my life to anyone.'

'I hope you think over what we've said, Alex.'

'Maybe I will.'

We shook hands and left Alex Smug to his analysis of others.

The Lounge Carriage

As Paul Comforter and I made our way towards the rear of the train, we passed through many carriages. The journey was difficult and we had to negotiate various items of luggage which were partially blocking the corridor and outstretched legs, and all the while the movement of the train seemed to want to throw us off balance. Occasionally, despite our best efforts, we did accidentally kick an item of luggage or an outstretched leg, apologising profusely as we did. Some of the people were none too polite. Many of the carriages we passed through were noisy, even raucous.

In time, we came to a lounge carriage with blue, lounge-style seating, such as you would find in a restaurant or in a home. A central bar sold drinks and snacks. It had a wider central corridor and was luggage-free which made it much easier to walk through. Although there were plenty of people in the carriage, the atmosphere was calm and classical music played quietly over the sound system.

'This looks like a good place to rest and relax,' I said.

Paul knew me well enough by now to know what I like. 'Okay, I'll get us a couple of coffees and croissants,' he replied.

Meeting Cheng Infidel

Paul returned a few minutes later with coffees and croissants and also with a tall, slim, sixty-something man with a thin, neatly-trimmed moustache. The man had a round-shaped face and eyes angled slightly downwards and looked Chinese. His name was Cheng Infidel.

Paul introduced us and said that Cheng was an inventor and held over one hundred patents for products as diverse as computer games and smart phones.

'Your friend has been telling me you both believe in God,' he said.

‘Did he?’ I replied, groaning inwardly. I could sense a question coming.

‘Tell me this then. I have invented a lot of things. You could say that I have created them. My question to you both is – who created God?’

‘What you have to understand, Cheng is that God, by definition, is uncreated. He had no beginning and He will have no end. He just is,’ Paul replied.

‘I thought you might say that but I find that answer very unsatisfying. To my mind, everything has a beginning. Everything is caused by something. It’s cause and effect.’

‘Everything which has a beginning is caused by someone or something. The universe – that is, matter and time and space – had a beginning so it must also have been caused. Things don’t come into existence by themselves. God caused everything to come into existence. But God Himself had no beginning, so He had no cause. He has no end either. God created time, so He is outside of time and therefore He had no beginning in time. He just is. In all the universe, only God is eternal. If something else or someone else had caused God to come into existence, then that something or that someone would be God. Everything was caused by something except for God.’

‘But quantum mechanics produces something from nothing all the time. Particles routinely pop into existence all the time. They are not caused by anything. Surely the universe itself could have just popped into existence?’

‘I would dispute that quantum mechanics produces something out of nothing. Any theory that the universe popped into existence as a result of a quantum fluctuation must assume that there was matter and antimatter there to begin with. Where do you think they came from? God created matter and antimatter.’

‘I invent things, Paul. That’s what I do. And I do it all the time. I bring things into existence that were not there before. I just can’t grasp the concept of anything – God in this case – not having a beginning.’

‘Cheng, when you bring things into existence, as you call it, you use materials like wood and stone that have already been created. And you use laws like the law of electricity. But God created all matter, all antimatter and all laws.’

‘Sorry, but my brain is hurting. I just cannot comprehend of everything being brought into existence from nothing by a supernatural being that has always existed.’

‘Neither can I, Cheng. As humans, our minds are finite and we are limited in our understanding. We can't conceive of a being like God having no beginning. But that's the way He is.'

Enter Ricky Revel

Sensing an impasse in the conversation, I was just about to suggest to Comforter that we get on our way when we saw Cheng wave at someone behind us and wave the person over. I looked round to see a handsome man in his thirties with black curly hair. He wore a black leather jacket with a red silk shirt. He was sitting with a group of other young men of about the same age. He excused himself from them and came over.

'Hi there, Cheng,' he said, easing his slim frame into the empty seat opposite Comforter and me.

The young man was instantly recognisable as Ricky Revel, the pop singer who had mesmerised a whole generation and inspired a legion of impersonators. This was the man with the raw, emotive and slurred vocal style which ranged from tender whispers to hoarse wailing and shouting. Single-handedly, he had made vulgar sexuality part of mainstream culture. His charismatic stage presence and colourful, elaborate stage costumes had made him like a god figure to his many fans. Seeing him up close, his physical attractiveness and sexual appeal were obvious.

'Ricky Revel!' Cheng Infidel smiled broadly. 'It's great to see you, son. You look great.'

'Thanks,' the young man replied.

He smiled and nodded at Comforter and me, as though inviting Cheng to introduce us.

'This is Paul Comforter and Simon Seeker. They are interesting fellows because they both believe in God.'

'Pleased to meet you, Ricky,' Comforter and I replied almost in unison as we shook hands.

'You believe in God?' Revel mused. 'So you must believe that there is a purpose to this life?'

'Indeed there is,' Comforter said emphatically.

'I have everything I've ever dreamed of in life. In fact, I have much more than I ever dreamed of. More money. More fame. More houses. More women. More of everything. But I still feel dissatisfied. I spend a lot of time on my own in hotel rooms and I do a lot of thinking about life and any possible purpose that it might have. I've come to the conclusion that there must be more to life than material things. I wish I could believe there is a purpose to this life but I don't think I could go that far. And I don't know if I can accept God's existence and the idea of a place called Heaven.'

'There is more to life than material things, Ricky. Much more. And there really is a purpose to this life and there really is such a place as Heaven,' Comforter responded. 'But to understand, you have to accept The Message.'

Infidel shook his head and frowned at the mention of The Message. 'I've heard The Message, Ricky, and I'm sure you won't be interested in hearing about it.'

'On the contrary,' Revel said. 'I've always been interested in spiritual things. Tell me about The Message.'

Comforter launched into an enthusiastic explanation of The Message, the need to accept Victor Love as King and the eternal kingdom headquartered in King's City, which lasted a good twenty minutes.

Revel listened with interest, interrupting to ask questions from time to time.

'That's about it,' Comforter concluded. 'Any more questions?'

'Would I have to give up everything I have?' Revel said thoughtfully.

'Ricky you don't believe this nonsense, do you?' Infidel protested.

Revel dismissed his comment with a wave of his hand.

'Would I have to give up everything I have?' he said again.

'This is a common question from people in your position. Let me just say that you have to be willing to give up everything,' Comforter replied.

'But I have so much.'

'If you put anything before the Kingdom, that is idolatry and idolaters can't enter King's City.'

'Idolatry,' Revel repeated thoughtfully. 'Isn't that just the worship of blocks of stone or wood that ignorant people did in ancient times? What exactly do you mean by idolatry?'

Comforter took a deep breath and began his explanation.

'An idol is not just the worship of some statue or image that is supposed to represent a false god. Idolatry today is more subtle and takes various forms. Idolatry is a matter of the heart. An idol is a spiritual addiction. An idol is something we can't live without. Idols fill a vacuum that was intended to be filled by God. Nowadays, we tend to worship at the altar of self to the exclusion of all others. For example, it can be ambition, careers, sports, entertainment, hobbies, relationships, addictions or an obsession of some kind. It can be pride, love of fame and wealth, love of possessions, greed, gluttony or our looks. Idolatry tends to leave little time for anything else. I believe that the worship of self is the basis of all idolatry today.'

'Ouch. Now you're getting close to home,' said Revel with a wry smile.

'Ricky, all of us believers have a continual struggle with idolatry in its various forms.'

'The way you describe it, idolatry is a subtle thing.'

'It is indeed, Ricky,' Comforter replied. 'To put it another way, idolatry is the thing or the person put in the place of God – loved more, enjoyed more, treasured more, wanted more than God. And only you can really say what that is or who that person is. God must come first. He must be number one in our lives.'

'Are there any other forms that idolatry takes?' Revel asked.

'Well one other form of idolatry is to idolise other people like scientists, successful business people or show business personalities like yourself.'

'I would hate to think that people were worshipping me.'

'Now there's a thought, Ricky. You could be the cause of other people worshipping you.'

'This conversation is making me feel depressed,' Infidel exclaimed with a loud sigh. 'Ricky, why are you listening to this rubbish?'

'Well, to tell you the truth, I have an interest in spiritual things but none of the guys around me are remotely interested in these things. So I don't get to hear this kind of thing.'

'Ricky, you should just enjoy your wealth and fame and not worry about things like this.'

I had noticed a tall, portly, middle-aged man sitting on his own, reading some papers and making some notes. He kept looking over at Comforter and I from time to time as though he was trying to figure out who we were and what we were talking about. Suddenly, he called out, 'Ricky. Ricky. Come over here for a moment, son.'

Ricky looked round and nodded at the older man.

He turned back to us and said apologetically, 'I've got to go. It's been interesting talking with you. I wished we'd had more time to talk. But I'll certainly think about what you've said.' With that, he joined the older man.

'Who is that?' I asked Infidel.

'That's Ricky's manager, Lars Greed. Greed is something of a legend in the pop music world. He has guided Ricky to become the highest paid entertainer on the train. Greed watches over Ricky like a hawk.'

'I hope Ricky thinks about what I've said,' Comforter said. 'He seems like a sincere young man who is imprisoned by his wealth and fame. He has everything this world has to offer and yet he really has nothing. I believe Ricky is seeking for the truth in his own way but that he is impeded by the distractions and temptations of the train.'

'Well it's been interesting talking to you guys,' Infidel said. 'I wish I could say it was enjoyable too but I can't. Goodbye and good luck. You're going to need it.'

We watched Cheng Infidel disappear down the corridor.

Meeting Fred Contentious

Hardly had Infidel gone when a smartly dressed fellow with a dark grey blazer and a bright blue tie approached us. He looked about sixty years of age. 'Excuse me. I hope you don't mind me saying so but I couldn't help hearing your conversation. I was especially intrigued to hear that you are believers.'

This man, Fred Contentious by name, then explained that he had formerly been in a religious cult and, on looking back, he was sure that he had been subjected to brainwashing techniques. There was a hint of bitterness in his voice as he recounted some of his experiences in the cult. He then looked intently at Paul and then at me. I noticed that he had a nervous twitch in his right eyelid. His voice became contemplative. 'I used to be like you once. I was so sure I was right. But it turned out that I had been cleverly brainwashed. Now I don't mean to be offensive, but what makes you think you have not been brainwashed too?'

'We believe that The Message is inspired by God and our faith is based on that belief. Brainwashing is carried out by men, who may or may not be well-meaning but we are able to read The Message for ourselves. We know what it says and what it does not say. It warns us to watch out for false teachers,' Paul responded.

'I used to think that myself. But sects and cults can cleverly lure you into believing that you are misinterpreting what you are reading in The Message.'

'How would you define orthodox belief, Fred?'

'That's a very good question, Paul. I believe that a simple and reasonable definition would be that orthodox belief holds to the original teachings of The Message. That being said, with the passage of time, denominations change for various reasons and changes are frequently divisive. Some see such changes as being at variance with the essential truths of The Message.'

'But what causes people to break away from the parent group?'

'They break away for a variety of reasons, Paul. Sometimes it's a simple disagreement over a doctrine or a tradition or whether sections of The Message should be taken literally or figuratively. The disagreement may have been caused by differences in interpreting one or more verses. On the other hand, it may be a battle of succession after the leader dies or leaves. Or it may be just a clash of personalities. It can be started by one person with, "a bee in his bonnet" about something. That person then argues with the church pastor and leaves, taking some supporters along. Religious groups can and have started like that.'

'Then how would you define sects and cults?'

'Defining sects and cults is notoriously difficult. Some definitions make them almost indistinguishable. But I will try to define them, based on my experience and study. Common definitions of "sects" and "cults" compare their teachings to generally understood teachings and state that they have departed from one or more of these. There are, of course, divisions between the mainstream believers groups but these tend to be relatively minor – at least compared to the sects and cults.

'Let's take the word, "sect" first. Some use the word to mean an enthusiastic splinter group with much the same beliefs but with different emphases from its parent religion. The beliefs and practices of sects are often more radical than those of the parent group. Sects tend to be exclusive. Members of sects can be expelled for contravening the group's rules. Members often consider themselves specially chosen for salvation.

'A cult is more complicated to define than a sect. In fact, there are three definitions of what a cult is. There is a psychological definition which sees cults as good organisations which benefit their members in various ways – helping them to give up addictions, providing them with stability and security, and so on. Then there is a sociological definition which views cults as social movements which affect not only their members but society at large. According to this view, all religions are pretty similar and no judgements are made either on the theological teachings of cults or on the moral behaviour of cult members. Finally, there is the theological definition which is more common. It views cults as dangerous organisations which can cause emotional and psychological harm to their members.'

'I would like to propose a simple two-part theological definition of a cult,' I interjected.

Fred nodded at me as if to give me permission to speak.

'A cult is firstly an organisation whose message promises salvation without the need for cleansing from sin and acceptance of Victor Love as King. And a cult is also an organisation which employs authoritarian methods of mind control and insists that their organisation is the only home for true believers.'

'That's a pretty good definition, Simon. Cults preach a different message and a different King,' Paul added. 'Cults either deny or misinterpret essential orthodox teaching.'

'Okay. You've explained the difference between a sect and a cult,' I said. 'Now are there any general characteristics of the leaders of these groups?'

Fred nodded as though to indicate that he was coming to that subject.

'Leaders of sects and cults tend to be charismatic in the sense that the members believe that he or she possess a special divine quality and, as a result, they are willing to grant that person authority over them. Not all these leaders are like this, but some are. Personally, I believe that there is nothing wrong in being charismatic in itself and that not all charismatic leaders misuse this special kind of authority, but some do.'

'Well, Fred, you have certainly given us a full explanation of sects and cults. So thanks for that,' I replied.

'Thanks to both of you for listening to me so patiently and taking me seriously. But I would like to return to my original question. How do you know that you are not brainwashed?'

'We know that we have not been brainwashed because we know that we have the truth,' Paul responded. 'The Message was inspired by God Who cannot lie. It contains the truth. We read it prayerfully every day. We pray for understanding. We are warned to watch out for deceivers and so we pray for protection from clever heresies. Yes, my friend, we know that we have not been brainwashed.'

'I can vouch for that, Fred,' I added.

Just then, a burly lady who may have been his wife, called out to Fred to join her where she was sitting with some friends. Fred bade us a speedy goodbye, saying he enjoyed talking to us, and then left to join the burly lady.

'You know, Simon,' Paul whispered confidentially, 'we must be aware of those who try to get us to doubt our faith and whether or not we have the truth. Fred is a nice guy and I don't think he was trying to undermine our faith but, whether deliberately or not, people will sometimes try to get us to doubt. We must constantly study The Message to have assurance that we are really in the true faith.'

Meeting Alison Apathy

As we sat there, Paul decided to have a nap. As I looked around at the other passengers, I noticed a plump lady who appeared to be in her early seventies struggling to put her suitcase on the overhead luggage rack. I immediately sprang to her aid.

'Here, let me help you with that.'

'Oh that's kind of you. My husband is off helping a friend to move some furniture.'

She looked like the kind of lady who liked to talk and she offered to buy us a coffee. I gladly accepted but, as Paul was sleeping, I didn't want to wake him up to give him a coffee. The seats reserved for her and her husband were only a little way along the corridor, so we sat there so as not to wake him. Her name was Alison Apathy and I got her whole life story. She was basically a cheerful person but, at that time, she was feeling sad because a close friend had just died.

'How long had you known her?'

'Over fifty years.'

'Where did you meet?'

'We met in a believers' group, a church of sorts.'

'Oh that's interesting. What kind of church was it?'

She looked at me and smiled.

'It's a long story.'

'I'm not doing anything else at the moment. I'd like to hear about your church.'

'Well, it's not my church anymore. And, as I think back to those years now, I'm not sure it was a proper church at all. My husband and I were in it for about forty years, and then we left.'

'Why did you leave, Alison?'

'At first they were a legalistic group, like a cult. It was unorthodox in its teachings. We were told not to keep orthodox festivals because they were pagan. We were told not to keep birthdays because that was vain. We were discouraged from having contact with non-members. You can imagine what that did for our relationships with family and friends outside the church. After a few years, the only friends we had were inside the church. We were told to pay one tenth of our income – a tithe – before tax, to the church. We had to save another tithe, again before tax, which could only be spent at church festivals. As you can imagine, that kept us poor.'

'What do you mean by, "at first"? Did things change?'

'Yes they did. The founder died and the teachings began to change. But each change just caused tension between those who were loyal to the teachings of the founder and those who wanted the church to become more mainstream. The tension grew. Even families were divided. We were pretty much split down the middle. It was distressing. I still have nightmares about those times.'

'That sounds terrible, Alison. Was that when you and your husband left that church?'

'We stayed for a while but eventually the tension got to us and we left.'

'How do you regard that church now?'

'I hate to say it, Simon but we both feel quite bitter. We denied ourselves and our children of things we could have bought and could have done, either because we couldn't afford it or because the church said it was wrong. We gave the best years of our lives to that church. They taught us things that just weren't true and we were stupid enough to believe them. We feel as though we've been emotionally abused. They have pretty much screwed up our lives.'

'That's awful, Alison. Do you think the leaders in that church deliberately taught errors for their own gain and sense of power or were they deceived to?'

'I don't know, Simon and, to tell you the truth, I don't care.'

'Did you join another church?'

'No we didn't. We tried going to a couple of other churches but they were so different from what we had become used to that we just couldn't adapt to them.'

'But what about your faith, Alison? Do you still have faith in God?'

'Well, as we don't go to any church now, I suppose our faith has pretty much drifted away.'

'That is tragic. But just because you've had a bad experience in that church doesn't mean that God is like that. What happened to you and your husband was done by men, not by God.'

‘I suppose so.’

‘Can’t you both put those things behind you and move on?’

‘That’s easy for you to say. You haven’t been through what we have.’

I nodded and thought it best not to reply. I felt sorry for her.

A thoughtful silence followed during which I wondered whether to mention The Message to this poor, disillusioned lady. I decided I had to.

‘Alison, have you ever heard The Message explained clearly?’

‘I don’t think so but I’ve become confused about what it actually is.’

‘So many people today, even church leaders, ignore it or distort The Message. I think that may have happened in that church that you’ve described. Would you like me to explain The Message?’

‘Look, Simon, I know you mean well but my husband and I have been duped once, with catastrophic consequences. We are not about to be duped again. We’ve discussed this often and we’re not interested in anything to do with religion anymore.’

Another silence followed. I couldn’t think of anything else to say.

A man with thinning black hair and a tartan shirt with a leather waistcoat appeared and smiled down at me.

‘Simon, this is my husband, Terry. I was just telling Simon about our time in that church.’

After exchanging a few pleasantries, I left and went back to my seat. Paul was awake.

‘I wondered where you’d got to. I think it’s time for us to get going, don’t you?’

‘Yes. Let’s get going.’

Terrorised by The Wolf Pack

Meeting Fellow Travellers

As we left the Lounge Carriage, Comforter and I came across a group of about twenty fellow believers, mainly married couples with children, who were also heading for the End Section. They were sitting in an otherwise empty carriage with their luggage on empty seats nearby. We had been told of a number of people who were making the same pilgrimage as ourselves and had hoped to meet some of them on the way but up until then we had not met any. They were seated together enjoying lunch when we happened to hear them speak enthusiastically of The Message as we were passing by. We introduced ourselves and were cordially invited to join them for lunch, which we did. We sat beside two married couples – a black couple called Daniel and Chloe and a couple of Korean appearance called Jin Soo and Yu Na. Both couples had two young children. What delight we felt as we shared how we had come to believe The Message! What pleasure we took in exchanging our thoughts on aspects of The Message! We also recounted our experiences on the journey, some interesting, some amusing, but many involving persecution of varying degrees. We discovered that some of them also had the dubious pleasure of meeting Nicole Enigma and had likewise firmly declined her invitation to blaspheme King Victor's name. We spoke of how sad we were at the thought of the loved ones we had left behind and how we hoped that they too would come to believe The Message. With much laughter, we spoke of the eager anticipation we felt at the prospect of arriving at the End Section, and especially King's City, and meeting up with many fellow believers, past and present. We speculated on how wonderful King's City would be and the people we expected to meet there. What pleasure we took in each other's company in that carriage! Strangers had quickly become like beloved and respected family members. We spoke of our plans for the journey and how much longer we expected it to take.

Kidnapped!

We had just agreed that it would be more enjoyable if we were to travel together, when we were suddenly surrounded by a group of about twelve stern-faced men holding semi-automatic pistols. They were mostly of Asian appearance but there were three white men among them. About half the men had beards of various types, some just looked unshaven with facial stubble and a couple were clean-shaven. They wore normal casual clothing and, individually, they would probably not have stood out in a crowd as being particularly ominous. About half of the men were young, maybe even teenagers. One of the men, who seemed to be the leader, was stockier than the rest, with lighter skin and thinner eyes. He stood in front of the others and looked around at us with a cold stare.

'Well, well, a group of believers on their way to the End Section! We've been listening to some of your conversation. So you are the poor sheep who are following the call of Victor Love their good Shepherd, eh? We are the Wolf Pack and I am the leader. We prey on sheep like you. You may have heard of us in biased reports in the media. Some people call us terrorists but we are soldiers of our god – the true god. We follow our holy book – the only relevant revelation from God. Our religion is the true religion and it is destined to prevail. We are freedom fighters. We are revolutionaries. This whole train will ultimately convert to our religion. We kill all those who will not convert. We take a special delight in making believers like you convert or die. You are now going to be escorted to our headquarters upstairs where you will be detained and used as bait while we negotiate the release of our fellow soldiers who are in prison.'

We were going to be hostages! Some of the women and children screamed. I had heard of the Wolf Pack but thought they had disbanded and were no longer operative. They were renowned for their ruthlessness, their desire to commit atrocities to further their aims and for their willingness to die for their cause. We were gripped by fear and dread. We rose up and prepared to go with the men. Chloe began to plead with the leader to let her and her husband and children go.

'Shut up,' the leader snapped. When she started to sob loudly, he slapped her hard on her face.

'I said, shut up.'

Her husband, Daniel punched the leader in the mouth, causing his lip to bleed. The leader staggered back. He put his hand to his lip and then looked at the blood on his hand. He grinned, pulled out his pistol and calmly shot Daniel dead.

Chloe's screams and sobs were truly heart-rending. Our group was horrified and in a state of shock.

'Throw him off the train,' the leader ordered and two of his followers picked up Daniel's lifeless body and carried it away.

'Anybody else want to argue?' The leader motioned to us with his gun to start moving.

Hostages

We were shown into a large upstairs room and ordered to sit on the floor in a corner. Husbands were separated from their wives and ordered to sit in an opposite corner. The children were allowed to remain with their mothers. Two women came from a side door carrying bunches of grey clothes which turned out to be prison uniforms, loose fitting jackets and trousers. We were ordered to put on the prison uniforms. A man with a video camera appeared.

'Now you are going to be famous,' the leader grinned. 'We are going to make a short video of you all and it will be uploaded onto the internet. It will be accompanied by a demand that our fellow soldiers are released from prison immediately. The train authorities will be given two days to comply with our demand. Failure on their part to release our brave warriors will result in one of you being beheaded every day. Your executions will be shown to the whole train on the internet. It will be the main feature in the evening news on TV. We hope that will persuade the authorities to be reasonable but it probably won't. You see, they don't care about you. All they care about is protecting their corrupt system.'

This shocking statement was greeted by gasps of horror. One of the young women vomited. Three soldiers entered the room carrying about six semi-automatic rifles which they gave to their comrades. The soldiers put on masks so that they would not be recognised and they each posed with the rifles.

Another masked soldier posed with a large sword, which I assumed was to be used to behead us. The cameraman began filming us, with his camera lingering in close-up shots of each of us, seeming to enjoy our fear.

After the filming, we men were taken to an adjoining room with mattresses on the floor. This was to be our dormitory. Two young soldiers armed with pistols stood guard over us. The women and children were taken to another adjoining room. We were only allowed to speak to those fellow captives on either side of us and we tried to encourage one another. This policy meant that I was not permitted to speak to Paul Comforter, although we frequently exchanged meaningful glances. We spent much of our waking hours in prayer and reading The Message, which we were allowed to do by our captors. As was to be expected under the circumstances, our prayers were more fervent than usual. Comforter and I also began to sing some hymns but, when the other brothers joined in, we were ordered to stop singing. I discussed with the two brothers on either side of me the possibility that the train authorities might give in to our captors' demands. However, we knew that the policy of the authorities was never to give in to the demands of hostage-takers. We did not expect any other outcome in our case. We wondered about the possibility of our being rescued by the train authorities but we considered it highly unlikely. And in any case, most of the attempted rescues in such hostage situations that we had heard about had resulted in the deaths of some, if not all, of the hostages.

'We must prepare to die, brothers,' I announced, trying to be brave but feeling scared. 'It's an honour to die as a martyr for King Victor.'

'But, Simon, they're going to cut our heads off,' one brother replied.

'It'll be over in seconds, brother. We won't feel a thing,' I assured him. 'And our reward will be even greater in Heaven.'

The other brother, who was married, said, 'I'm not worried for myself. It's my poor wife and children. How can they execute children?'

'Shut up!' one of the guards ordered. 'You are afraid to die but we are willing to die as martyrs for our god.'

'It is not being a martyr if you go on a suicidal mission that is bound to end in your death, as your group does. That is suicide under another name. A martyr is when you are killed for your religious beliefs,' the brother argued.

'Shut up! What do you know about our motivation?'

They fed us with meagre rations of rice, cheese, beans and stale bread. I found it hard to eat or sleep. All hopes of rescue were soon abandoned. I resigned myself to dying sometime within the next few days. I thought of all the things I had planned to do with my life which would never be accomplished now. I thought of my family and some of my friends. They would surely have seen me on the video when it was reported on the evening news. My poor mother would be so distressed. Other relatives and friends would say that it was my own fault and will speak of how they tried to warn me but I wouldn't listen.

Taunted by Our Captors

'Why are you killing us?' one brother asked our guards in a plaintive voice.

One refused to answer but the other said roughly, 'Because we hate believers and because, by killing you, we are doing our god a service.'

'But why do you hate us?' the brother persisted. 'We don't hate you. We haven't done you any harm. We are peace-loving people.'

'I hate you because you are so sure your religion is the right one and that everyone should worship only your god. I hate you because you say your god is so loving and powerful. If He is so loving and powerful, why doesn't He help you now? I hate you because you go around telling everyone about your faith and it keeps growing. I hate you because you are identified with imperialism and democracy and human rights. We've deprived you of your human rights and your god does nothing to help you. Where is He now, this god of yours? You say you walk by faith and not by sight. I say you are fools to believe in this god who does nothing to help you.'

At this point the other guard joined in.

'And I hate you because you oppose violence and corruption and exploitation of the poor. You are upsetting the status quo in a lot of places by promoting these things and you are making it harder for groups like us to operate. You are gullible idealists who stand up for the poor. Only the strong survive on this train.'

Then the other guard joined the attack again.

'I hate you because your allegiance is to another kingdom, the kingdom of your King, Victor Love. This means you can't be controlled by us or by anybody else. We just can't seem to get through to any of you because of your mind set. Personally, I think you are all insane.'

We thought it best to remain silent. There didn't seem to be any point in trying to reason with them. They laughed at us and went to a corner where they could keep an eye on all of us. A brother next to me whispered to me, 'They need our prayers. They are not our real enemy. Our real enemy is Prince Nicholas Rebel.'

Executions

After two days, the leader entered our room at noon with three of his soldiers and looked around at each of us. We were sitting on our mattresses. We became tense, fearing the worst. He looked at us for around two minutes, appearing to enjoy our fear. The tension was unbearable. In a calm voice, as though he was announcing a change in the lunch menu, he said, 'I have to inform you, gentlemen that, as expected, the train authorities have refused to meet our demands. Therefore, one of you will now die.'

He looked at each of us again and pointed to one man.

'You!'

Immediately, the three soldiers grabbed the man and forced him to his feet. They started to drag him to the door. I learned that his name was Joseph.

'Be brave, dear brother Joseph,' one brother said.

'You don't have to use force. I'll go to my death willingly for my King,' Joseph said to the guards.

There was a calmness, even a cheerfulness in his voice which appeared to take the soldiers by surprise. They let go of him and pointed to the open door.

It was only about two minutes after they entered the other room that we heard Joseph shout, 'Praise God! Don't lay this sin to their charge!'

There was a terrible swishing sound and then silence. A couple of us brushed away tears. The two young guards then returned and closed the door behind them. We noticed that they looked pale and one of them was trembling a little. We guessed that neither of them had witnessed someone being beheaded before or, if they had, they still found the sight repulsive. I was inspired by the way our brother Joseph had bravely faced death. I decided that was the way I would try to conduct myself when my turn came.

Profile of a Terrorist

That night after our meal, I sat chatting to a brother called Bruce. He had worked as a newspaper reporter and was quite knowledgeable about terrorism. We were out of earshot of our guards but even so, we spoke quietly.

'What kind of people become terrorists, Bruce?' I asked.

'Those who indulge in religious terrorism like these guys often have middle-class or even upper-class backgrounds and are well educated. Some of them have university degrees. A "good" terrorist has to be dedicated, strong, intelligent, brave and totally loyal to the leader. They need to lack any pity or remorse for their victims, even though they are likely to include innocent men, women, and children. They must be able to blend in without drawing attention to themselves. They must be ordinary-looking, with no distinguishing birthmarks or scars. They must avoid anything that would draw attention to themselves. They must be inconspicuous and anonymous.'

'Where do they get recruited from?'

'Often from university, Simon. It is not unusual for up to half of the membership of these groups to be students. Highly educated recruits are usually given positions of responsibility and leadership.'

'Are they groomed or brainwashed?'

'Basically, yes. I believe they are. When they show an interest in the violent ideology of the group, they become isolated from their family and friends. This enables the grooming process to take place unchecked. They are trained to use explosives, guns, knives and whatever else they will need. The dynamics of the group are usually very powerful and the individual is likely to meet the violent demands of the group.'

'But many of the people you describe seem to have so much going for them, Bruce. They could live successful lives. Why do they want to risk death by becoming terrorists?'

'From what I've read, terrorists usually feel alienated from society. It might be because they have some kind of grievance or see themselves as victims of an injustice.'

'Are they mainly single?'

'In some groups, yes. But many are married with children. This helps them to blend into society.'

'Do they ever disguise themselves?'

'If they feel they need to, they will. They may even resort to plastic surgery.'

'Do you know what proportion of terrorists are women?'

'It's impossible to give a figure, Simon. In the past, women have tended to function in supporting roles but that seems to be changing. There is some tactical value for terrorists groups to have female operative, simply because an attack by women is less expected. Also, women terrorists can be more ruthless and single-minded than men.'

'What motivates women to become terrorists?'

'A number of things. Revenge. Idealism. Even companionship, believe it or not.'

'Do terrorists regard themselves as criminals?'

'No I don't think they do. They are devoted to their political or religious cause and they feel this justifies their actions.'

'Not much point in trying to reason with these guys then, Bruce?'

'No indeed, Simon.'

One of the guards came over.

'You two seem to have a lot to say. What are you whispering about?'

'We were just talking about what makes people become terrorists,' Bruce replied in a reasonable voice.

'What do you know about what makes us terrorists?' he snarled. 'You believers are fools! You will die tomorrow,' he sneered at Bruce.

When the guard walked away, Bruce said quietly to me, 'At least it will soon be over for me.'

'Be strong, brother,' I replied tenderly.

At midday the following day, the leader entered the room again and Bruce was then roughly hauled away to the next room.

'Goodbye, brothers. Keep the faith,' he called out to us as he was led away.

We heard Bruce shout, 'King Victor, receive my spirit.'

We then heard the dreaded swishing sound, followed by an awful silence.

The Deadly Schedule

Day after day, at noon, the deadly schedule continued. One brother and sister after another was executed. One mother was executed along with her two young children. Nearly all went to their deaths bravely and with a calm dignity. I wondered whether witnessing the calmness in the face of death that these brothers and sisters displayed had any effect on our guards. Did it make them wonder about whether The Message might possibly be true? Or were they so brainwashed that these deaths had no effect on them? Eight of our brothers and sisters and two children had now been executed. That was half of those in our group. It was the worst nightmare I could imagine. I felt weary with the daily tension and, although I was afraid, I wished they would pick me next to deliver me from the horrific situation.

Staring Death in the Face

Like my fellow prisoners, I had a lot of time to think about my situation. I found the contemplation of my own death to be a very daunting occupation for, despite the numerous assurances in The Message and from fellow believers, this situation was not speculative, nor distant, nor about someone else. It was real, it was imminent and it involved me. Death for me was now a certainty although the details about it were hazy in my mind. I was sure that it would be a conscious continuation and that it would be far better than this life. I consoled myself with the thought that it would be a new beginning, not a tragic ending. I had read and been told that, when we close our eyes in this world, we open them in Heaven. I imagined King Victor taking my hand and smiling at me while He led me gently to Heaven. I tried to instil in my thinking the excitement and anticipation I would feel when going on holiday. I found these thoughts immensely comforting. I knew that I had to feed my soul with thoughts like these to prepare myself for the ghastly thought of my execution. In my mind, I began letting go of my present existence. I thought of a couple of people that I had never forgiven and I forgave them from my heart. Everybody I could think of with whom I had ever had any disagreement was now totally forgiven. I found that thought liberating and cleansing. I resolved to try to face death with as much courage as I could muster. My main focus would be on worship and prayer. I even tried to anticipate death with joy. I decided to get my mind off the things that are seen and onto things that are not seen. As I contemplated death, God seemed closer than before. I surrendered myself to Him and was comforted.

Rescue!

One evening around midnight as I lay awake, I heard a loud bang, as though a distant door was being kicked in. This was immediately followed by loud shouting, then what sounded like a number of dull thuds like gunfire. Suddenly, the door to our room flew open and a masked soldier with a bullet-proof vest stood in the doorway holding a semi-automatic rifle.

'Get on the floor,' he screamed. Looking at our two guards, he yelled, 'Lie face down on the floor. Spread out your arms.'

One of the guards picked up his pistol and was immediately shot dead. The other shouted, 'Okay. Okay. Don't shoot!' as he lay spread-eagled face down on the floor. About a dozen other masked soldiers then entered the room, each holding a rifle. The guard was frisked and hustled out the door by three soldiers.

'Are you guys okay?' one of the soldiers asked us.

What a relief! We found it hard to speak. The unbelievable had happened! We had actually been rescued! We managed to assure him that we were all unharmed. We stood up and hugged each other. Some of us shed tears of relief. There were only eight believers and two children left alive from our group. The soldiers continued to ask us questions about the guards. Just then, the soldiers stopped their questioning and looked towards the door. The figure of a woman stood in the doorway, unmasked but wearing a bullet-proof vest and holding a rifle. It was Nicole Enigma!

She came to each of the brothers and asked us if we were okay. When she came to me, I said, 'I never thought I'd say this to you, but you sure are a sight for sore eyes.'

She didn't reply but turned to address all of us.

'I'm sorry that it took us as long as it did to locate you. I wish we could have gotten here sooner. But the terrorists are all dead now, apart from the one who surrendered. You can relax. You will now be taken to a reception centre where you will be given a medical examination and then you will be interviewed by the media. Sorry, but we have to do this because your kidnapping was such a high profile event. After that, there will be a debriefing by train security. We have some questions that we need to ask you about the terrorists.'

The Debriefing

After the amiable chaos of the media circus, during which we were able to pass on messages to our families, the eight of us who were left alive, including a married couple with two children, were gently ushered into an office. We sat in a semi-circle in front of a large desk. Nicole Enigma came in and, instead of sitting behind the desk, lifted the chair from behind the desk and placed it in front of the desk and immediately in front of us. She had a note pad on her lap and proceeded to ask us questions about the terrorists. But this was a very different Nicole Enigma from the one I had encountered before. She spoke in a quiet, gentle voice. She even smiled a little. She treated us with respect. It was like another person had entered her body. Did any of the terrorists let slip any information that might be helpful to her enquiries? Did we catch any of their names or where they were from? Did we overhear any conversation about what they were planning? When she had finished her questions, she asked us if we were still planning to go to the End Section. We all confirmed that was our destination. Emboldened by her change of approach, I said. 'The last time I met you, you tried to get me to blaspheme my King. Will you try that now?'

She smiled faintly. 'No, I won't try that again. As you know, I've been studying a great deal about the theology of believers. And now I've seen how bravely some of you have faced a brutal death at the hands of these morons. It made a big impression on me. It caused me to take a fresh look at your teachings. I used to think you were a dangerous cult. But now I've changed my mind about you. I admire you for your faith. I admire the teachings of your religion too. Any society would derive benefit from people who share your moral values. You are a credit to your religion. And I know how difficult this journey has been for some of you and I know I've played a part in that. Now you've had to endure this very traumatic experience. You've suffered enough. So I and a couple of my officers will escort you to the End Section. I will make sure that you get there safely. There's just one condition I will have to make. In order to guarantee the safety of all of you, I will have to insist that we stop only at places authorised by myself and that there are no more discussions and delays on the way. We must get there as quickly as possible. Is that agreed?'

We all expressed our grateful appreciation for our rescue and her offer to escort us to our destination. We readily agreed to her condition which seemed reasonable to us.

'When would you like to leave?' she asked.

We unanimously declared our intention to continue our journey as soon as possible.

‘Won’t you need any counselling first?’

We thanked her but assured her that we wanted to leave as soon as we could.

‘Then we shall leave tomorrow morning,’ she said with a smile. The next morning, our party left for the End Section.

Calvary Junction

With our armed escort hurrying us along, we made rapid progress. Many fellow passengers looked quizzically at us, as though wondering if we were criminals or hooligans who were being arrested or if we were celebrities who were considered worthy of an armed escort. They would probably have been disappointed to know the truth. Our accommodation and refreshment stops had been arranged in advance. Everything was highly organised. I wondered if the motivation of the authorities was to get us to the End Section as quickly as possible so that they could be rid of us. We might then be considered to be not their problem anymore. As we drew near to the End Section, an announcement was made over the sound system that the train was approaching Calvary Junction where the last two carriages would be separated from the main part of the train. That announcement spurred us on to make faster progress. Within a short time, we finally arrived at the End Section. What excitement we felt! What relief! We had just made it! We couldn’t help cheering loudly as we entered the End Section.

Drama!

We turned to thank Nicole Enigma and her two officers for getting us there safely but she held up her hand to silence us and turned to her two officers. She beckoned to them to move a little further away from us. She then removed her pistol with its holster which was around her shoulder and handed it to one of them along with what looked like an identity badge of some kind. Both of them looked shocked. They seemed to protest and then be firmly overruled by Enigma. Voices were raised. We heard Enigma say, ‘It’s no use. I’ve made my mind up. Now go.’ We had noticed that one of the officers had been carrying a small back pack and we assumed it must contain items that he needed for the journey. However, he removed it and gave it to Enigma which she promptly put on. She then appeared to dismiss them for they walked quickly back down the train. We were puzzled.

'What's going on?' I said. 'Aren't you going back with your officers?'

'No, as a matter of fact I'm not. I'm coming with you.'

'Why? We surely won't need to be protected from persecution in the End Section.'

'No you won't need that kind of protection from now on but the truth is, you see… I've become a believer too.'

'You've what?' I gasped incredulously. 'Are you serious?'

'I've never been more serious in my life.'

'This is amazing!' Comforter shouted. 'What a miracle!'

Those in our party were stunned at this dramatic news! Could this really be true? Could someone who persecuted us so zealously and so mercilessly have undergone such a massive change of direction? Could someone who persistently tried to make us blaspheme King Victor's name really have surrendered to the King's authority? But as she gently assured us that she was serious, we were reminded of the recent changes we had observed in her. We soon became convinced that her conversion was genuine and we rejoiced at the news. Our astonishment was replaced by great joy. We all exchanged warm welcoming hugs with her.

'Well, Ms. Enigma, I guess you're one of us now,' I said, beaming broadly.

'Call me Nicole,' she said with a warm smile.

Even then, when we thought she wasn't looking, some of us would sneak questioning glances at her, as though expecting her to reveal a darker side. But she never did. It really was the most amazing turnaround. We invited her to join us as we sought accommodation in the End Section, which she accepted.

Arriving at the End Section

We entered the first of the two end carriages and found that it was almost full. Every skin colour was on view and people were dressed in accordance with the various cultural norms of their origin. The atmosphere was very different from any of the other carriages that we had passed through. It was just as we had expected it to be. The atmosphere was peaceful and pleasant and polite. The passengers were smiling. There was a lot of laughter. They looked happy and content. I noticed several copies of The Message lying around on the tables between the seats. That was reassuring. It seemed to us that we were where we belonged, where we were meant to be. We were with fellow believers, people that we would someday spend eternity with. We exchanged smiles of acknowledgement with those fellow passengers who watched us enter the carriage. A few of them waved at us and we waved back. We introduced ourselves to some of them and they to us. However, there were some who recognised Enigma, for she had been a high profile persecutor of believers and, in this capacity, had appeared frequently on TV and the internet. They quickly became alarmed at her presence, doubting that she was a genuine believer and that she must be engaged in a covert operation to arrest as many of us as possible by posing as a believer. Despite our assurances, they still did not trust her. It was then that Enigma herself intervened.

'I think I may be able to convince you that I am on your side,' she said, pulling a document out of her inside pocket. 'This is the official document giving the following men an early release from their prison sentence. Their names are, Luke Watchman, John Herald, Harold Horrid, Sam Cynic and Delroy Wrath.'

When Comforter and I heard the names of Harold Horrid, Sam Cynic and Delroy Wrath, we shouted out in delight.

'So Harold Horrid really did accept The Message after all. I was never sure if he really understood what we were saying. How wonderful!' I said to Comforter.

Comforter replied, 'You can never judge by outward appearances. I told you all those protests from Sam Cynic and Delroy Wrath might be covering up a real interest in the faith, didn't I? Imagine Sam Cynic and Delroy Wrath becoming believers! Amazing, isn't it?'

Enigma paused briefly, smiled at our outbursts and carried on.

'You will notice my signature at the bottom of the document authorising this action. I managed to persuade the train authorities that it was no longer safe for these men to be in prison after the awful attack on believers. It was not so easy to obtain the release of Luke Watchman and John Herald because, as leaders in the community of believers, they were considered to be a particular threat to public order. However, I managed to persuade a couple of doctors that I'm friendly with and who owe me a favour, to recommend their immediate release on the grounds of their poor health. If you have seen either of these gentlemen recently, you will know that they are in excellent health, as are the other three men. The five of them must be here somewhere because I sent an armed escort with them too to make sure they got here safely.'

On making enquiries from nearby passengers, it was confirmed that all five men had indeed arrived safely at the End Section. This news was received with great jubilation and was more than enough evidence to convince the doubters that Nicole Enigma was indeed a genuine believer. We looked forward to seeing the five men again.

The married couple with the two children whom we had befriended just before we were kidnapped, Jin Soo and Yu Na, went off with another married couple with children who had offered to help them find suitable accommodation. The single men left us to join other single men whom they knew previously. Nicole Enigma, being a strong-willed, independent person, also left us to seek her own accommodation.

'Well, it's just you and me again, brother,' I said to Comforter.

'Come, let's sit down for a while and watch as we reach Calvary Junction. We'll soon be there. We can look for accommodation later,' he replied.

We managed to find two empty seats together and plonked ourselves down. We were tired after what seemed like a very long and difficult journey but we were happy and excited to have arrived at our destination at last.

After what seemed to be only a few minutes after we arrived at the End Section, the announcement was made that the train had now arrived at Calvary Junction. It is the busiest railway station in the world and it is where all mankind separates – the believers from the non-believers.

The Separation of Mankind

Calvary Junction! What a joy to be there! This was the point at which believers were separated from those who reject King Victor. This was where mercy and justice met. This was where love and wrath collided. This was where righteous judgement was satisfied. This was where the seriousness of sin was dramatically portrayed. This was where the solution to the corrupt nature of man was presented. This was where forgiveness was offered. This was where straying sheep must venture. This was where the success of the human race project was guaranteed. This was where the power of Prince Nicholas Rebel ended. This was the central issue. This was where the answer to all our problems could be found. There was no other way. This was where our relationship with God started in earnest. This was where our eternal destiny was sealed. It was there that the few were saved to enjoy eternity in King's City and the many were lost forever – doomed to spend an eternity cast out from the presence of God. This was where two paths separated. Two destinations. Two roads. One led to King's City, which would be transformed into Heaven. The other led to Hell.

We watched a couple of dour looking uniformed railway men directing operations as the last two carriages were decoupled. There were some clanging noises and a sudden jolt and then we were aware that we had been separated from the rest of the train. We watched as the locomotive moved the main part of the train away, slowly at first then gathering speed. As it sped away, it sounded a loud blast of the train's whistle. The whistle sounded joyful, jubilant. It was as though the main part of the train was glad to be rid of the End Section.

'Those poor people,' Paul said sadly as he watched the train pull away. 'They don't know what lies ahead for them.'

'It is tragic,' I replied. 'These are they who have rejected God and King Victor and accepted Prince Nick Rebel. Those are they who hate their friend and love their enemy.'

'Yes, Simon, there go those who hate King Victor without cause. There go the haters of The Message. There go those who have rejected their only hope of salvation. Onward they go to their miserable fate, those people who have loved lies rather than truth, those who have exalted folly above wisdom. And it's permanent. There's no turning back now. Words fail me to adequately express the tragedy of it all. Tragic indeed.'

As we watched the main part of the train disappear beyond the horizon, another locomotive appeared from a siding with another driver in control. A couple of attendants, recognisable by their uniforms, were in attendance. The locomotive then reversed slowly out of the siding onto the main track and proceeded to reverse towards the two carriages and was coupled to the front carriage. This connection was much smoother than the de-coupling had been and we were hardly aware of it being carried out. We received a cheerful greeting from the driver over the sound system and with several triumphant blasts of the train's whistle, we started moving. The sound of cheering from the passengers was even louder than the sound of the whistle. At last we were headed in the right direction! King's City here we come!

The Contented Carriage

As Comforter and I relaxed in the End Section, we reflected on the fact that the End Section was composed of two carriages. We assumed that must be because a single carriage would not have enough space for the number of believers expected.

After our eventful journey, we felt exhilarated and excited to have arrived, so much so that the tiredness we both felt quickly vanished. We hoped to meet up with some of the believers we had met on the way. We wondered if Mark Waverer had made it to the End Section. Mark had left us at the Quiet Carriage in some distress regarding the high cost of following the requirements of The Message. However, he had later come to visit us in the Hospital Carriage, in high spirits and full of deep conviction, telling us that he had since learned some valuable lessons about his own character weaknesses and he told us of his intention to journey to the End Section, whatever the cost. We looked forward to meeting Luke Watchman and John Herald, who had both been instrumental in our conversion. We both felt that we still had so much to learn from these men. We had been so excited and inspired to learn that Harold Horrid, Sam Cynic and Delroy Wrath had become believers and we wanted to meet up with them as soon as possible. Their testimonies would be sure to be an inspiration to other believers. We were still in some incredulity and excitement about the dramatic conversion of Nicole Enigma. We eagerly anticipated getting together with her too.

Welcomed by Martha Disciple

We had only been there for about a half hour, when we were approached by a pleasant, burly lady wearing a blue apron that was heavily stained. She introduced herself as Martha Disciple. 'Welcome to the Contented Carriage!'

she smiled. 'It's great to see people arriving here and to know that our numbers are still growing.'

'The Contented Carriage?' I replied. 'Why do you call it the Contented Carriage?'

'Oh, because we are all contented here. Many of us have had a difficult journey to reach this place and now we just want to relax and be content with what we have here. Although many different denominations are represented, most of us are content with our understanding of The Message and content with the differences between us. We are not perfect of course, but most of us have a niche that suits our abilities reasonably well and that makes for a contented atmosphere. I'm sure that you two gentlemen will soon be given responsibilities according to your abilities and that you will quickly settle into a routine here that you will be content with.'

'That sounds like a good recipe for harmony,' I said.

'It sure is,' she replied.

Comforter looked pensive. 'I hope you don't mind me saying this, Martha, but I'm just a little concerned about your frequent use of the word, "content",' he said. 'Actually, to be honest with you, it makes me feel a little discontented. Believers ought to be content with their faith of course, but it seems to me that, in such an atmosphere, believers could be at risk of becoming complacent.'

'Why do you say that, Paul?' I asked hesitantly.

Comforter seemed to weigh his words carefully before replying. 'Harmony between believers is certainly a good thing, Simon. In fact, when believers love each other that is a strong indication that they are true believers. However, there are a number of exhortations to believers in The Message which require effort and these exhortations seem to rule out comfortable thoughts of contentment. For example, we are exhorted to grow in our understanding of our faith, to make every effort to show ourselves approved to God and to examine ourselves to see if we really are true believers. These things are not easy and frankly, they don't make me feel content with the way I am at present. The word, content, implies to me that it's all right to stay just as you are in your spiritual journey. But I do not believe we should stay just as we are. The Message exhorts us to grow in maturity and to become more like King Victor Love. That means examining ourselves and changing the things in our understanding and character that need to be changed.'

Martha looked at Comforter quizzically but said nothing.

I asked Martha if she had seen Mark Waverer and described him. She said that she had seen a young man of that description but that he hadn't stayed long. She suggested that he may have returned to where he came from or that he might possibly have gone on to the last carriage. The thought that Mark may have returned concerned us greatly. We also enquired if she had seen Luke Watchman, John Herald, Harold Horrid, Sam Cynic and Delroy Wrath, describing each of them. She replied with some enthusiasm that she had seen Watchman and Herald around and that they had each been very active in teaching The Message and also in social activities. She also confirmed that she had seen Horrid, Cynic and Wrath in the Contented Carriage.

'Well it was nice to speak to you both but I have so many things to do and I need to get going. I hope to see you both later,' Martha said.

Comforter and I lapsed into a thoughtful silence.

Meeting Bishop Arthur Manpleaser

Soon after, we were approached by a jovial, charming man with a ruddy complexion who introduced himself as Bishop Arthur Manpleaser. His white clerical collar stood out against his scarlet vestment and dark blue jacket.

'Hello. It's always a special joy to welcome newcomers to the Contented Carriage,' he beamed. He had a loud voice and spoke with the confidence and authority of a man used to preaching to people.

'It's wonderful to be here,' I replied with a smile. Comforter nodded in agreement.

'Please tell me how you each came to accept The Message,' the bishop enquired. 'I've often found such testimonies to be an inspiration and an encouragement as well as a fruitful source of sermon material.'

'My corrupt nature was directing my life and I was depressed when I heard The Message,' Comforter responded with passion. 'What joy it brought to me to discover that there really is a god who loves sinners like me and directed me to His servant King Victor so that I can go to the glory of King's City instead of spending eternity being tormented in Hell, which is what I deserve.'

I was also moved to respond with enthusiasm. 'In my case, when I heard The Message, I was convicted of my corrupt nature and was deeply moved to learn that God loved me enough to offer me the opportunity to be forgiven and spend eternity with Him in King's City and the Heaven that it will be, delivering me from having to endure the horrors of Hell for eternity.'

Bishop Manpleaser listened attentively. 'Hmm. You both mentioned Hell in a way which leads me to think that you both understand Hell in a literal way. In speaking of Hell, I believe we should make it clear that it is a difficult subject which is best viewed in a metaphorical way. We don't know what Hell is like or even if it is a literal place. We must avoid any interpretation which suggests that God is punishing people. The god who is revealed in The Message is a gracious god – a loving god. A god who is not willing that any should perish. Not a vengeful god. The idea of God punishing people forever in Hell is like a relic from the past. Most modern preachers would back away from saying such a thing. Speaking personally, I regard that concept as repulsive.'

Comforter frowned and then looked puzzled. 'I think that most believers feel that Hell is an uncomfortable topic, Bishop. But I don't believe that we should reject a literal view of the verses which deal with Hell in The Message simply because they are repulsive to us. There are many references in The Message to things that many of us find unpleasant, like God punishing rebels. I believe these accounts have been included in The Message to warn us of the dangers of straying from the right path. I don't think preachers should shrink from declaring just how terrifying the judgements of God can be. He is loving and merciful, but He is holy and righteous. He hates sin and will punish sinners. God is also described as a consuming fire whose very presence is terrifying.'

The bishop began to look somewhat flustered. His assured smile and authoritative tone had disappeared and been replaced by an embarrassed hesitancy. It seemed to me that he was unaccustomed to being challenged on a theological point.

'We must be careful not to cause offence,' he replied rather lamely.

'Did I understand you to say that you don't know whether or not Hell is a literal place?' I asked.

'That's right. I don't know. And even if it is a literal place, I don't believe anyone can know what it's really like. In my view, it is better to regard those verses which refer to Hell as metaphors, that is, language that should not be taken literally. One reason that I regard these verses as metaphors is that conflicting language is used to describe Hell. It is described as a fire, but it is also described as darkness. How can it be both?'

'I agree that fire and darkness are both symbols but I believe they describe different aspects of Hell,' Comforter said. 'I see no contradiction in taking both symbols literally. Besides, since we agree that they are both symbols, we should ask what they are symbols of.'

'If you don't know whether Hell is a literal place, how do you understand the punishment that people receive in Hell?' I enquired. 'I understand that this punishment is punitive rather than redemptive.'

'Yes I agree with you, Simon that the punishment described is punitive and not redemptive but I believe that it is better to understand this punishment as separation from God and a terrible eternal burning in the hearts of those who have been lost for God.'

'But surely that would still mean that people are being tormented severely and endlessly? There would still be pain, even though it is mental pain rather than physical pain,' Comforter reasoned.

The bishop nodded and said, 'Hmm. I suppose so. I hadn't really thought of it that way before.'

'Do you believe that people can repent of their sins in Hell and be saved?' I asked.

'Knowing that God is patient and merciful, I think that is a distinct possibility.'

'But that would mean that the vast majority of people who have ever lived would be saved but The Message tells us that it is only the few who will be saved and that the many will perish.'

The bishop nodded. 'I don't know the answer to that one but I read a survey recently which indicated that most believers are Universalists, that is, they think everyone will be saved eventually.'

'Maybe that's because prominent preachers like you are influencing them to believe that,' Comforter replied.

'But what about those in Hell who refuse to repent of their sins? Do you believe that their punishment will be eternal?' I asked.

'Actually, no I don't. I think that those in Hell will eventually be annihilated after an appropriate period of punishment. I don't believe they will suffer for all eternity. I believe they will eventually be put out of their misery and will simply cease to exist.'

'Does your interpretation of the verses on Hell not raise questions about the accuracy of The Message?' Comforter asked.

The bishop hesitated. I felt I had to support Comforter on this point.

'It seems to me, Bishop Manpleaser that we are speaking with the authority of The Message but that you are using human reasoning to avoid a topic that you find difficult to explain – namely, the topic of God's judgement and Hell. I think you are dumbing down The Message in an attempt to please people. I feel there is a danger that your interpretation will weaken the impact of The Message to those hearing it.'

The bishop looked at his watch. 'It has been most interesting hearing your views, gentlemen. I'm afraid we will be unable to reach agreement on this matter at this time. I hope you don't mind but I would like to give each of you a piece of advice.'

We both indicated that we were always ready to listen to advice.

'I think you are taking The Message rather too seriously if you don't mind me saying so. You need to lighten up a bit. Learn to be more accepting of views which differ from the traditional understanding.

'As for me, I will continue to do what I have always done and that is to emphasise the love of God in my sermons and avoid any mention of judgement and punishment. Now I really must be on my way as I have some important pastoral matters to attend to.'

We wished each other well and said we hoped to continue our discussion further at a later time. Comforter and I exchanged thoughtful glances but said nothing. It was clear to me, however, that we were both disappointed by our conversation with Bishop Manpleaser. We rejected out of hand his advice that we should not take The Message so seriously.

Enter Reverend Abigail Backslider

Comforter stood up suddenly. 'I've been sitting long enough. I think I'll have a walk along the rest of the carriage and perhaps I'll be able to become acquainted with one of our fellow believers.'

'Okay. I'll just sit here and read some of the believers' literature that is lying on some of these unoccupied tables.'

After about ten minutes, Comforter returned with a diminutive lady with a broad smile. She wore a white clerical collar with a black vestment and a pink jacket that seemed to be a size too small for her.

'This is my friend Simon Seeker. Simon, this is Reverend Abigail Backslider.'

'Call me Abigail,' she smiled as she sat down beside us.

'Abigail is the Chairperson of an inter-denomination committee and she and I were just discussing the importance of unity in diversity amongst believers,' said Comforter.

'Unity in diversity? What do you mean?'

'Abigail, would you care to explain unity in diversity to Simon here?'

'Of course. The members of our committee come from different denominations and each of them hold views about our faith that differ in various ways. Most of these differences concern relatively minor doctrinal points but other differences involve basic doctrines. These differences have the potential to divide us, especially when we hold joint worship services but we agree to respect the views of other members.'

'But what does this mean in practice, Abigail?' I asked. 'I mean, how can you hold joint worship services if you disagree on some basic doctrines?'

'We just avoid topics that may offend others.'

'But, if you are saying that you have to avoid some basic teachings of The Book, doesn't that involve compromising?' I asked.

'Yes, that's what I was thinking,' Paul added.

'Well, to tell you the truth, gentlemen,' she said, 'it does take some compromising but the committee members and I strongly believe that it is worth some compromising if it helps to maintain unity among the denominations.'

'Compromising in spiritual matters is never a good thing, Abigail,' Paul responded. 'And unity is not always a good thing. People have to be united in a way that aligns with the teachings of The Message. Unity that is not in line with the teachings of The Message is not in line with the will of God and will ultimately do more harm than good.'

'I agree with you in theory, Paul. But I could never advocate going back to the days when the denominations were divided and we all did our own thing. What kind of example is that to unbelievers? No, we have to be pragmatic. We must be seen to be working together.'

'Well, it's good to see the different congregations working together to undertake various projects that benefit others,' I said, trying to achieve some kind of unity among the three of us on the topic of unity.

'Yes that is certainly good to see,' Paul conceded.

On that point of agreement, Abigail took her leave of us, saying she had to chair another meeting of the inter-denominational committee.

As we watched Abigail weave her way hurriedly along the aisle, I said, 'You have to admit, Paul, she means well.'

'Yes she does, Simon. Still, I have concerns about the practice of compromising with the teachings of The Message. Peace at any price is not real peace.'

Dr. Rashid Flatterer's Lecture

Not long after we arrived at the Contented Carriage, Paul and I were invited to a lecture on persuading unbelievers to accept The Message. It was to be held in a large upstairs lecture room and given by a Doctor Rashid Flatterer. The room was full. Dr. Flatterer was a television evangelist and pastor in a church with a very large congregation. He had a charismatic personality and his lecture was full of humorous anecdotes, some involving the many celebrities he had met. Consequently, the lecture was accompanied by much laughter and spontaneous applause. Flatterer had the audience in the palm of his hand. He spoke of the success he had in attracting people to his church. His view was that the emphasis in preaching should be on love and not on telling people they need to repent of their faults. He advocated the use of some psychological methods to attract people. He told them they would be blessed in material and financial terms if they gave generously to his church. As a direct result, the finances of his church were healthy and growing steadily. He told them they were fine people who were in good standing with God. He said their future in King's City and Heaven was assured. The growth statistics of his church that he quoted were impressive. Every week new people started to attend.

After the lecture, a number of fellow attendees gathered around Dr. Flatterer to ask him questions. As far as we could tell from the body language, there did not appear to be much, if any, disagreement about what Dr. Flatterer had said.

'You know, Simon, I totally disagree with Dr. Flatterer,' Comforter said to me as we walked out of the lecture room. It seems to me that he has watered down the truth of The Message to attract such a vast congregation. He is telling people what they want to hear not what they need to hear.'

'I think you're right, Paul.'

Professor Alistair Mocker's Lecture

Soon after, we were invited to another lecture in the same large upstairs lecture room. This time, the lecture was given by a noted scholar on The Message, Professor Alistair Mocker. Again the room was full. Professor

Mocker took the view that The Message is not adequate to instruct believers. He insisted that it is necessary to consult other traditions within various communities of believers in order to arrive at a full understanding. He also stated that some parts of The Message need to be interpreted in the light of modern historical and scientific discoveries.

As with the previous lecture, a number of fellow attendees gathered around the lecturer afterwards to ask him questions, all appearing to be impressed by Professor Mocker's lecture.

Again Comforter and I expressed our concerns about the lecture as we left the lecture room.

'I am sure that The Message has been inspired by God and contains no errors either, scientific or otherwise,' Comforter said.

'So am I and I'm surprised and disappointed that so many people seemed to agree with him,' I said.

A Discussion with Amir Manlover

As we left the lecture room after Professor Mocker's lecture, deep in conversation, we met a young man that we had met on a number of previous occasions in the Contented Carriage. His name was Amir Manlover. He had certain distinguishing features – thick, curly light brown hair, a short beard, arched eyebrows, a rather long, curved nose and an olive skin tone. Amir was openly affectionate in public with other men that he liked and always greeted us with a hug and two kisses on the cheek.

'Great lecture wasn't it? What a gifted teacher Professor Mocker is! It was as good as the recent lecture by Dr. Flatterer. We are certainly blessed with some fine speakers here,' Amir enthused.

'I agree that both men are gifted teachers,' Comforter replied rather stiffly. I just smiled but did not reply.

Manlover looked intently at each of us, his green eyes darting from Comforter to myself and back again, as though sensing some reservation about the lectures.

'I've only been a believer for about three years and I'm still learning. But Dr. Flatterer's views on the need to make The Message more attractive to more people seemed reasonable to me. And Professor Mocker's opinions about interpreting The Message in the light of modern historical and scientific findings appeared perfectly sensible to me. After all, The Message was written a long time ago. We won't attract people to the faith if we don't move with the times.'

Manlover had a habit of placing his hand over his heart and bowing his head slightly to emphasise his sincerity.

Comforter suggested we find the nearest seats and have a chat.

'Amir, the way to King's City and Heaven is described in The Message as narrow and difficult. Only the few ever travel that road. Even some people who call themselves believers do not go that way. On the other hand, the way to Hell is broad and easy and the many, the vast majority, travel on that road. Just because someone calls himself or herself a believer doesn't mean that they are. This train has some fake preachers and fake believers who preach and teach a fake message. I think Dr. Flatterer has watered down the truth to make it more acceptable to more people. That is dangerous. It is vital that people are told that they need to repent of their sins, otherwise they will end up in Hell.'

'But we need to show love to people, Paul,' Manlover protested.

'It's not showing love to people if you let them carry on in their sins thinking they are going to Heaven when you know that The Message teaches something different. They could end up in Hell. That's not love. Those who love us warn us. Those who don't love us don't warn us. Love always warns of dangers ahead.'

'But you have to admire Dr. Flatterer's popularity and his success in building a megachurch.'

'Popularity with people means nothing, Amir. What counts in the end is having favour with God. Numbers mean nothing. God has to be involved not clever psychological techniques.'

'But what about Professor Mocker's views that The Message is neither scientifically accurate nor adequate to instruct believers? Surely that is a reasonable stance to take?'

'We believe that The Message has been inspired by God and contains no errors either, scientific or otherwise,' Comforter said. 'If we can't trust the accuracy of The Message, we have no authority for teaching and preaching it.'

'You certainly speak your mind, Paul,' Amir replied. 'I'll think about what you have said and I'll discuss it with my pastor. Thanks for sharing that with me.'

He didn't look convinced. With that, Amir Manlover walked briskly away.

Facing an Uncomfortable Truth

Following a long period of thoughtful silence, Comforter said, 'You know, Simon, I've been doing a great deal of thinking and praying and studying since we arrived at the End Section.'

'So have I, my friend. And have you come to any conclusions?'

'Yes, Simon I have, but it is difficult for me to say it.'

'Go ahead, Paul. Take your time. I'm listening.'

'Simon, there is much to appreciate about this environment. The people are friendly and sincere. There are enjoyable social activities here. Most of the leaders work hard. They do and say many things that are good. They regularly visit the other carriages on the train to assist others in various ways and to invite them to join us here. I have heard some helpful sermons. I have been inspired by the worship – well, some of it anyway. They call this the Contented Carriage and it's true that the people here are generally contented. But maybe a more accurate word to describe them is complacent. It sounds harsh but I believe that most of the people here are rather complacent with regard to their understanding of The Message. And I would have to blame the leaders for this. Some of them have become liberal. I feel they have lost sight of some of the basic truths of The Message. I feel they are compromising The Message by focussing only on the love of God and refusing to mention His holiness and His righteous judgement. They are not declaring the whole counsel of God. This is not the right message. It's a false message. And it's having a negative effect on their members.'

'What do you mean, Paul?'

'Some of the members seem to be hardly distinguishable from unbelievers. They look like the real thing but their lives often don't match up with what they say they believe. When a person becomes a true believer, that person becomes noticeably different from the way they were before. There is evidence of a spiritual rebirth. There is a fundamental change in that person's life, with a changed heart, not just a different language and lifestyle.'

'True, but I'm sure that every group of believers has nominal members. You know, people who profess to be believers but are not.'

'Yes but such people need to be confronted with their error. The leaders have to teach the people the truth without fear or favour and to rebuke and correct when necessary. I'm beginning to think the biggest danger facing believers today is from within our own ranks. We tend to expect challenges to The Message from outsiders but I think the worst kind of challenges come from insiders. These challenges come from sincere people who might mean well but who are wrong.'

'But how could such well-meaning people pose a bigger threat than some of the hateful cynics who want to destroy our faith?'

'Don't misunderstand me, pal. The people I'm talking about will usually not criticise The Message openly. The problem as I see it is that they treat The Message as a kind of therapy. The way they come across is that The Message will help you to make wise decisions, to be a success in this life, to have a better marriage, to be a better parent and a better work colleague and so on.'

'I can see that would appeal to a lot of people, Paul.'

'That's true but The Message is not about any of that – well not primarily anyway. The Message is about a god who is holy and righteous, sinners who deserve His judgement, His sinless servant, King Victor and the promise of forgiveness and eternal life to all who repent and believe. It's not about appealing to what people want to hear.'

'You're spot on, Paul. No one can ever improve on The Message, no matter how eloquent a speaker they are. I think the Contented Carriage needs a spiritual awakening.'

'I agree. Frankly, pal, I don't believe that this is the right environment for us.'

'I've been thinking about and praying about this subject for quite a long time myself, Paul. I didn't want to mention it first because I thought I could be misunderstanding something. Or I was afraid that I might be being self-righteous and judging people wrongly. But, before I make a final decision, I would love to know how Luke Watchman and John Herald feel about the Contented Carriage. They're both men of great wisdom and understanding. We've been trying to catch up with them since we arrived here but have only managed a few words of greeting in passing. I would like to counsel with them about this matter.'

'I've been making enquiries about them and I've been told that they have recently moved on to the final carriage, citing doctrinal and pastoral concerns. So we know what their view is, my friend. Simon, it's one of the hardest things I've ever had to say but I think we should move on to the last carriage.'

I lapsed into deep thought. If Luke Watchman and John Herald were dissatisfied with the Contented Carriage, and possibly Mark Waverer too, there must indeed be serious problems with it.

'To think of all that you and I have sacrificed and suffered to get here, Paul, only to find that many, if not most, of the believers are spiritually asleep and have embraced false teachings!'

'It's a tragedy, Simon.'

'I agree with you, Paul. We should go to the final carriage and check it out. I don't know if it will be any better than this one but we have to hope that it will be.'

We then made our way without delay to the final carriage.

The Contrite Carriage

Paul Comforter and I entered the last carriage with some trepidation. Leaving the Contented Carriage and breaking fellowship with such fine folk was probably the hardest thing that either of us had ever done. We had gained some respect there and we had built up good friendships with some of those people. Now it wouldn't be the same. We would try and keep in touch with them but would they want to keep in touch with us? Now we had to start all over again. We were trading in friends for strangers, familiarity for unfamiliarity. Would we be able to fit in? It might be that we would discover that the problem lay with us, not the people in the Contented Carriage. We were concerned. Really concerned.

Greeted by Mary Disciple

We sat down in the first two empty seats and looked around. The Contrite Carriage contained far less people than the Contented Carriage but every type of race you could think of was well represented and the atmosphere was just as friendly. After a few minutes, we were approached by a pleasant, burly lady with a wide grin. She wore a white, knitted woollen top and a plain, black skirt. 'Hello. It's lovely to see new people arrive. My name is Mary Disciple.'

'We met a lady called Martha Disciple in the Contented Carriage and you remind me of her,' I replied.

'Yes, she's my sister. Anyway, welcome to the Contrite Carriage!'

'The Contrite Carriage!' I exclaimed. 'Why do you call it the Contrite Carriage?'

'The believers here are focussed on The Message and King Victor. This has made us keenly aware that we are wretched sinners who deserve to go to Hell and that it took the willing sacrifice of our sinless King to save us from that terrible fate. So we are contrite – apologetic, ashamed, remorseful – about our sins. We devote ourselves to prayer, meditation and study of The Message. That doesn't mean we don't have many happy social activities, we do. But it's probably fair to say that we have less social activities than the Contented Carriage. Although we will readily admit we are far from perfect, we strive to identify and root out any remaining faults. This contrite approach to The Message has given us peace and joy and assurance that we are loved and forgiven by God. I think this shows in our happiness and in the way we conduct ourselves. We regularly visit people in the other parts of the train to serve them in various ways and to evangelise.'

'This sounds like the ideal environment for a believer to grow in the faith,' commented Comforter.

'But how is your relationship with the fellow believers in the Contented Carriage? Is there any tension between you?' I asked.

'If I'm honest there is a little tension at times. There are some big differences in our understanding of The Message and this makes it difficult for us to co-operate in most outreach ventures. But we try to show love to each other and most of the time we manage to co-exist without problems. My sister Martha and I get on fine though.'

I asked Mary if she had seen our friend Mark Waverer, describing his appearance. To our delight, she confirmed that Mark had recently arrived in the Contrite Carriage. We determined to look out for him and try to meet him as soon as we could. She confirmed that both Luke Watchman and John Herald were now resident in the Contrite Carriage too. Somewhat anxiously, we enquired about Harold Horrid, Sam Cynic, Delroy Wrath and Nicole Enigma and to our delight she told us that all those people had recently arrived in the Contrite Carriage.

Enter Rev. Graham Good

As we were talking to Mary, a man came alongside her and greeted her with a friendly, 'Hello, Mary. Nice to see you again.' He looked as though he could be in his early thirties although he was bald. He had a polite, if rather formal, disposition and looked like a man with something on his mind. He wore a clerical collar and a beige-coloured jacket. Mary introduced us to him and he to us. His name was Reverend Graham Good.

‘You look like a busy man, Reverend Good,’ I smiled.

‘Yes I am, Simon,’ he replied. ‘Every now and then I have to confront and refute some heresy or other. And this is one of those times.’

‘How would you define heresy?’ I asked.

Reverend Good thought for a minute. ‘To put it simply, heresy is opposed to orthodoxy and, before you ask, I will tell you what orthodoxy is. Orthodoxy is right belief whereas heresy is wrong belief. Heresy is an obsession with a particular doctrine or part of a doctrine in The Message. An undue emphasis is then placed on it at the expense of the rest of the doctrines in The Message.’

‘What causes people to have such an obsession?’ I asked.

‘Very often, the obsession is fuelled by a desire to teach something that nobody else teaches. In other words, it is a desire to be original. This desire then develops a momentum of its own and it becomes increasingly significant to those involved. It becomes even more important to them than the truth. The obsession might also be caused by a desire for recognition and the wealth that can result from such recognition.’

‘But are those who teach heresy knowingly teaching lies or are they deceived themselves?’ I enquired.

‘It could be either, Simon. But my experience indicates that those involved have convinced themselves that it is true. So I suppose the answer is that, in most cases, they are deceived themselves. But what does it matter whether they believe the heresy themselves? Heresy is heresy and it’s a very serious matter.’

The expression on Reverend Good’s face became more intense. ‘You know, Simon, I would say that the biggest problem facing believers today is not persecution, it is false teachers who pollute The Message. These false teachers sometimes creep into our meetings unnoticed. Sometimes their errors are obvious but at other times, they can be quite subtle.’

‘That must make your life difficult?’

‘That’s my job and I’ve been blessed with some discernment. I’m ready to contend for the faith and I’m not complaining.’

‘Is there a simple way for ordinary believers like myself to recognise false teachers?’

‘Basically, all teaching must be in agreement with The Message. If you are not sure if it is or not, then look at their lives. Is this teacher in question a person of character? Many, if not most, false teachers live lives that, at times, are seriously inconsistent with the standards given in The Message. They pervert the grace of God and turn it into a license to live immoral lives.’

'That's so true. King Victor told us we would recognise false teachers by their fruits,' Comforter added.

'Yes and false teachers and false religions nearly always pervert what The Message says about King Victor,' Reverend Good continued. 'We must also remember that The Message has not changed. It was delivered once for all time. So it doesn't need some smart aleck to come along and tell us we've all been wrong all this time. The Message does not need to be updated or qualified in any way.'

After a little more conversation, Reverend Good left us, saying that he had important pastoral matters to attend to. Comforter and I were impressed and encouraged by Good's sincerity and his desire to defend the faith. I couldn't help but compare him with some of the teachers and preachers we had listened to in the Contented Carriage. The difference was like chalk and cheese. The man was like a breath of fresh air.

Enter Bishop Zimuzo Faithful

As we continued talking to Mary Disciple, a black man in a clerical collar approached and greeted Mary. He was middle-aged with wavy hair which was greying at the sides. He had a cheerful personality and a pleasant smile. As before, Mary introduced us to him and he to us. His name was Bishop Zimuzo Faithful. Mary wished us well as she had her duties to attend to and she left us in the company of the bishop.

'I haven't seen either of you before. Have you arrived here recently?' the bishop enquired with a smile.

'Yes, we were in the Contented Carriage for a while but then we decided that we needed to move on,' I replied.

As soon as I had spoken, I wished I hadn't worded it the way I did. It gave the impression that we were not impressed with the way things were done in the Contented Carriage. Although this was the truth, I didn't want to give a negative impression about the other carriage. I felt bad. The bishop smiled and nodded his head but tactfully said nothing.

'The atmosphere in this carriage is what I would expect of a place where believers are gathered. It's peaceful, polite, enthusiastic, busy and happy,' I said, in an attempt to say something positive.

'That's good to hear,' the bishop replied.

I expected him to say more but he didn't.

Not knowing quite what to say next, I said, 'What do you put it down to?'

The bishop paused to consider my leading question. 'I could mention a number of things. But if I had to pick on just one reason for the atmosphere you describe, I would say that everyone here is on a quest for personal holiness.'

'Holiness? I'm sorry to show my ignorance but what is holiness exactly? I've heard the word many times but I really don't know what it means.'

'The word, "holiness" basically means separation. It means detached. It means different. When the word, "holy" is applied to God, it refers to the fact that He is different from us. He is detached from mankind because He is in a different category. He is far superior in every respect – His greatness, His nature, His righteous character. God is glorious and majestic and awesome. That's why He is holy. In fact, Holy is one of His names.'

'But we humans can't be holy, surely?' I enquired.

'No. Not like God is holy. You see, Simon, God is holy with an absolute holiness. But we believers are also holy. The Message refers to us as holy people. You could call this a reflected holiness. That is to say, we are what we are because God is who He is. We are holy because of His holiness. This makes us different from unbelievers. Holiness is at variance with the standards of this train.'

'But what does the holiness of believers look like in practical terms?'

'We have to live holy lives. The holiness of believers signifies that we are set apart for God's service. This holiness makes us different from unbelievers because we reflect the holiness of God to some degree.

Our standards are not those of unbelievers. We strive to reflect God's standards.'

'But we are not to be isolated from unbelievers, are we?'

'That's right. The holiness of believers means we are to be different from unbelievers but not isolated from them. In fact, we are to be involved in serving them.'

'This holiness you describe, Bishop Faithful is daunting for a new believer like me. I don't feel I can live up to this holiness.'

'Simon, don't be discouraged. All believers feel that way. I feel that way too. Although we are holy now, we are to pursue more holiness. We are to grow into more holiness and that's a life-long process.'

'But holiness sounds so serious and so spiritual and I feel so unspiritual.'

'Simon, pursuing holiness does not mean you must be serious all the time. It doesn't mean you can't enjoy leisure time or sports or hobbies. It doesn't mean you can't wear bright colours, for example. It does mean that, in your heart, you have a deep desire to please God and that affects the decisions we make. Holiness is something that all true believers want more than anything else. And I can tell from speaking with you for just a few minutes that that is something you want more than anything else too, my friend.'

'Yes indeed, sir. But I slip up sometimes.'

'We all slip up at times, Simon. When that happens, we repent and pray for the strength not to repeat that mistake again.'

At this point, Comforter joined in the conversation.

'Bishop Faithful, is there not a danger that the pursuit of holiness can approach legalism? It seems to me that, if we produce a list of things we cannot do, that can become a form of legalism.'

'Paul, the reason we pursue holiness is because we want to please God. It is not because of legalistic tendencies.'

'But we still have sin lurking within us from our former nature, don't we?'

'Yes, Paul that is true. The pursuit of holiness does not shut out this indwelling sin. It means there is a battle within us between this desire in our minds and hearts for holiness and the presence of our old nature. May God grant all of us a hunger for holiness.'

On that note, Bishop Zimuzo Faithful wished us well and left. I felt edified by our conversation. Here was a true leader of the faith. A man beyond reproach. A man you could trust.

Enter Julia Joy

In the middle of the Contrite Carriage there was a small cafeteria and Paul and I decided to go there for a coffee. As we stood chatting, we began talking to a retired missionary lady called Julia Joy. She had been a missionary for many years in various parts of the train and had never married. I asked her about her experiences as a missionary.

'There have been so many experiences, both good and bad, but there is one particular experience that stands out in my mind. In my experience and in the experience of other missionaries I have spoken to, the biggest problem for believers everywhere is discipleship. Believers are disciples of King Victor and this should be reflected in the way we talk and act. But sadly, the lives of many believers don't seem to be much different to the lives of the unbelievers around them. They seem to separate their lives into two separate compartments – the holy and the secular.'

'That is so sad,' I replied. 'How would you describe a disciple?'

'Well firstly, every believer must think of himself or herself as a disciple of King Victor. The Message is a message of the grace of God towards humans. But grace without discipleship cheapens the wonder of God's grace. Believers must obey the ethical and moral standards taught by King Victor in The Message. It is essential that King Victor must also be the Lord Whom we obey.'

'Julia, are you saying that some believers do not regard King Victor as their Lord also?' I said.

'That's exactly what I'm saying, Simon. In fact, I would say that, if He is not our Lord, then He is not King either.'

'That's a sobering thought.'

'Yes it is indeed, Simon. Secondly, every believer must love the King above anyone else, even more than family members and even more than one's own life.'

'So it requires total dedication then?'

'Yes, total dedication. Being a disciple demands everything of us. It demands our heart and mind. It demands our time, our energy, our property. It means we are willing to put up with any hardship, including persecution. We must be willing to die for our faith.'

'You make discipleship sound very expensive, Julia.'

'It is very expensive, Simon. Salvation is free but discipleship costs us everything we have. We must be willing to forsake everything we have for our faith. We must make time every day to pray and to read The Message.'

'That takes dedication.'

'Indeed it does. But thirdly, every believer must be radically changed and bear fruit. We can't just carry on as we did before. Our previous desires and hopes and dreams must come to an end. It's like a new birth. The person we used to be no longer exists. The believer now has a relationship with God and with the people of God.'

'I can see that I need to do some serious self-examination.'

'We all need to examine ourselves regularly, Simon.

'A fourth and final sign of a believer is that every believer must be involved in sharing The Message with unbelievers. This is called mission and it is a great test of the quality of our discipleship.'

Julia's description of a true believer left me speechless. My mind was working overtime trying to process the information and asking serious questions of myself. Paul had listened in silence so far but he finally responded. 'I really appreciate listening to your description of a disciple, Julia.'

As Julia left, she left Paul and I with much to think and to pray about.

Reunited with Mark Waverer

As we were thinking about our conversation with Julia Joy, I felt a tap on my shoulder. I looked up to see the smiling face of Mark Waverer. We embraced each other and greeted each other warmly.

'It's been a long, hard journey to get here, friends,' he said with a broad grin.

'It sure has. But it's all been worth it,' I replied, to which they both nodded in agreement.

'We looked for you in the Contented Carriage and were told that they hadn't seen you for a while. It was suggested that you had either returned back or that you had moved on here. We were worried about you and are so glad to see that it was the latter,' Paul said.

'I began to feel that the Contented Carriage was rather liberal in its approach to The Message. I wasn't comfortable with that, so I came along here.'

We were delighted to learn that Mark had taken the same view as ourselves regarding the Contented Carriage. He had gone through a hard time of doubt and despair from which a confidence in the authority of The Message had emerged. It was this confidence which had caused him to be perceptive with regard to false teachings.

Meeting Other Old Friends

During our time in the Contrite Carriage, we regularly met up with the friends we had met in prison, Harold Horrid, Sam Cynic and Delroy Wrath. We were delighted and relieved to see that they had all accepted the truth of The Message and had progressed from the Contented Carriage. It was obvious to us immediately that a great change had come over all three of them. We found this change to be inspiring. In the trying prison conditions, we could not be sure whether we had been able to fully convince them of the truth of The Message. Harold Horrid looked a changed man. Gone was that sad, dishevelled look. He was an enthusiastic student of The Message and a regular attendee at our meetings. He was outgoing and friendly and smiled frequently. He had even cut his hair and he looked quite handsome. Similarly, Sam Cynic and Delroy Wrath had discarded their tough gangster appearance and had become humble and gentle and polite, as believers ought to be. Any lingering tendency that they had to be confrontational and forthright was reserved for any who dared to dilute The Message. We enjoyed our fellowship with them and spent much time recounting our experiences in the prison. Comforter and I did have some initial concerns about Nicole Enigma, mainly because she had remained somewhat of a mystery to us. With the benefit of hindsight, we both agreed that we should have known that the intense study that Nicole had undertaken in order to try to prove us wrong when she worked for Train Security would serve her in good stead. She came to understand The Message so thoroughly that she would not be taken in by any false teachers. We spent much time with Nicole and never tired of listening to her account of how she came to accept The Message. We regularly spoke with Luke Watchman and John Herald and continued to learn much from both of them. Although Comforter and I fully expected two such giants of the faith to be saved, it was a relief to see them in the Contrite Carriage all the same. We also regularly met six adults of the eight people and two children who accompanied us to the End Section. However, the married couple and their two children had remained in the Contented Carriage.

'It's wonderful to see these old friends here with whom we have gone through so much,' Comforter said with evident satisfaction.

Joseph Trustworthy's Correction

Comforter, Waverer and I were in the habit of attending worship services together and, after one particular worship service, as the three of us mingled with other members of the congregation over coffee as usual, we got talking to an elderly black deacon called Joseph Trustworthy. Joseph looked as though he was in his seventies. We were talking about the decline in the morals of society in general. We agreed that at this was most clearly demonstrated in the films which are shown on television. I confessed that I had watched a film the previous week that I now felt I should not have watched. On reflection, I felt it was bordering on pornographic.

'Why didn't you turn it off?' Joseph asked.

'Films have been gradually becoming more violent, with more bad language and blasphemy, and I suppose I've just gotten used to it. What would've shocked me once doesn't shock me so much anymore.'

'Simon, you need to be careful, my friend,' Trustworthy remarked with a sudden intensity in his voice.

'It is very important not to override your conscience. The conscience is a wonderful gift from God. Every person has a conscience and every culture recognises right and wrong, at least in some sense. The conscience has imposed a kind of natural law in every one of us. It's an inbuilt ability to sense what's right and what's wrong. It rebukes us when we dabble in things we shouldn't. It makes us feel guilty. It's like an automatic warning system that tells us to change our course of action. But it can become de-sensitized.'

'How does the conscience become de-sensitized?'

'If a believer's conduct is at variance with his or her faith, it will result in the conscience becoming de-sensitized and defiled. If you keep overriding your conscience, it will become hardened so that it no longer functions as it should.'

'But won't we be safe if we continue to follow our conscience?'

'No, Simon, I wouldn't go that far. You see, the conscience is not infallible. It judges our thoughts and actions according to the moral standards we've been taught. But the conscience can be hardened by wrong moral teaching and false ideas. Basically, if you've been taught wrongly, your conscience will be wrong too.'

'But isn't it possible for a conscience to be hyper-sensitive, so that it tells you something is wrong when it isn't?'

'Indeed it is. That's a weak conscience and it's the opposite of a hardened conscience. A weak conscience can condemn you for something that isn't wrong. It might even be the right thing to do.

You have to guard your conscience, Simon.'

'Guard my conscience? How do I do that, Joseph?'

'It might be helpful to think of the conscience as a roof light. It lets light into the mind but it doesn't produce its own light like a light bulb does. The effectiveness of the conscience is determined by the amount of good teaching we expose it to. Basically, the conscience must be informed by The Message, then it will function as it was designed to do.'

'It sounds like you are saying we have to educate our consciences, Joseph.'

'Exactly, Simon. But there are strong consciences and weak consciences and those with strong consciences must never encourage those with weak consciences to overrule their conscience. Instead, they should defer to concerns of the person with the weaker conscience whenever possible.'

'So, to go back to where we started, I must be careful about the programmes I watch on television?'

'Exactly, my friend.'

I thanked Joseph Trustworthy for his wise advice. And I meant it. I had been becoming too lax and it was important for me to be told about the conscience.

Philip Gentle's Rebuke

Small groups of believers met regularly to discuss various parts of The Message or specific topics. There were usually around twelve to fifteen people in each group and they were normally led by a member who was considered to have the necessary experience and understanding. We had three different groups to choose from and Paul, Mark and I decided to attend separate groups. Our thinking was that we could tell each other about our groups, who attended, what was discussed, and so on. The group that I attended was led by a deacon called Philip Gentle and we met in his cabin. On one occasion, the group was studying the subject of forgiveness. As Philip directed us to various sections of The Message which dealt with forgiveness, I began to feel somewhat uncomfortable. Forgiveness had been a problem that I had been wrestling with since I had become a believer. I found it difficult to forgive certain people in my past who had mistreated me. I didn't want to tell the group about this problem so I remained behind after the others had left in order to discuss it with Philip privately.

'Philip, I find it so hard to forgive certain people in my past because of the way they treated me. I might find it easier to forgive them if they apologised to me but no apology has ever been made.'

'Simon, you must forgive them. The Message is clear about this. It doesn't matter whether or not they have apologised to you. God has forgiven you and you must forgive them.'

'This must be one of the biggest challenges that believers face?'

'It is. Forgiving those who have wronged us is the greatest challenge any of us face. The society we live in has made revenge one of the most popular themes in films and books. So many stories are about getting even, settling the score. We can all identify with feelings of revenge but you must resist these feelings. How can we who cling to God's forgiveness refuse to forgive others? Forgiveness is probably the most God-like act we can do. Refusing to forgive is a hate crime.'

'That's interesting, Philip. How would you define forgiveness?'

'It might be easier to say what forgiveness is not, Simon. It's not overlooking or condoning or excusing. I would say forgiveness is being prepared to give up one's right to resentment and retaliation towards somebody who has treated us unfairly, and, at the same time, cultivating kindness, compassion, generosity, and even love, towards that person.'

'Phew! That's hard to do.'

'It is hard, Simon. To forgive an offence, especially a serious offence, might well be the hardest thing any of us can ever do. And forgiveness usually takes time. Most of us can brush off minor upsets, but when a more serious thing happens, we usually need to take time to wrestle with our feelings.'

'It sounds to me that forgiveness is a decision we make.'

'That's right, Simon, and it's a life-long commitment. And don't go around telling other people what this person has done to you. That won't help. If you still have contact with the person who wronged you, try to defuse the situation as best you can. Try to be gracious towards them. Let them save face if you can.'

'Should we ever set conditions before we forgive?'

'No. If the person has apologised, then it's easier to forgive them. But, even if they don't apologise, even if they don't deserve to be forgiven, we must forgive them. Now, although we should not set conditions for forgiveness, we might need to set conditions for reconciliation. For example, if a person sexually abused a child in the past, then conditions might need to be put upon any future contact that person might have with children, even though forgiveness has taken place.'

'So basically, you are saying that nothing is unforgiveable, even very serious things?'

'Yes. No matter how serious the offence is, no matter how much you've been hurt, it will hurt even more if you hate someone for it. If you allow yourself to become bitter, you'll find yourself reliving the offence over and over. If you give in to bitterness, you'll become a prisoner to your emotions. Set yourself free, my friend. Forgive. Then you'll have peace.'

‘But I still say it’s so hard, Philip.’

‘Forgiveness is not weakness. You have to be strong to forgive. To overlook an offence is a glorious thing. But to forgive very serious things, you’ll need God’s help.’

‘Thanks for your guidance, Philip. I’ll remember what you’ve said and I’ll try to forgive from now on.’

‘Remember, Simon, we are never more like God than when we forgive. God is the only One who can decide when or if there should be vengeance. Vengeance belongs to God alone.’

We continued to look for Luke Watchman and John Herald but we only saw them either in the distance or as they passed by quickly on the way to an appointment. We concluded that their skills were much sought after.

Conclusions on the Contrite Carriage

As Comforter and I reflected upon our time in the Contrite Carriage, we concluded that we had been and continued to be much encouraged and edified by the experience. Topics that were difficult or unpopular, which had been avoided in the Contented Carriage, were dealt with openly and honestly in the Contrite Carriage. The integrity and authority of The Message was much in evidence in all our conversations and in all the teachings. And, most importantly, teaching about King Victor was central. We were being gently corrected, warned about the subtlety of sin, encouraged to pray and study The Message more – but we were also loved. We were convinced that, in the Contrite Carriage, we had an environment in which we could thrive as believers.

A Town Called Tribulation

Separation!

Comforter and I were enjoying coffee and pleasant company with some of our fellow passengers in the Contrite Carriage when suddenly, and without warning, the train slowed and stopped. Conversations ceased as passengers looked out their windows to try to see why the train had stopped. We had stopped at a town called Tribulation.

We next became aware of the two carriages which comprise the End Section being detached from each other in a deliberate and decisive way. The mystery deepened. Many became alarmed. Why were the two carriages being separated? It was surely a temporary situation. Some technical problem, perhaps? A routine maintenance programme maybe? It couldn't be anything serious because we were believers after all. We were on our way to King's City. All of us. Nothing could change that. There must be a simple explanation.

A solemn announcement then informed us that the passengers in the Contented Carriage were being left at the town of Tribulation and must experience the horrors of tribulation for a period. Providence had decreed that they were only nominal believers, not genuine believers. As such, they could not be taken to King's City. They would have to be tried and tested through persecution at the town of Tribulation. Unknown to us, a divinely appointed separation had been taking place between the two carriages. Only those of us in the Contrite Carriage were accounted worthy to go to King's City. The passengers in the Contented Carriage would now be required to examine themselves. All sins would have to be confessed and repented of and forgiveness earnestly sought. They would have to face suffering, much of it severe, and even death. However, those who remained faithful in the face of death would be accounted worthy to be taken to Heaven. The others would be rejected and taken to Hell. Loud gasps and cries sounded throughout our carriage. Many wept uncontrollably. Some trembled with distress. It was a truly shocking and frightening announcement. The announcement had caused great torment among the passengers in the Contented Carriage and we could hear their loud cries of anguish and pleas as they pleaded not to be left there. They were far from contented now.

The locomotive started to move slowly forward. On looking back, I could see a large army of armed soldiers approaching the Contented Carriage. They were led by several men who appeared to be wearing some kind of clerical apparel. As we pulled away, the cries from the Contented Carriage became fainter. In our carriage, many passengers sat in stunned silence as though in a state of shock. It was distressing beyond words to know that our fellow believers were in such anguish. I could not bear to think about what lay in store for them.

My anguished voice cried out to Comforter. 'What's happening, Paul? Why are we being separated from those other believers?'

'It's just like the announcement said, Simon. Those who have been accounted worthy are being taken to King's City. Those who have been left behind will face a time of great tribulation. It will be the time when God pours out His wrath on the train because of their sins and because they have rejected The Message. We are being removed so that we are not affected by this judgement. True believers are not appointed to the wrath of God. We will be protected from it.'

'But where did they go wrong?'

'Only God really knows the answer to that. But judging from what I read in The Message, it could be that they lost sight of the basis of The Message. This could happen to anyone who doesn't give sufficient attention to prayer and diligently reading The Message. The end result is that people are not true believers anymore, if indeed they ever were. They are only nominal believers, professing believers.'

'Professing believers? That is shocking! To think that they are not true believers is truly shocking!'

'That's right, Simon. God saves all who respond to His call, who accept King Victor and who are willing to follow Him, no matter what. But not everyone who claims to be a believer really is a believer. Some will wander back into their former way of life that leads to Hell. They start off being zealous about their new faith. They can't get enough of prayer, worship, fellowship with other believers and reading of The Message and other explanatory literature. But they don't continue like that. They become lukewarm and reduce the amount of time they spend doing what they should do. Slowly but surely, they lose their faith and finally they give up altogether and they return to the ways of the train. It's a bit like a dog returning to eat his own vomit or a pig that was washed returning to wallow in mud. They may even be seduced by counterfeit versions of The Message from false teachers. A number of false prophets have arisen who are doing notable signs and wonders. It's only genuine believers who will not be taken in by them.'

'We all need to examine ourselves, don't we?'

'We sure do, pal. It's necessary to protect us from self-deception too. We need to be sure that we are genuine believers.'

'What sort of things would assure us that we are genuine believers?'

'There are a number of things that assure us but I'll mention a few of them. Genuine believers don't habitually indulge in wrong habits that we are aware of. Sin can be very subtle. We hate it in all its forms. When we are made aware of some fault, we repent of it immediately. We are zealous for good works. We have a high view of The Message. We venerate and love King Victor. We seek to glorify God in all we say and do.'

'But those people in the Contented Carriage seemed to me to be genuine believers, Paul.'

'It's hard, if not impossible, for any human being to tell who is a genuine believer and who is only a professing believer, Simon.'

'You mentioned a time of great tribulation. But everything seems to be going on as it always has. When will this tribulation happen?'

'Now that we have been removed, it will happen very quickly.'

'But wasn't this separation foreseeable, Paul? I mean, shouldn't all believers have been prepared for it?'

'It was foreseeable, Simon in the sense that The Message warned us that a great separation would happen at the time of the end.'

'But I understood from the announcement that professing believers are not eternally lost. They will have another chance to get to Heaven, won't they?'

'If they earnestly turn from their errors and seek forgiveness, they will be forgiven. But, as the announcement said, they will have to face that time of great tribulation. They may have to give their lives in martyrdom. But God is merciful and they might yet be saved.'

'Oh I hope they are saved, Paul.'

‘So do I, Simon. But you and I ought to be so grateful that we have been accounted worthy to enter King’s City.’

‘Yes indeed, Paul. And we must remember to pray fervently for the people in that carriage that they will ultimately be saved.’

Thanks to Paul Comforter

In thinking about the journey to the End Section, with all of its trials and tribulations, it occurred to me that Paul Comforter had been by my side almost every step of the way. I didn’t know what I would’ve done without him. He was there to guide and encourage me, and to exhort me when I needed it. His knowledge of The Message and his understanding of its application proved invaluable. I wasn’t sure if I would’ve made it to the End Section and the Contrite Carriage without him. And I hadn’t even thanked him.

‘Thanks, Paul. It was largely because of you that I made it here.’

‘That’s okay, pal. You’ve been a big help to me too in a number of ways. Don’t underestimate yourself. Anyway, God was in it all the time helping both of us. Thank Him, not me.’

With the passage of time, the shock of the separation gradually passed but we continued to pray for the people who had remained at the town of Tribulation. The certainty of our destination multiplied our joy and love for each other. Our love for God and the intensity of our worship increased also. So it was with great joy and excited anticipation that we settled down again on our journey to King’s City.

Arrival at King's City

It was clear that each of us in the Contrite Carriage felt unworthy to enter the transformed King's City and the fact that we were certain to do so was attributable solely to the amazing grace of God. Our sins really had been forgiven! All of them! Oh the bliss of that glorious thought! And all because of the work of our King Victor! The grand redeeming work had been accomplished. All guilt and pain were now at an end. The reign of sin and death was over and was swallowed up in victory. Prince Nicholas Rebel the enemy of believers had been totally defeated. Even the sorrow caused by the memory of those loved ones who had rejected The Message had faded. It was as though the distressing thought of their appalling eternal fate had been automatically ejected from my memory. Spontaneous cries of praise were heard. Songs of joy and worship reverberated throughout the carriage. Many tears of joy were shed.

King's City, restored to what it was meant to be! Capital city of the whole world! Heaven on Earth! What a magnificent concept! Throughout the carriage, excited, animated conversations erupted. We were about to see what no human eye had ever seen and to hear what no human ear had ever heard and to behold what no human mind had ever conceived, namely what God had prepared for those who loved Him. Would there be a welcoming committee?

Our weak bodies were about to be changed! Glorified! Made suitable for eternal life! What a thrilling thought that was! It engendered such thrilled speculation! What would our bodies be like? Would we really still be ourselves? Would we be capable of sinning? What age would we be in human terms? What new information would we have? Would there still be things we didn't know? Would we be able to eat and drink? Would there be entertainment, and if so, what kind? Would there be sports? Would we be able to have animals as pets?

And didn't The Message indicate that we would be given new names? We happily joked about names that we felt would be appropriate for each of us. Shrieks of laughter accompanied the whimsical suggestions proposed for each of us. Surely I wouldn't be called Seeker anymore because I had now found that which I was seeking after? Mark Waverer would likely have his name changed to something more suitable. Our prison friends Cynic, Wrath and Horrid would have their names changed too, as those names were no longer suitable. The same applied to Nicole Enigma. She was no longer an enigma to us but a loving, dependable, transparently open sister in the faith.

The thought of being reunited with loved ones again who were also believers evoked such joyful anticipation! Surely we would recognise each other? We would have the whole of eternity to be with them. We would surely have so much to talk about. We would be able to explore the wonders of Heaven together. Maybe we would even tour the universe together. And what about those family members that died before we were born? I didn't know much about my family history. I wondered whether some of my relatives of the past became believers too. Wouldn't it be fascinating if they did and I met them in King's City? Our reunions with loved ones would be likely to be filled with recounting the grace and glory of God in our lives, His wondrous love, and His mighty works. We would surely rejoice all the more because we would be able to praise and worship God in the company of other believers, especially those we loved on Earth. And when would King's City itself be transformed to make it Heaven on Earth? And to see the beloved King Victor Love face to face! Ah, that was the sweetest thought of all! We were about to see Him as He really was! What an utterly compelling thought!

After the dreadful experience at the town of Tribulation, days turned into weeks and weeks became months and there was not one day that I didn't grieve over our poor fellow believers at the town of Tribulation. Finally, the glorious announcement was made that we were approaching King's City! A triumphant blast sounded from the train's whistle! Many eager voices cried out that they could see the beloved City come ever closer! Nothing had prepared me for the sight. It had been miraculously transformed. Such magnificence! Such splendour! Such glory! As the train drew nearer, we saw people waving at us! Who were they – angels or saints who had gone on before us? As we drew even closer, we could clearly make out the smiling faces of our dear brothers in the faith who had been killed in the prison, Manchu Humble, Arthur Gentle, Hammad Peace, Walter Mercy and Rohan Patience. Some cried out that they could see believing relatives who had gone on before. The noise of joyful shouting from every person in the carriage was deafening.

And wait – who was that glorious figure who looked so dignified and splendid? Could it be Him – the One Who made our rescue possible? Had King Victor come personally to welcome us? Who else could it be? The train came to a gentle stop and the blessed announcement was made – 'You have now arrived at King's City!' Home at last!

Reflections

'Breakfast!' I was woken by someone calling out, 'Breakfast!' in a rough, Scottish voice, accompanied by loud knocking on the door. The door flew open, banging on the side of my bed and a small waiter came in.

'Good morning, sir. Here's your breakfast. We've just arrived in Aberdeen. It's another cloudy day I'm afraid but at least it's not raining. Not yet anyway.'

I blinked and stretched and yawned. I quickly got dressed and pulled up the window blind. It was 7.00am and Aberdeen Station was quiet. I looked out the window thoughtfully as I sipped my tepid tea and ate a soggy croissant.

What was that all about? A lucid dream? An out of body projection? A vision? Was I experiencing dream-reality confusion? Who was this Simon Seeker guy? That's not me. That's not my name. So who was he supposed to be – my alter ego? Who were those characters called Luke Watchman, John Herald and Paul Comforter and all the others? And who were Prince Nicholas Rebel and King Victor Love? Fictitious characters plucked from deep within my psyche?

Did some external force insert this – whatever it was – into my brain to tell me something I need to know? Or was it a message meant for someone else but delivered to me by mistake? It was over whatever it was. But what brought it on? The incessant onslaught of bad news in the media? Seeking answers to questions like, "who am I?" and "what am I?" The frustration of reading a book called *The Meaning of Life* before going to bed – a book that promised answers but delivered only more questions? Physical, emotional or mental busyness? Was it nothing more than my brain's way of dealing with stress? Or, on a more mundane level, did it have something to do with those sleeping pills? Whatever it was, it had a happy ending for those who believed this thing called The Message. For those who didn't, it was tragic. They faced a catastrophic fate. It was over whatever it was. But was it supposed to mean something? What if it did have a meaning? The arguments for the existence of God had been compelling. And the world was in such a mess that it needed a benign dictator like King

Victor Love to sort it out. What if there really is a god out there who gave it specifically to me? What if He's trying to tell me something? Could there be a lesson in it for me? Am I supposed to do something now?

It was over whatever it was. It was time to get on with the business of life that passes for reality. I had to stay anchored to reality. The pragmatism of this existence was about to kick in. What would this pragmatism tell me? I'm a grown man and I must start acting like one? I must accept that life is meaningless and get over it? It was ended whatever it was but I sensed that something had begun. Something that wasn't there before. Something deep within. Something life-changing.

My search for meaning would continue but now it would have to be more focussed than before. More diligent. More urgent. I would need something to believe in, something bigger than myself. Something like The Message or its equivalent. I would need Someone to believe in too, Someone like King Victor Love. Maybe that's what I've been seeking all these years. If there is a god out there who sent me this dream or whatever it was, and if it does have a meaning, and if He wants me to understand it, surely He will help me to understand how The Message applies to me. In the meantime, I would have a lot of thinking to do. A lot of studying. A lot of counselling. And a lot of praying.

Lightning Source UK Ltd.
Milton Keynes UK
UKHW04f0617250718
326252UK00001B/99/P